Seek Her Like Gold

by

Caitlyn Callery

Copyright Notificaiton
This is a work of fiction. Names, characters, places, and incidents are either the product of the author's imagination or are used fictitiously, and any resemblance to actual persons living or dead, business establishments, events, or locales, is entirely coincidental.

Seek Her Like Gold

COPYRIGHT © 2025 by Caitlyn Callery

All rights reserved. No part of this book may be used or reproduced in any manner whatsoever without written permission of the author or The Wild Rose Press, Inc. except in the case of brief quotations embodied in critical articles or reviews.
Contact Information: info@thewildrosepress.com

Cover Art by *The Wild Rose Press, Inc.*

The Wild Rose Press, Inc.
PO Box 708
Adams Basin, NY 14410-0708
Visit us at www.thewildrosepress.com

Publishing History
First Edition, 2025
Trade Paperback ISBN 978-1-5092-5837-6
Digital ISBN 978-1-5092-5838-3

Published in the United States of America

Dedication

To my friend and fellow author, Belinda E Edwards,
without whom I would have been lost.

~

And to my wonderful editor, Nancy,
who makes my books the best they can possibly be.

Chapter One

Rotherton, Sussex. May 1818

Eliza Rolfe—Rawlins! How many times must she remind herself that she should only ever use her assumed name, even in her private thoughts? Otherwise, she ran the risk of giving herself away, and there was far too much at stake to allow that.

Eliza *Rawlins* stood with a group of Rotherton residents at the wall separating the road from St. Bartholomew's churchyard. They all stared at the Norman church, with its squat tower and red, gabled roof, which shone in the early summer sun. A flagstone path led from the front door, through the grassy churchyard dotted with ancient gravestones and an occasional chest tomb, to the lych-gate.

"Not long now, I reckon," said a woman of mature years. She nodded as if agreeing with herself, and the ends of the bright green ribbon she'd tied around her bonnet fluttered with the movement. "Then, our Miss Catherine will be a lady." A couple of women murmured agreement, their smiles broad.

A man wearing a laborer's smock and breeches sniffed, clearly unimpressed. "She allus was a lady," he answered, pushing back the front of his hat brim, presumably so he could see better. "She don't need no toffee-nosed baron to make her one."

That caused a stir. "Lord Abberley is not toffee-nosed," objected the woman with the green ribbon.

"He's a very nice man," agreed her companion.

"No airs and graces to him," said another woman. "And," she blushed, "he's very handsome."

"He can afford to be handsome," said the laborer. "Got the blunt to pay for it, and a valet to help him." He sounded the T at the end of the word valet. "Don't make him special, though, does it? If you ask me, he's lucky to have our Miss Catherine. Not the other way around."

There was a general murmur of agreement before Mrs. Green Ribbon asked, "you've not gone and become one of them whatchamacallits, have you? You know, them radicals?"

"No." The laborer bristled defensively. "I was just saying, that's all."

Mrs. Green Ribbon snorted in derision. "I was just saying," she mimicked. "Go and say it somewhere else, to people what are interested in 'earing you."

The laborer scowled at her, but he didn't try to argue. Eliza wasn't surprised. Mrs. Green Ribbon was almost his height and considerably stouter than he was, and she held her arm just so, with her fist curled in a manner that suggested she knew how to use it effectively.

"Although," said a tiny, birdlike woman in a brown dress, which she had adorned with a sprig of flowers, "I do wonder at the rightness of it. I mean, should Lord Abberley be getting married today at all?" Mrs. Green Ribbon glared at her, and the birdlike woman's voice faltered. She swallowed, hard. "That is," she said, and she looked around as if seeking support. Eliza saw that some of the people scowled at her; others wore blank faces. Nobody rushed to agree with her. "That is," she repeated, face pale and chin quivering, "Lord Hadlow was his friend, and he's hardly cold in the ground yet, and..." She shrugged and let her words tail off into the silence.

"They do it different to us," said the laborer.

"Don't be ridiculous," answered Mrs. Green Ribbon.

Fearing the two might come to blows soon, Eliza moved discreetly until she was a few feet away from them. The last thing she wanted was to become embroiled in a street fight.

"There's nothing to worry about on that score," said someone else, patting the nervous birdlike woman on the arm in a reassuring manner. "There was nothing old Bertie—I mean Lord Hadlow—liked more than a celebration. Why, I've heard that man could celebrate anything and everything. He once celebrated the fact that grass was green."

"That's right," said another person. "Lord Hadlow would have hated to think his friend had not celebrated his wedding because of him. In fact..." She chuckled. "...if there was any such thing as ghosts, ol' Bertie would be here, right in the thick of it."

"No, he wouldn't," argued the laborer. "Not unless the wedding was at Saint Simon and Saint Jude's in Crompton Hadlow." The women eyed him skeptically. "What?" he continued. "That's where he's buried. Everybody knows ghosts can't move from one place to another."

"Everybody knows no such thing," argued Mrs. Green Ribbon. "Since there are no such things as ghosts."

"Oh, but there are," said the birdlike woman. She

nodded emphatically. "Saint Simon and Saint Jude's is full of them. Most haunted church in Sussex, if you ask me."

"Bertie'll be happy there, then," said the laborer. "Plenty of souls to make up his parties."

"Poppycock!" said Mrs. Green Ribbon.

Shaking her head at the absurd turn the conversation had taken, Eliza moved further from the crowd. She slipped through the lych-gate and stood just inside the churchyard, half hidden in the shade of a yew tree. Here, she hoped, she would be able to see the bride as she left the church, without being too obtrusive.

A rattling of leaves startled her, and she turned sharply, then breathed a sigh of relief when she saw it was only Ned Fellowes. A young man of indeterminate age, Ned lived somewhere in the district, although Eliza had no idea where. He didn't seem to have any family and fended for himself, which was probably why he was so incredibly skinny, his arms and legs spindly, elbow, wrist, and ankle bones showing clear through his grubby skin. His cheeks were hollow and his eyes sunken, so that he looked more like a skeleton over which someone had stretched skin than an actual living person. His hair was cut into uneven clumps and his clothes, which were too small for him, were little better than rags. Eliza had the thought, no doubt brought on by the preposterous talk of ghosts, that Ned could well have been mistaken for a resident of this churchyard.

Shaking away the fanciful thought, she smiled at him. He hunched his shoulders and curled his spine, the way a dog would do if it feared a beating. His lack of trust saddened her. "It's all right, Ned," she said in her most soothing voice, "I won't hurt you."

He eyed her for a moment longer, then seemed to relax.

"Have you come to see Miss Ashton and her new husband?"

Ned's closed lips widened in a semblance of a smile. He peered at the church door.

"Stand by me, then, and we will see her together."

He took a step nearer to Eliza and purred like a cat. Seemingly unable to speak in actual words, Ned was a talented mimic, and his impressions of animal sounds had Eliza in awe of him.

"Here they come," said Mrs. Green Ribbon. Everybody turned to the church door.

There was a joyful peal of bells as the newlywed couple came out into the bright sunshine. Catherine looked resplendent in a gown of cerulean blue silk overlaid with a fine voile that made it shimmer. The hem was adorned with lace frills like those that also edged her bonnet. Fashioned in a deeper blue than the dress, the bonnet matched her high-waisted, long-sleeved Spencer. She carried a simple posy of countryside flowers in one hand, while her other hand was firmly placed in the crook of her new husband's arm, and both wore wide, happy grins that made Eliza sigh with longing and, she was ashamed to admit, a tinge of envy.

Which she had no business feeling at all. At six-and-twenty, Eliza had long ago accepted that the bridal path was not to be hers, and she had made her peace with that. Still, a woman could dream.

Beside her, Ned gave a soft whimper. Eliza glanced at him, and he smiled, showing badly cared-for teeth, some black, others broken. There were gaps where some teeth were missing completely.

"They are a lovely couple, are they not?" asked Eliza. Ned whimpered again, then resumed his purring. Eliza reached out cautiously, not wanting to scare him, and patted his arm. Knowing how skittish the boy could be, she felt ridiculously pleased that he let her do so. Then, she turned back to the wedding party, which was now emerging from the church behind the happy couple.

Immediately behind the newlyweds were the bride's parents. Mr. Ashton seemed to have grown several inches taller at the marriage of his only daughter into the nobility, and his head was held high with pride. Mrs. Ashton dabbed at her eyes with a lace handkerchief, then grinned broadly for the benefit of the spectators.

Behind them came the two bridal attendants. Both ladies wore empire-style dresses in soft gold, trimmed with silk flowers in the same blue as Catherine's gown. They wore dainty blue bonnets and long blue gloves, and looked so beautiful that Eliza could not help but look down at her own ensemble with dismay.

She wore a black dress made of stiff, uncomfortable bombazine, topped with an equally stiff black coat, fastened with large jet buttons. Her black bonnet was heavy on her head, and the heat of it made her hair itch. The uncomfortable outfit was the only set of mourning clothes she'd been able to afford when she decided on her persona for what she had hoped would be a short stay in Rotherton. In the winter months, when she had arrived here, these clothes had been eminently sensible. It had never occurred to her then that she might still be wearing them as summer started five months later.

How she longed to wear something lighter, both in material and in color. A pastel cotton perhaps, or sprigged muslin. She had dresses made of both packed away in paper in her trunk, but she could not wear them. One did not announce to everybody in the neighborhood that one was a grieving widow, and then cast off one's weeds before a respectable amount of time had passed. But, oh! how she wished she could.

The newlyweds came closer. Eliza took a step back, further into the shade of the yew tree. Beside her, Ned did the same. She smiled at him, but she knew, despite her best efforts, it was a sad smile. It went with the dull ache in her chest as she accepted her role: she was a widow who had never been, and never would be, a bride.

Once she had hoped to be. When she was a girl growing up in her father's vicarage, she dreamed of her wedding day. In those dreams, her groom had been tall and handsome, although his features were always undefined, waiting for her to draw them in when she met the right man. Her dress, likewise, had not been rigidly decided upon, and it changed each year with the pictures in *La Belle Assemblée*, the fashion magazine she and her sister pored over, getting pleasure from seeing the outfits even though they knew none of them would ever be theirs to wear.

But the wedding day itself—that Eliza had seen clearly. In her dream, it had always been a gloriously sunny day, like today, warm but with a hint of fresh breeze that blew the perfume of roses toward her. Full bloomed, red roses, that was, because Eliza's wedding day had always been planned for June. No other month had even been considered. As for the church, well, that had been similar to this one, for her father had held the living in a rural parish not unlike Rotherton.

Still, she thought now, there was no point in dwelling on it. Childhood dreams needed to be put away at some point. With a heavy sigh, she turned her attention back to the wedding party.

The bridesmaids left the church on the arms of two handsome and distinguished-looking gentlemen. One of those escorts was a viscount, Lord Fremont. Eliza understood him to be a colleague of the groom, but she had never met him. She only knew his name because she'd heard it whispered by the women who now stood at the church wall, clapping and cheering for all they were worth.

The other escort was known to her, although they had not actually been introduced. Mr. Finch was the second son of the Earl of Seaford, and the groom's closest friend. He had come to Rotherton a few weeks ago, with Lord Abberley and Lord Hadlow, ostensibly on a repairing lease following some disastrous results at the gaming tables in London. Although, since Lord Abberley had proved not to be a gambler after all, and had not even been in debt, Eliza found herself wondering whether Mr. Finch was in such dire straits as reported, either.

If he was, you certainly could not have known from the cut of his coat. Eliza didn't know much about gentlemen's fashion, but even she could see Mr. Finch was dressed impeccably, and the work of his tailor was of the highest quality. His dove-grey pantalons looked equally expensive, and fitted him as closely as a second skin, while his black boots shone like dark mirrors. Eliza had a disturbing vision of some poor servant sitting up half the night, just to create that deep shine for his master.

She frowned, wondering if the man actually had a valet. She knew he had brought no servants when he first arrived—none of the gentlemen in that party had brought anyone. In the weeks since, she had not seen or heard of anyone arriving, either, but he must have someone to do for him, surely? He would need an experienced gentleman's gentleman to achieve not only the shine on those boots but the perfect starching of his blindingly white cravat above his striking silver silk waistcoat, and the expert cut of his honey-colored hair into that carefully tousled style.

Eliza felt the prickle of a blush heat her cheeks as she realized she was taking altogether too much interest in the gentleman. The gentleman who, at this very instant, was showing an equally inappropriate interest in her. Their eyes met, his grey and fathomless, seeming to see right through her, able to know her every thought, her every feeling.

She swallowed hard at the idea. The way he grinned, she would swear he knew what she imagined. Nonplussed, she turned her head and made a show of watching the other guests, although, in reality, she saw none of them at all.

Which was why she was not prepared for the arrival of Miss Burgess.

In her early thirties, the curate's sister was just five feet tall, but she had a presence that made her seem much taller. She was slender and narrow-hipped, with straight shoulders and a way of holding her head that suggested a great deal of self-assurance. Her cheekbones were high and well defined, her eyes wide, and she could have been considered a beauty were it not for the expression she constantly wore, which indicated that the world, and everything in it, smelled rotten, and she was gamely trying not to take offence.

As she approached, Ned's purring changed to a low growl. Eliza turned, just in time to see him duck under the lower hanging branches of the yew tree, scramble over the churchyard wall and disappear.

"Was he bothering you?" asked Miss Burgess. She stopped three feet from Eliza and gave her a cursory bow. "He really is the outside of enough."

"Not at all," answered Eliza. She returned the bow.

"Somebody ought to take the boy in hand," continued Miss Burgess. "He is a nuisance. I spoke to Lord Rotherton about him, but you know how men can be." She shook her head, as if she despaired. "They never see the whole, do they? Of course they don't. The boy has committed no crime—that we know of—so his lordship will not curtail his freedoms. Never mind that he is an affront to decent people, or that he cannot properly look after himself. No, just let him run wild. That's his lordship's verdict for you." She rolled her eyes. "I ask you, did you ever hear the like?"

Eliza could see nothing wrong with Lord Rotherton's verdict, but all she said was, "He wasn't troubling me."

"You have a big heart, Mrs. Rawlins." Miss Burgess patted her arm. "It does you credit. But you should temper it with a little..." Miss Burgess wiggled the fingers on her free hand, as if trying to snatch at the word she wanted, "...wariness. We live in a sinful nation, amongst a people laden with iniquity, evildoers and corruptors who have forsaken the Lord."

Eliza gave a smile she hoped covered her feelings about that pronouncement. "We should pray for them," she said.

Miss Burgess nodded, enthusiastically, almost toppling her purple bonnet, and causing a few wisps of her white-blonde hair to escape its confines. "You are a good Christian woman, Mrs. Rawlins. I knew that about you the moment we were introduced. But then, I always say we become that which surrounds us in our formative years. With a father and two brothers who are men of the cloth, to say nothing of your dear, sainted husband—how you must miss him."

Elizabeth cleared her throat and let that be her answer.

"They make a lovely couple, don't you agree?" Miss Burgess watched as Catherine and Lord Abberley moved past them, toward the lych-gate and their carriage, which had just pulled up there. The rest of the wedding party followed in their wake, smiling and laughing, cheering and calling out felicitations. A few ribald comments came from the crowd of well-wishers at the churchyard wall, along with shocked admonishments to behave from some of the women there.

"Yes, they do," Eliza agreed with Miss Burgess's pronouncement.

"I had my doubts at first. A gambler can make a wife miserable, and leopards find it difficult to change their spots. However, I am assured that I was mistaken in his character. Although, he should take care." Her lips became even more pinched and she sniffed for good measure as she watched the two gentlemen escorting the bridesmaids. "When a man lies down with dogs, he will get up with fleas, as the saying goes." She nodded, as if agreeing with her own sentiments, then sighed and curved her lips in a semblance of a smile. "But, my dear, why are you here in the shadows? Come closer and you will see much more of the wedding. Miss Ashton—Lady Abberley," she corrected herself, "is a picture of radiance, is she not?" As she said this, Miss Burgess took

Eliza's arm in her surprisingly strong grip and drew her out into the sunshine. Eliza could not pull back without creating a scene, so she let herself be moved onto the path and into the midst of the wedding-goers, whose colorful clothes and pretty jewels left her feeling dowdier than ever in her widow's weeds.

She stood behind the bridesmaids and watched the happy couple go through the lych-gate. Holding on to the arm of the shorter bridesmaid, Mr. Finch half turned, made sure to catch Eliza's eye and winked mischievously at her. She felt the heat of a blush in her cheeks, and the infuriating man grinned. Eliza glowered at him in a way she hoped showed disapproval and discouragement, then made a show of turning her attention back to the newlyweds.

Mr. Finch chuckled. Lord Abberley may not have been the rake and wastrel he had originally portrayed, thought Eliza, but his friend, Mr. Finch, most definitely was. She determined to ignore him.

Lord Abberley handed his new wife into the carriage. She paused on the top step, looked around the crowd on the churchyard path, saw her bridesmaids, and threw her wedding flowers toward them. The two gentlemen stepped sharply away, as if both were terrified of being touched by the bridal bouquet. More surprisingly, the taller of the two bridesmaids also moved out of its way, leaving the shorter lady, Miss Potter, to reach up for it.

However, Lady Abberley had thrown the bouquet too high and Miss Potter could never have reached it, even had she been able to jump like a horse at a hedge. It sailed right over her stretched arm and grasping fingers before beginning its descent, coming down at just the right angle to land squarely against Eliza's chest. Instinctively, she raised her free hand, the one not held by Miss Burgess, and caught the bouquet.

The crowd cheered and applauded. Even Miss Potter clapped congratulations.

"Well caught, Mrs. Rawlins," called Mr. Ashton, and others echoed his words.

"You'll be next then," said somebody else.

Miss Burgess squeezed Eliza's arm. "Superstitious nonsense, of course," she whispered. "But they are pretty flowers."

"And not mine." Eliza's murmured reply was filled with her embarrassment. She was not a wedding guest, just an interloper, and she had no right to this bouquet. She offered them to Miss Burgess, the nearest unmarried *invited* guest.

"Oh no, they are not for me." Miss Burgess grinned, and it transformed her face. It surprised Eliza to see she really was a very pretty woman when she wasn't scowling and pinching her lips.

"But they should go to a guest."

Miss Burgess shook her head. "Not only did I not catch the flowers, but they would be wasted on me, even if I had. The whole point of the ritual is to make people think they know who will next be a bride. In which case, it would disappoint them to see me catch them."

"But—"

"They know, and I know, that I will never be a bride. I accepted that fact a long time ago."

"Surely—"

"In truth, I am happy about it. I am married to my faith. No man could match that. Besides, everyone saw you catch them. Therefore, the flowers, and the superstition that goes with them, are yours."

"It is not seemly for me to keep them when I am not even a guest." To say nothing of the fact that she was a plain woman of six-and-twenty, who had realized long ago that she would never succeed in the marriage market, and who was, to boot, wearing widow's weeds, which of themselves meant she could not encourage the advances of any eligible man anyway.

"Nonsense!" The voice from behind her startled Eliza. She turned, then made her curtsy to Mrs. Ashton, the mother of the bride, who smiled benignly at her. "You caught the flowers, fairly and squarely, my dear," said the lady. "You must keep them." She leaned forward and added, conspiratorially, "I wouldn't worry too much about all that next-to-marry flummery, if that's what concerns you."

"Quite so," agreed Miss Burgess. "Stuff and nonsense, as I was just telling Eliza." She turned to Eliza and tittered. "I may call you 'Eliza,' I hope? We have been friends for some time now, and 'Mrs. Rawlins' seems so formal."

Eliza opened her mouth, could not think of anything to say, closed it again, and gave one short, noncommittal nod.

"And you shall call me Prudence. We shall be Bosom Belles from this time on."

Eliza frowned. That was, surely, not a correct phrase.

Mrs. Ashton raised an eyebrow. "Surely," she said, "it is Bosom Bows?"

Miss Burgess—Prudence—sniffed. "Not if you speak French. *Beaux* are gentlemen. *Belles* are ladies."

"But surely, it doesn't mean 'beaux' as in…" began

Mrs. Ashton.

She was cut off by Prudence, who gave her a smile that could only be described as smug. "I was educated beyond the scope of most ladies. So I know these things, whereas others, only versed in the usual, empty pastimes such as watercolors and dancing, cannot be expected to do so."

Eliza closed her eyes for a moment, shocked at the woman's rudeness.

"I see," was Mrs. Ashton's frosty reply.

"Thank you for allowing me to keep the flowers, ma'am," said Eliza, more to change the subject than because she was genuinely grateful. Although, she had to admit, the blooms would look nice in a jug on her parlor table, and they would certainly brighten that rather austere room.

"You are more than welcome." Mrs. Ashton's smile became genuine again. "And you never know your luck. They may work their magic for you after all, and guide you to another husband. I think your mourning period must be reaching its end soon?"

Eliza smiled vaguely and said nothing. According to what she had told her new neighbors about her husband's demise, she should have been out of full mourning some time ago, moving into half mourning and exchanging the black bombazine for more comfortable dresses in lavender, grey, and other muted colors. Which, considering the heat of this day and the threat of more warmth in the oncoming summer, might not be a bad idea.

Prudence pursed her lips. "We should be careful not to encourage too much belief in superstition," she said.

The twinkle in Mrs. Ashton's eye was decidedly

naughty as she replied, "Not even a lovely superstition such as this one?" She glanced at Eliza and actually winked. Eliza fought down the answering chuckle, though her lips did twitch into a small smile.

Prudence did not see the funny side of it. "Refuse profane and old wives' fables, and exercise thyself rather unto godliness," she quoted.

Mrs. Ashton's demeanor grew icy. She glared at Prudence for a few seconds, before answering, "As you say." She turned back to Eliza. "Nevertheless, Mrs. Rawlins, I would like to think you will soon find yourself in company with the special person who holds your heart."

"On that we can agree," said Prudence, her grin signaling a truce in their hostilities. "I, too, would like to think that person is out there, waiting for you."

Eliza prayed they were right. Although both these ladies might be shocked to discover the 'special person' they wished she'd find was not somebody she could marry. It wasn't even a man. But, in her search for Claire, Eliza would accept every wish and prayer she could get.

****

Who was she? Freddy could not help but be distracted by the woman in the severe black coat. Several times, over the past few months, he had seen the young widow walking through Rotherton and the wider district, though never anywhere he might engineer an introduction. But, he had to admit, each time he'd seen her, she had left quite an impression upon him. There was just something about her that drew him in.

It wasn't her looks. Oh, she was not unattractive. But she wasn't an outstanding beauty, either. Her nose was too long and thin for her face, and her lips were too narrow. Her hair, what he could see of it under that awful black bonnet, was a nondescript brown with curls and waves which must be natural, for no lady would deliberately give her hair such abundance of life. She was tall, although not freakishly so—if he had to guess, he would say about five and a half feet, although, because she was slender almost to the point of gauntness, she seemed taller. He had no idea whether her figure was androgynously straight under that heavy coat or whether she had feminine curves, so it could not be her shape that drew him.

It was probably her eyes. Big and almond-shaped, with long dark lashes, their irises were an arresting light blue, surrounded by a narrow rim of indigo. They could easily trap the unwary and hold them in thrall. Yet there was more to those eyes than just their hypnotic beauty. They held humor and intelligence, too. A man could stare into them forever and never grow tired of it.

Hark at him! Freddy looked around quickly and was relieved none of his friends seemed to have caught him staring at her. He didn't want to have to explain his interest to anybody else, especially when he could not really explain it to himself.

He glanced at Fremont. His fellow groomsman was more usually to be found in London, where he held some shadowy post in the government machine. Charged with keeping king and country safe, Fremont recruited retired military men like Freddy and Adam for his secret missions. Fremont missed little, so if anybody saw Freddy's interest in the widow, it would be him.

Nothing about Fremont said he had noticed anything worthy of comment, although that didn't mean he had not seen the way Freddy watched her, and simply decided it was unimportant. After all, both men knew any attraction Freddy felt for her was unlikely to lead to anything. Unlike the widows he knew in London, this lady did not look as if she would welcome a dalliance. There was an air of innocence about her, something in her demeanor that was almost virginal. If he hadn't heard she was a widow, he would have thought her a maiden, and one who had never been kissed, at that. Nothing about her suggested his flirting would be welcome.

Even so, he had been unable to refrain from giving her a saucy wink today. There she'd stood, trying to blend in with the shadows, while all around her brightly dressed people basked in the sunshine. She had looked so wistful, and he'd felt a need to cheer her up, to let her know he saw her, even if nobody else did and, what was more, he liked what he saw.

He'd been emboldened when he caught her watching him. She looked as if she'd been appraising him, and he found he wanted her to approve of him. In hindsight, a wink was perhaps not the best way to gain her approval, although he fancied he'd seen the ghost of a smile as she blushed and turned away. And God knew, the woman needed something to smile about, after being accosted by Miss Burgess. Even Ned Fellowes had had the horse sense to make himself scarce as *that* woman approached. Not that the widow could have followed Ned's lead—she would not have looked particularly elegant, scrambling over the dry-stone wall that bordered the churchyard. The image that conjured made him smile.

"It is good to see our friends so happy, is it not?" asked the bridesmaid on his arm. Miss Potter was petite, so petite that Freddy, almost six feet tall, had to bend to talk with her. She was also, he guessed, exceedingly shy, since those were the first words she'd voluntarily spoken to him since they'd been introduced at dinner two nights ago. She blushed and averted her eyes as she continued, "I am glad you, too, are happy for them. I know sometimes gentlemen profess to pity their friends for..." she blushed again, "entering Parson's mousetrap. Isn't that the term you use?"

Ah. She had seen him smile and thought it was because of Adam and Catherine. He would not disabuse her. "It is," he answered. "Although, between you and me, once they meet the right lady, most gentlemen do not mind being caught as much as they say they do." A shadow passed across the young woman's face and he wondered whether she'd had her hopes dashed by some unworthy suitor. He hoped not. She was still very young, hardly out of her schoolroom, and it would be a pity for her to become jaded before she had the chance to taste life properly.

They lapsed into silence once more.

Freddy glanced at the widow again, talking now with Catherine's mother, smiling at something Mrs. Ashton said, and cradling the bridal bouquet in the crook of one arm. The colorful flowers relieved the darkness of her clothing and enhanced her natural charms. He wished he could march over now and ask Mrs. Ashton to introduce them. Then he could get to know her, learn about her...

For what reason? What possible good would it do to be introduced to her now? Besides, it would be unforgivably rude to abandon Miss Potter and embroil both ladies in a scandal that would dog them for months, if not years. He wouldn't even be here to help them weather the storm he caused. With the smugglers caught, his job here was complete. Now, Freddy would leave for London, probably never to return. Which meant, before long, the pretty widow of Rotherton would be no more than a pleasant memory.

Reminding himself of that, he turned away, resolved to leave the woman in peace.

Chapter Two

After talking with Mrs. Ashton for a minute or so more, Eliza made to leave the churchyard. The happy couple had gone, and other carriages were being summoned to transport the wedding guests to the breakfast, which was to be held at the Ashton estate. Those still waiting for their vehicles mingled and chatted in small groups, while the villagers drifted away. Eliza planned to go back to her cottage, take a dish of tea, and reflect quietly on the morning.

Prudence, however, had not finished with her. "I have the perfect solution to the dilemma," she announced in that forceful way only a clergyman's female relatives seemed able to adopt. "Eliza is uneasy about taking the bouquet, which she caught and *should* keep. That uneasiness stems from the fact she is not an invited guest of the wedding. So, there is a simple answer, is there not?"

Mrs. Ashton looked blank, her expression mirroring the one Eliza was sure she wore.

Prudence's smile widened, and she nodded, clearly pleased with herself. "You could invite her."

Eliza gasped, horrified at the woman's rudeness. Mrs. Ashton's smile slipped, and her eyebrow raised, although almost immediately, she set her face to benign neutrality once more.

"I persuade myself it would be no hardship to bring

Eliza to the breakfast," continued Prudence, apparently oblivious to the reactions she had garnered. "She *did* catch the flowers. Is that not a sign from God that He wishes her to be part of this?"

Eliza's cheeks burned and tears of embarrassment and humiliation pricked the backs of her eyes. She hoped Mrs. Ashton did not think she had encouraged Prudence in any way.

That poor woman was now placed in an impossible situation, for if she said no, she would insult Eliza, and must wonder if bad feeling would ensue. *Eliza* knew she would feel no ill toward Catherine's mother, but Mrs. Ashton could not know that. Besides, she suspected Prudence would be offended on her behalf, and she was certain Prudence's offence could be an enormous obstacle to have to overcome.

On the other hand, if Mrs. Ashton said yes, she risked making chaos of her carefully planned catering arrangements, causing the seating to be uneven and heating the tempers of harried staff.

Since Mrs. Ashton could not easily solve this problem without upsetting somebody, Eliza would do it for her. She pasted on an apologetic smile. "I am afraid I cannot. I have other things which I must do today."

For the briefest of instants, Mrs. Ashton looked relieved. Then she smiled and said, "I wish you would come. It would be an honor to have you." Her tone was so convincing, Eliza might have believed it if she didn't already know better.

"You are very kind, ma'am," she replied. "But, alas, I truly do have other things I must do. Besides," she indicated her heavy black clothes, "I am not dressed for a wedding."

"That is not an insurmountable obstacle," argued Prudence. She clutched her fingers together in front of her waist, the picture of pious propriety. "With God, all things are possible."

Slightly to the side of Prudence, and momentarily out of her sight line, Mrs. Ashton rolled her eyes. Eliza bit her lip and looked down to avoid laughing.

Prudence continued, "If we put some flowers in your hair, and…" She thought for a moment, her index finger tapping at her top lip. "A shawl! You may borrow my shawl. It is lavender-colored, so still in keeping with your mourning, and yet it will take away the darkness of your dress."

"I have an amethyst brooch to hold it in place," agreed Mrs. Ashton, surprising Eliza with her sudden enthusiasm. "I absolutely insist you come, my dear," she continued. "I will not hear a word of your refusal. In fact, I am certain I did send you an invitation when I put out all the others." She nodded, agreeing with herself. "Yes. I recall now. I was not sure if you were out of full mourning yet and did not want to torment you with an invitation you could not accept, so I kept it back until I could ask you. Now, though, it is several months since Mr. Rawlins' unfortunate demise. You are surely able to move to half-mourning? Which, of course, means you may rejoin Society. Oh, I do not say you should go to a ball or a rout, of course. But we hardly anticipate any such thing today." She chuckled.

Eliza was tempted. She would dearly love to go and mingle with the other guests. She knew few people in this neighborhood yet, thanks to the isolation of bereavement. It would be nice, finally, to laugh and smile and talk with people other than her maid. As well as which, it must surely be of benefit in her search for Claire to meet people, observe them, listen to them and, perhaps, even subtly question them.

She did not resist when Prudence shoved her arm through Eliza's and grinned. "There. That is settled," said the curate's sister. "I knew there would be a solution. If God wishes something to happen, he always finds the way. My brother and I can take you in our vehicle. To be sure, it is not the grandest vehicle here, but it is comfortable and well appointed, and will easily carry three of us." She giggled. "I am so glad Mrs. Ashton invited you."

She led Eliza along the churchyard path in such a way that Eliza could not stop, or even slow down, without causing a scene. Eliza glanced quickly back at Mrs. Ashton, and hoped her expression adequately conveyed her apology to that lady. It must have done so, for Mrs. Ashton's answering smile was warm, and genuine. It even reached her eyes.

"Not dressed for a wedding, indeed! Utter garbage," said Prudence. "The color is, obviously, not what one would usually wear to such an occasion, but we have taken care of that. And it hardly matters, for you look so elegant in it." She giggled again, a high-pitched noise which made Eliza cringe. "I should dislike you for that alone, you know. You are always so effortlessly elegant."

"Thank you." It was all Eliza could think to say. Not that she needed to say anything, for Prudence continued, showing that she needed no answers.

"All your concerns being met, shall we join my brother? I see he is already at his vehicle. He will not like to keep his horse standing for long."

The curate's vehicle was a surprise. Eliza's father,

who had been vicar in a rural area not unlike Rotherton, had driven a gig, small and light and easy to handle, with a seat just big enough for two people. Such a vehicle was inexpensive to buy and maintain, and ideal for a man of limited finances, such as a country clergyman. Eliza had, therefore, expected Mr. Burgess to drive something similar, and she was taken aback to see him beside a Berlin phaeton, its body painted a deep, gleaming red, which was echoed on the wheel spokes. It had a black leather hood that was presently folded back, concertina style, to allow the driver and his passengers to take in the sunshine and fresh air.

It was roomy, too. Eliza had dreaded the ride, thinking that three adults would be a squeeze in a clergyman's cart, but the seat in this vehicle was wide enough to fit them all comfortably.

"Come along, dear sister," Mr. Burgess chided Prudence. "We do not want to keep everyone waiting. They all want their breakfast and they cannot eat until I have blessed the food."

"Silas," Prudence replied, completely ignoring what he had said. "This is my friend, Mrs. Rawlins."

"Yes, I know. We have met at the church porch on many a Sunday." He bowed, politely. "How do you, Mrs. Rawlins?"

Eliza curtsied to him. "I am well, sir. And you?"

Before he could reply, his sister interrupted. "I have told Mrs. Rawlins—Eliza—that we will take her to the Ashtons'. I was sure you would not mind."

Mr. Burgess frowned. "Of course I don't mind. I didn't know you were invited, Mrs. Rawlins. That is, I didn't see you in the church."

"A misunderstanding." Prudence dismissed the

topic. "Are you going to help us into the vehicle, or do we clamber up by ourselves?"

"What? Oh, of course. My apologies." Mr. Burgess held out his hand and helped first his sister, then Eliza, up to the seat, which was beautifully upholstered in red leather, the same shade as the outer woodwork. Once they were seated, he moved to the driver's side, climbed in, and fidgeted to make himself comfortable, which made Eliza and Prudence jolt and bounce. Eliza gripped the side rail in a vain attempt to keep from crushing into Prudence.

"Silas!" Prudence was clearly losing patience with her brother now.

"I have to be comfortable before I drive," he said, and he unwound the reins and set off at a sedate pace, restricted by the slowness of the carriage in front.

"Yes, you do," said Prudence. "But you don't have to send us flying out of our seats. Poor Eliza and I nearly ended sprawled in the dirt with our clothes ruined and our limbs on display."

Silas Burgess eyed his sister, appalled. "I don't feel there's any call for lewd remarks." He leaned forward and spoke directly at his horse. "On you go, Balaam." The horse maintained its steady plod. Mr. Burgess then peered around his sister to bestow a friendly smile on Eliza. The man looked very much like his sister, slight and bony, but his smile rose more readily and the crinkles around his eyes suggested he found good humor more easily than Prudence did. "Are you comfortable, Mrs. Rawlins?" he asked.

She nodded and thanked him.

"Good, good. I chose this vehicle expressly for the comfort of the seat. If one is out and about, in all weathers, at all times of the day or night, one should not also be dealing with aches and pains in unmentionable places."

Eliza nodded again, unsure how to respond. It wasn't the sort of conversation she expected from a clergyman, especially one she barely knew.

"I expect your husband made the same complaint. And your father. Am I right, he was also a man of the cloth?"

"He was." Papa had retired now, although that was not what she had told her new neighbors. She hadn't exactly lied to them, she told herself, trying, vainly, to assuage her conscience. But when they assumed her parents were dead, she had not corrected them, for they would have wondered why, if he still lived, she hadn't returned to him when her husband died. That wasn't a question she could easily answer without making known her search for Claire, something she did not wish to do yet.

"He had his own vehicle, a little dog cart," she continued to answer the reverend's question. "Nothing as beautiful as this," she went on. The curate beamed, clearly proud of his conveyance.

Briefly, she did wonder how he had come to have it, though. A clergyman's living was not well paid, and certainly Papa could never have afforded anything this grand. But then, for all she knew, the Burgesses came from a moneyed family and had no need of anything but the basic stipend. Many clergymen were the second and third sons of nobility and gentry, the "spares," whose families saw either the church or the army as a perfect place for them.

As if she had asked her questions aloud, Mr. Burgess

answered them. "I daresay you wonder how a man such as I can afford this beautiful phaeton on my less-than-generous stipend?" He smiled. "Let me put your thoughts at rest. I have not been raiding the poor box." He chuckled. "It was a gift from an anonymous benefactor. Someone whose life was changed by one of my sermons." His grin broadened. "Knowing that he found the narrow path through what I said is, of course, the true reward for my efforts, but I am human, and flawed enough to admit, I am very grateful for this token of appreciation as well."

"Let's keep the token of appreciation on the highway, shall we?" Prudence reached out and touched her brother's hand, steering him away from the pavement, where a pedestrian scrambled out of his way.

Silas Burgess waved an apology at the man. "It is a beautiful day, is it not?"

"Indeed it is, sir." Eliza smiled. "But then, do they not say the sun always shines on the righteous?"

He nodded and smiled.

Prudence pursed her lips. "A frequent misconception. One I am astounded you would make, dear Eliza."

"I'm sure Mrs. Rawlins was simply quoting common parlance," her brother defended.

"It is our duty to ensure Biblical quotes are used correctly. The verse is, 'He maketh the sun to rise on the evil and on the good, and he doth rain on the just and the unjust.'"

"My apologies." Eliza felt like a naughty schoolgirl at the headmistress's door.

"Think nothing of it." Mr. Burgess frowned at his sister, then corrected the direction of his vehicle once again. Eliza gripped the side rail and thanked God they were moving so slowly.

The Ashtons' home was large, although not ostentatiously so, well kept, and old. Eliza guessed it was built in the seventeenth century, before the introduction of the window tax, judging by the number of embrasures that had been bricked up. Even so, it still boasted a fair number of windows, and a forest of chimneys on the roof. The large wooden entrance doors stood open, and several servants waited there, ready to welcome guests and take their coats and hats.

No expense had been spared for Catherine's wedding. Over the next hours, the guests were treated to a wonderful breakfast of freshly baked bread and hot rolls, buttered toast, selections of tongue, ham and eggs, salmon, beef, lamb, trout and cod, as well as oysters and lobster, pork pies and chicken. After the meat courses were taken back to the kitchens, there were generous portions of fruit cake, shortbread biscuits and marchpane balls, together with syllabub, gooseberry fool, and even ice cream. It was all washed down with wine and brandy for the gentlemen, Madeira for the older ladies, and orgeat for the children and nondrinkers among them.

More than once, Mr. Burgess reached for a glass of wine, glanced sideways at his sister, saw her pinch-faced look and picked up orgeat instead, then grimaced at each sip. Eliza sympathized. She did not drink alcohol herself, but she loathed orgeat, and found its sickly sweetness nauseating. So she smiled at a footman and whispered, "I don't suppose I might have a cup of tea instead, please?" He returned her smile with a kind one of his own, bowed and turned to fetch it for her.

"I'll have the same," decided Prudence. The

footman bowed his head in acknowledgement.

Finally, after everybody had been fed to the point of discomfort, two servants carried in a massive, three-tiered cake, each tier covered in pristine white icing, sugar flowers and leaves, each of which must have taken a steady hand and eye, and a lot of time. It was worth it though, if the gasps of delight from the appreciative crowd were anything to go by.

The top tier was soon sliced into portions for everybody present, while the rest was taken back to the kitchens, where it would be cut and parceled and sent to friends and family who had been unable to attend.

Once the cake was consumed and the toasts made, the bride and groom took their leave. They planned to go north to the groom's estate for a few weeks, after which they would travel to France and Italy on what sounded like a perfect honeymoon trip. Eliza stood with the crowd at the door, waving and wishing them well, and she sent up a silent prayer that they would always be as happy as they were today.

Many guests, especially those who needed to travel some distance to their homes, took the couple's departure as their own cue to leave. Eliza fully expected she would also go home now, but she could not leave without Prudence and her brother, and they seemed to be in no hurry to depart.

"Shall we take advantage of this lovely day and stroll through the gardens?" Prudence phrased it as a question, although it really wasn't. Other people were already outside, wandering around in twos and threes, or gathering in small groups on the lawns. Mr. Burgess soon found a knot of gentlemen he could converse with, and Prudence and Eliza strolled on without him.

The gardens were certainly enjoyable. A sandstone path wound its way past carefully shaped lawns on which were statues on plinths, ornate sundials, even a fountain. Here and there, colorful flower beds boasted Allium Gigantium, and Bearded Iris, purple and yellow pansies, and red poppies, blue Jacob's Ladder and pink sweet peas. The hedgerow flowers and the curved paths gave the gardens a carefree, natural appearance, and the floral scents mingled, perfuming the air and attracting honeybees, which droned sonorously.

Beyond the gardens was a park, and a wooded area which provided welcome shade. It was here that Prudence and Eliza strolled, where the leaves dappled the light and birds sang to one another from their hiding places in the canopy.

"It really has been the most pleasant of days," said Prudence, as they turned another corner, "made even better by being in company with someone of like mind to myself. All too often, people who show promise as friends prove disappointing once one gets to know them more fully."

Eliza had no answer.

"Whereas you... I feel we shall become bosom belles."

Eliza examined the bark of the nearest tree, softly running her gloved finger across it. It saved her from replying. Not that Prudence seemed to need a reply.

"Elizabeth." The curate's sister said the word as if she was tasting it. "I wanted to be called Elizabeth when I was a child. Such a pretty name. You should wear it more proudly, you know. Not diminish it to Eliza."

"I do not. Eliza is my name."

"I do so hate abbreviations," continued Prudence, as

if Eliza had not spoken. "If the Lord led your parents to call you by a name, it should be honored in its fullness."

Eliza smiled with her lips, though her teeth were gritted behind it. "My parents called me Eliza." She worked hard to keep the irritation from sounding in her voice. "They did not call me Elizabeth."

Prudence raised her eyebrows in surprise. "Truly? You are baptized Eliza?"

"I am."

"Oh." Prudence took a moment to assimilate that information. "I daresay they had their reasons."

"I daresay they did." Eliza turned away and made a show of inspecting the convolvulus, which had somehow escaped the gardener's notice.

"Your parents are not with us anymore, are they?"

My father is, although he lives a long way from here, in the parish of my oldest brother, but my mother has gone to her reward.

At those thoughts, Eliza felt a sharp pain, as if somebody had grabbed at her heart, twisted it and squeezed it cruelly. It had been seven years since Mama's death, but the loss still hit hard. It pained her even more to pretend she no longer had her father either, and she offered a quick arrow prayer for his safekeeping, as if allowing people to believe him dead was tempting fate and needed to be warded off. It was a terrible lie, she knew, but, she told herself, it was for the greater good, and Papa would understand. Besides, it was not forever. Once she had Claire safe and well, Eliza would see the truth told.

"Of course they are not." Prudence spoke and it took a few seconds for Eliza to work out that she was answering her own question about whether Eliza's parents were still alive. "Forgive me," said the curate's sister, with a small smile. "Where are my wits? If your parents were still here with us, you would not be in Rotherton, with not even a companion to give you countenance, would you?"

Eliza said nothing and let Prudence jump to her conclusions.

Chapter Three

Freddy had steered clear of Lord Fremont throughout the wedding festivities. The man was supposedly here to support Adam, and he'd been an admirable groomsman, attentive to every detail of his duties, but Freddy had his doubts. He didn't think Adam knew the viscount well enough to ask him to stand up at his wedding.

His suspicions were confirmed just before Adam and Catherine left for their honeymoon. Adam drew Freddy aside, under the pretense of lighthearted banter, and then murmured, "Watch yourself, my friend. I think Fremont has something for you."

Freddy groaned inwardly. They had only just finished mopping up after their last assignment. He'd hoped for a week or two of respite before plunging back into the murky waters of government work.

"He turned up late last night and asked to be included in the wedding party," Adam continued. "Luckily, Catherine takes things in her stride. Although," he grinned, "she did warn him that if he intended to send me somewhere during my honeymoon, he might put his own affairs in order first."

Freddy laughed. "I like your bride."

"He assured her he has no plans for me. Which leaves you."

"No rest for the wicked." Freddy slapped Adam's

back. "Enjoy your wedding trip."

Along with the other guests, Freddy watched the couple leave. After they had gone, he found himself caught in conversation with Mr. Ashton, followed by a talk with Mr. Potter, then various other guests. All the time, though, he was conscious of Fremont standing nearby, waiting for him.

Finally, Freddy turned to Fremont, who indicated they should walk in the gardens. They strolled along the paths toward the park, their appearance that of two friends enjoying the sunshine.

"I want to congratulate you," said Fremont. "You and Abberley did a good job of rooting out the vermin infesting this area."

"Thank you." Freddy tensed, knowing Fremont's congratulations were never the final word.

"There is more to it than simply catching rats that one can see, though. One must also starve the hidden nest of nutrition. Deprive them of the things they need, so the whole infestation dies."

Freddy sighed and nodded. "Where is the infestation you wish me to deal with now?"

"Here."

"Here? But I thought…I thought we caught all the—rats that were here."

"You did."

They walked a few yards in silence. Fremont looked around as if admiring Ashton's estate, although Freddy knew he was really checking that they were alone. What he had to say next was obviously going to be said plainly, with no euphemisms employed, so it was imperative that there were no eavesdroppers.

Once he was satisfied that nobody lurked in the

flower beds, Fremont said, "You caught the local ringleaders. We believe there are others, elsewhere, people higher up the chain. But we are satisfied there's no more treason in this area."

"Then what am I looking for?"

"Gold."

Freddy's eyes widened. "Gold?"

Fremont nodded. "Specifically, the chest of it that was delivered last month."

The Bonapartists had taken delivery of a chest of gold, which they intended to send to France to help pay for an army loyal to the former emperor. They'd been thwarted, but the chest had disappeared.

"We looked for it," said Freddy. "But..." He shrugged.

"You didn't find it."

"We were thorough." It irked Freddy that he sounded so defensive.

"It has to be somewhere. Chests full of coin do not vanish into thin air." Fremont gave a long-suffering sigh. "Most of the traitors were killed or arrested, but there are always more. And if they can retrieve that gold... We cannot allow it. I need you to find it."

Freddy gave Fremont a sidelong look. "If it's still here."

"It can't be anywhere else. We had men watching the roads. They saw it brought in and waited to see where it was taken. It never came out. Ergo, it must still be here." He took out his fob watch and checked the time. "It's gone three already. I hoped to be back in London tonight. If I leave now, I might still make it."

"Not before dark, you won't."

Fremont grinned. "Worried I might fall prey to

highwaymen?"

"Only if they are stupid."

That made Fremont laugh, briefly, before he frowned and said, "Find that gold, Finch."

Freddy nodded, though he took the job reluctantly. He and Adam had searched Hadlow Hall, where, supposedly, it had been delivered, and they hadn't found a single coin. Looking again would not make it reappear. Besides, Freddy did not enjoy the country. He much preferred the hustle and bustle of the city where there was an abundance of life and activity, varied entertainments and delectable company. He wanted to go home.

"Wouldn't you be more likely to succeed with someone local?" There had to be someone. Fremont must have a whole network of spies, the length and breadth of the country. Probably in other countries too. And a local man would know of hiding places Freddy could not begin to imagine.

"I don't have anyone else," said Fremont. He glanced at Freddy and smiled. "You don't believe me. But it's true. I keep my operation small. Secrets lose their secrecy much more easily if too many are party to them. So you're it, I'm afraid."

"I don't have anywhere to stay after tonight." Freddy had paid his shot at the Golden Goose that morning, telling the landlord he would stay one more night, then move on. There was no plausible reason for him to change his mind without raising suspicions. The landlord knew Freddy had only stayed in the area as long as he had because Adam was about to wed, and because Lord Rotherton, the local magistrate, had investigated the apprehension of the traitors and had required all involved to remain here while he did so. But now, the enquiries were finished and the wedding was over.

Nor could he go to Hadlow Hall, where he had originally been. Lord Hadlow, his erstwhile host, had been killed fighting the traitors, and the house was now shut up, pending the arrival of his heir.

"All arranged, dear boy." Fremont gave a dismissive wave of his hand. Freddy gritted his teeth against the irritation of being called "boy" by a man who was no more than five years his senior. "Rotherton has offered to put you up. You accepted his gracious invitation just this morning. Looking forward to a couple of weeks' fishing, I believe. And grateful for the opportunity. After all, you still need to avoid the duns in Town, do you not, dear chap?"

Freddy groaned. "Is this assignment never going to end?"

"Yes. When we find the gold."

Freddy sighed heavily. "I'll begin a new search tomorrow."

He watched Fremont leave, then started back to the house. He should find Lord Rotherton and thank him for his kind invitation. And perhaps apologize for Fremont's imposition on the man.

Not for the first time, he wondered just how much Rotherton knew of their work. The earl gave off an air of insouciance and acted as if every duty was an annoying interference to his pursuit of pleasure, but his eyes were bright with intelligence, and Freddy didn't think he missed much.

He was halfway across the garden when he heard someone call him. He turned and saw Miss Burgess wave at him. "Yoo-hoo, Mr. Finch," she called again. She even smiled, something he could not recall having seen her do before. Miss Burgess always seemed far too taken up in her pursuit of heaven to have reason to smile at people here on earth. Perhaps, he thought, she'd had a glass of Madeira and it had gone to her head. Immediately, he chastised himself for his lack of charity.

The usually dour spinster held the elbow of the widow from the churchyard, and pulled her toward him. It seemed, he thought with some satisfaction, he was about to be given an introduction to her after all. Although, he was also surprised. He hadn't realized she was a guest. He had thought her merely an onlooker, standing with the villagers at the lych-gate. She certainly wasn't dressed to attend a wedding.

She also did not look happy to be dragged toward him. Freddy swallowed down the hurt he felt at that and wondered why she seemed reluctant to meet him. Had she heard stories that gave her a disgust of him? He hoped not, though there were plenty to be heard, thanks to Fremont.

Perhaps it was simply that she was more aware of protocol than her friend. After all, it really wasn't done to shout across a garden to a gentleman in the way Miss Burgess had just done. But then, if she had been tippling at the wine… But, since she was about to introduce him to the striking widow of Rotherton High Street, he could forgive her a few *faux pas*.

He smiled and waited for them to catch up to him. Miss Burgess breathed heavily, and her cheeks were pink with her exertion. By contrast, her friend's cheeks were a bright red, making her blue eyes brighter and enhancing the prettiness of her features.

"My, Mr. Finch, you do walk so fast. Not all of us

have such long legs as you," admonished Miss Burgess.

"I do beg your pardon."

"No matter. Have you enjoyed the day?"

"I have, I thank you. Have you?"

"Immeasurably. Not least because I was able to spend it in cozy conversation with my dear friend Eliza. Mrs. Rawlins," she corrected herself. "May I make you known to her?"

He said nothing would give him greater pleasure, and she effected the introduction he had wished for earlier. Mrs. Rawlins looked less than comfortable as Miss Burgess told him the woman was the daughter of an esteemed, though sadly departed, clergyman, and that she had recently lost her equally esteemed husband, another clergyman.

"I am sorry to hear of his passing," said Freddy, with a slight bow of his head.

"Thank you." Her voice was deeper than he expected, and husky. If it had been a color, he thought, it would have been a deep, rich chestnut.

The thought worried him. He had never had such an absurd notion in his life. What was the matter with him, to come up with something so asinine?

She looked away, uncomfortable. For a moment, he thought he had made his remark aloud, until Miss Burgess tittered and he realized it was her friend's forwardness that had put Mrs. Rawlins to the blush.

"We are very pleased to have her settled here," Miss Burgess said now. Freddy forced himself to concentrate on her words. It wouldn't do at all to be perceived as giving all his attention to the respectable widow. Miss Burgess continued, "She's very interested in the church, you know."

A strange thing to say. Freddy smiled his most charming smile to hide his surprise at her words. "As the daughter and widow of esteemed clergymen," he said, using Miss Burgess's own fulsome praise for the late, lamented ministers, "I would imagine such an interest is to be expected."

Mrs. Rawlins' color deepened. Miss Burgess tittered again.

"No, no," she said. "Well, that is, yes. My dear friend is interested in the spiritual aspects of the church. Of course she is. That, however, is not what I meant. I meant Mrs. Rawlins is interested in the architecture and history of the churches and chapels of Sussex. Is that not so, Eliza?"

The lady nodded once. "I find them fascinating, yes." She smiled at him then, and it was as gracious as Miss Burgess's grin had been disconcerting. He suspected Mrs. Rawlins' smile was a ready one, and appeared often. He smiled back.

"There are several good examples near here," he said. "Some have a great deal of history attached."

"I have already told my friend as much," said Miss Burgess. Was it his imagination, or was there a slight emphasis on the word "my"? She looked around. "I saw Viscount Fremont leave. Is he returning home?"

"Yes, he is."

"I am surprised you did not go with him. Journeys are always more pleasant when shared with a companion."

Freddy couldn't think of anything to say to that comment. He felt his eyebrows raise in surprise. Mrs. Rawlins looked mortified.

"What I mean is," continued Miss Burgess, clearly

realizing she had spoken out of turn, "since you are returning to London too, it would have been nicer if you…" Her words trailed off, awkwardly.

"I am not returning to London, or I would certainly have gone with Lord Fremont. Lord Rotherton graciously asked me to stay with him, so it seems I shall be here a while longer."

"Oh," said Miss Burgess, her smile pinned firmly in place. "That is… I dare say it will be a boon to this area. Gentlemen of…" In the space of an instant, she looked him up and down, pursed her lips against a bitter taste, then smiled again, wiping away all evidence of her disapproval. "…quality," she continued, "are in short supply in Rotherton. I do hope you plan to stay until after the next assembly. We ladies need partners to stand up with us." She punctuated her words with another titter.

Freddy was about to say he was unsure of his plans while silently vowing to be gone before the dance she seemed to have claimed for herself, but he was silenced by the approach of her brother. The curate was dressed in black except for his simple white neckcloth. He was thin to the point of being skinny, and his legs, encased in knee-length breeches and stockings, didn't look strong enough to hold him up. With his soft-brimmed hat and the long tails of his loose-fitting coat, he resembled a crow. That thought had Freddy fighting to keep his amusement hidden.

"Mr. Finch," he said, and made a polite bow, "I do beg your pardon, but I must take these ladies away. Are you ready to leave, Mrs. Rawlins?"

The widow said she was ready, and Freddy expressed the necessary regret at the loss of the ladies' company. Miss Burgess did not seem so happy to go, however.

"Surely it is not as late as all that," she said. "I thought I heard Mrs. Ashton mention tea."

"Forty minutes ago, my dear," replied the curate. The 'dear' did not sound like a term of endearment.

"Oh. Oh, I see. Where does time fly to?"

"Do come along, sister. I've had them put the horse into the traces and it's not good to leave the beast standing." He took her arm and gently but firmly steered her away. A few yards on, she shook his hold off and strode away from him.

Mrs. Rawlins went with them. They had not gone far when he heard the clergyman speak to her in a low tone, though not low enough for someone with such a strong voice. "Mrs. Rawlins, if I may ask you, how many glasses of orgeat has my sister imbibed?"

Nonplussed, she replied, "I hardly know, sir. I don't see…"

"It is just that she seems unable to take too much of it. It has a strange effect on her, as you may have seen. I have found it is worse when she also eats sweetmeats, cakes and other such things. It changes her entire way of being."

"I…" Mrs. Rawlins seemed at a loss to know what to say. Freddy surmised she was being polite. He had noticed the change in the lady's behavior, so it was certain her friend must have done. "I am sorry. I did not know," she finished, with a helpless shrug.

"No reason you should, dear lady. If anyone is at fault, 'tis I. I should have kept a closer watch on her."

As he spoke, Miss Burgess strode back to them. "What, Silas? Are you your sister's keeper?" She tittered again, but this time it had a brittle, malevolent timbre.

"Does your sister's blood cry out to the Lord from the ground?"

Clearly, this was not the first time she had acted thus, for the curate said nothing, nor did anything in his manner suggest her behavior was out of the ordinary, or *de trop*. He merely took her arm and secured it in his own, then walked her to the front of the house, and his waiting vehicle. As they walked away, Freddy could hear her rambling about being under a curse and driven from the ground, which she said had opened, for some reason. Freddy vaguely thought she quoted the Bible, but he couldn't be certain, nor could he fathom why she chose those verses. They didn't seem to have any bearing on anything here and now.

As they reached the path that would take them out of the garden, and out of his sight, Mrs. Rawlins turned and looked over her shoulder at him. She saw him watching her and turned back, nonplussed. Her reaction made him smile. It was a far more pleasant memory to keep of the end of this day than the bizarre demeanor of the curate's sister.

****

Lord Rotherton made Freddy welcome, giving him a comfortable suite of rooms with a decidedly masculine feel. The furniture was solid, dark wood, the top halves of the walls painted in a pale grey, the lower walls in burgundy, with a dado rail between the two. The thick carpet was grey, as were the heavy floor-length curtains, while the bedding was burgundy to match the walls. As well as the bed, which was high enough to require a step, there was an armoire, a dresser, a desk and a captain's chair, two armchairs, and a nightstand on which stood a white porcelain bowl and ewer. On the desk was a decanter, half full of brandy, a rummer beside it. A fire played merrily in the grate.

"Hope all is to your satisfaction," said Rotherton. "Best I could do at such short notice."

"It's perfect," Freddy assured him.

Rotherton smiled, lazily. "Compared to the creature comforts at Hadlow Hall, the cowshed would be perfect," he said. "Bertie was many things. A decent host was not one of them." He smiled, sadly, then shook his head, as if dispelling the mood. "Anyway," he went on, "come and go as you need to."

Once again, Freddy wondered how much the earl knew about the work he did for Fremont.

"I assume you'll start whatever you're doing in the morning, though. So, do you fancy a game of billiards before dinner?"

****

Anybody who believed Freddy's portrayal of the idle gentleman who spent his evenings carousing and his days recovering would have been astonished to see him let himself into Hadlow Hall at eight the next morning. He had borrowed the keys from Lord Rotherton and now stood in the hallway, wondering where to begin.

The place had the feel of vacancy, a certain flatness of the air that only came when no other living creature was nearby. Already, just weeks after Bertie's death, it smelled musty and unloved. The atmosphere was not helped by the fact that the only light came from the open door, all windows having been shuttered and secured against intruders, wildlife, and the elements. The black-and-white checkered floor was chipped and cracked, the sheen worn from it in places, and the shapes of pictures stained the walls, indicating where lost treasures had once hung. Freddy did not envy the new Lord Hadlow. He would have his work cut out, making this place habitable.

"Rather him than me," he murmured. His words echoed softly.

He lit a candle and closed the door, casting the hall into a gloomy darkness that tempted him to open at least some of the shutters. He decided against it. He didn't want his presence here to be immediately obvious to anybody who passed by. Although, a little more light would be welcome; Freddy was not a man given to flights of fancy but there was a definite spookiness about the old building. He almost expected to hear footsteps on the stairs and the rattling of chains.

"Fustian!" he scolded himself. "There were no ghosts here before, and they haven't moved in over the last few days." Even if two people had died violently here recently. He shivered, then squared his shoulders. "And why chains, for crying out loud?" Ghosts were always portrayed as rattling chains. The people hadn't carried chains around with them in life. Why on earth would they need them in death?

"Pull yourself together, man," he said and looked around, trying to decide where to begin his new search. He and Adam had already scoured the Hall and found nothing, but he could look again. He would examine every nook and cranny from attic to cellars, check every cupboard, knock on every wall looking for hidden spaces. When he left, he would be able to report, with confidence, the gold was not here.

It took him several hours to work through the entire house. He found chests of clothes from a bygone era in the attic, and a small space he suspected was a priest hole behind one of the guest bedrooms, plus a servants' corridor that ran behind the walls of the chambers and took him down to the kitchens. There was evidence of mice in the kitchen, and woodworm holes in the wainscot in the dining room. The parlor reeked of stale alcohol, while the library smelled of dusty paper and cracked leather, though most of the books were long gone. The pantry was bare, the stove cold, and old pots hung from the kitchen ceiling. Most drawers and cupboards were empty, although the armoire in Bertie's room still held his clothes, and there was some linen that had seen better days in a cupboard in the corridor. Enough coal for perhaps one fire lay on the main cellar floor, and there were a few dusty bottles of wine on the racks in the wine cellar.

There was, however, no gold. No chest. No coins. Nowhere to hide them.

Satisfied it was not in the house, Freddy searched the outbuildings. There was a gardener's shed and a herb room, a space that might once have been an office, a cold-store, vegetable-store, stables, a tack room, kennels, and a carriage house with a coachman's rooms above it. All were well on their way to rack and ruin. None held anything of note. In the stables, he found a trap door that led to a tiny space beneath the floorboards, but the space was empty and looked like it had been for some time.

"I don't think it's at Hadlow Hall, Fremont," he muttered. He clapped his gloved hands together, trying to dislodge cobwebs, thick with dust and age. "Thank you so much for thinking of me for this task," he said, as he brushed more evidence of where he had been from his clothes and ruffled it free from his hair.

In the estate office, he found rolls of paper and

realized they were plans of the estate. There were five of them, dated every ten years, showing updated changes. Farms were marked, the tenants' names written in a flowing cursive. The house was there, its floor plans laid out. He saw the outbuildings he had searched, the park, the woods, arable land, a river winding its way through to a lake. And there, beyond the park but still on Hadlow's land—a mark that looked like a church.

Freddy frowned. He didn't recall any mention of a church on the property. It had clearly fallen into disuse, because Bertie and all his tenants attended the Saint Simon and Saint Jude church in Crompton Hadlow, which was where Bertie had been laid to rest.

Still, this church was marked as being there, and Freddy could not say he'd completed the job properly if he didn't search it. Carefully, he extinguished his candle, which by now was little more than a stub, made sure the house was securely locked, and set off across the grounds to the church.

It was an old building. He could see that as he approached. At one end was a small, intact building with a ridged roof and two small, arched windows. From outside, it looked as if it would comfortably hold about thirty people.

The other end of the church was in ruins. There was a squat stone tower in the Norman style, and half a wall on either side, all that was left of the nave. The roof and glass from the windows of the nave were long gone.

He walked into the tower through an open arch and looked around. About ten feet square and perhaps thirty feet high, it had no roof. The floor was hardened mud, with here and there a dip filled with rainwater, and the walls were slick with years of neglect and being open to the elements. There was no way to get to the top of the tower, that he could see, any steps having long gone, and it was obvious the ground had not been dug recently. The chest was not in the tower.

The nave was, likewise, undisturbed. A breeze blew through glassless windows and over the tops of ruined walls and whispered its way around the forlorn space. The flagstone floor made it seem even colder.

The chest was not in here.

He crossed the nave to the ancient wooden door leading to the still-intact part of the church. The wood of the door was warped, making it stiff to open, and he had to put his shoulder to it. It scraped across the stone floor.

He stepped into a plain room, its walls whitewashed. The windows let in a surprising amount of light, which played on the high-walled pews, each with a latched door. The central walkway was gray stone and led to a small table against the far wall, on which was a tarnished cross between two equally tarnished candlesticks. A lectern stood to one side of the table, but the Bible it had, presumably, once held was gone. A pulpit took up the other corner. On the wall beside the pulpit was a marble tablet, faded lettering on it commemorating the first Viscount Hadlow, who had lived in the sixteenth century and received his title for some service he had done Queen Elizabeth. There was also a plaque listing all the priests who had officiated here since that time. Freddy perused it idly, noticing the long gap between the man in charge from 1643 to 1644 and the new incumbent, who took the post in 1658. A period of political and religious unrest in the country, if he remembered his history lessons correctly.

There was nothing else of interest in the building.

After a cursory look under the seats inside all the pews, Freddy left the church, pulled the door to, and made his way across the park to the woods at the side of the estate. He planned to head toward the lake he'd seen on the plans, where there might be a boathouse, or even an island, to search.

He reached the tree line, turned for one final look at the dilapidated church, and saw someone beside the building. Because of the angle of the sun, the light was in his eyes, so he could not immediately see who it was, but it was a given that they should not be here. The estate was closed to visitors, and it could not be a groundsman—Bertie hadn't had the blunt to pay for one for years.

Freddy stepped back into the shadow of the trees and watched the intruder.

Chapter Four

Eliza had woken early, keen to get on with the task she'd set herself. She knew she couldn't check the interior of the church in the town of Rotherton today, for it would be locked. She could ask the curate or his verger to unlock it for her, since she had made her interest in church buildings plain, but she didn't think it would do her any good. She had asked for access to the churches at several different villages in the neighborhood in the past few weeks, and while she'd not been refused access, the people who unlocked the doors never left her alone, although she'd given strong hints that was what she wanted. They had talked about the buildings and their histories, pointed out what they thought were notable features, or told stories of things that had happened there in the past. Eliza had feigned interest and hidden her frustration at the inability to search for the clues she needed to find Claire.

She sat at her writing desk and massaged her forehead with blessedly cold fingers. "Please, Lord," she whispered, "guide me. Take me to the church I need and help me get inside."

A memory flashed into her mind then. Her father, catching Peter Owens, young son of a local farmer, picking the lock of the church at dusk one evening. Where other men would have hauled Peter up before the magistrate, Papa had filled him with the fear of God before confiscating the set of lock picks and sending him home in the knowledge he had had a lucky escape, and he had better use the chance wisely. To Eliza's knowledge, the boy had stayed honest from then on.

Now, she wished she'd had the presence of mind to get him to teach her how to use those lock picks. Then, perhaps, she could gain access to church buildings at dead of night and search for the clues she needed.

Eliza looked around her, guiltily, then sent up a prayer of apology. She was certain the Almighty would not take kindly to someone wishing they could burgle His house, even if her motives were pure. Wishing someone else had continued in sinful behavior to benefit her would probably not help her cause with the Lord, either.

"And it's not like I knew such a skill would come in handy one day," she muttered.

"Beg pardon, mum?" Betty's question made her jump. She'd forgotten the maid was cleaning and re-laying the hearth.

"I was thinking aloud," said Eliza, with a sheepish grin.

"I'll finish this and make you a cup of tea, shall I?"

The last thing Eliza wanted was a cup of tea. Especially since Betty would insist on accompanying it with her rock cakes. Eliza wasn't certain the treats were meant to be rock cakes, to be honest, but since they were invariably hard enough to break teeth, that's what she had christened them. Because she was unkind, she chided herself, and in need of a lesson in Christian charity.

"No, thank you." She smiled and tried to look regretful about her refusal. "I think I'll take a walk around the neighborhood while the weather is good."

"Very good, mum." Betty piled the wood onto the hearth but didn't light it. "You must know the area like a born local now," she went on. "Better'n a local, even, what with all the walking and exploring you do. Where will you walk today, do you think?"

In most households, Betty would be considered too forward, impertinent in the way she spoke to her employer, but Eliza didn't mind. For one thing, if the girl never spoke to her, hers would be a strikingly lonely existence, and anyway, she had grown up in a home where servants were not exactly friends, but they were treated with respect.

"Our Lord came to earth as a humble Carpenter, son of poor parents," Papa had taught her and her siblings. "Who knows but that the person you disdain may turn out to be Him, coming again, or at least one of His angels? Treat everyone as if they are Him, and you cannot go wrong."

Eliza smiled at the memory. "I don't know," she answered Betty. "I shall see where the wind takes me."

That wasn't exactly true, she admitted to herself, just over an hour later when she walked across the Hadlow estate toward another place of worship on her list.

She had made her way along the High Street, stopping several times to exchange pleasantries with neighbors, to agree that yes, Miss Ashton-that-was had made a lovely bride, and yes, the weather was taking its time to become warmer, though, no, it wasn't as wet and cold as the last two summers had been, and the bonnet Miss Louisa Bell was wearing was very pretty, and had she decorated it herself? She made several promises to come for tea later in the week, and avoided answering when asked if she would attend the assembly in a fortnight's time.

When she finally left Rotherton behind her, she took the list of local places of worship from her reticule and decided the best place to attempt to search today was the little church on Lord Hadlow's land. It was, to the best of her knowledge, not in regular use, and from what she had been told, in a state of disrepair. That might mean it was easier to access. It also might indicate it was a likely place to find what she was looking for, since, she reasoned, villains who stole and sold children would want somewhere they were unlikely to be disturbed. Really, when she thought about it, she couldn't say why she hadn't begun her search there. In her defense, although the church had always been on her list, she had only recently learned of its abandoned state.

The list of churches and their whereabouts in the Rotherton area had been given to her in Rye in January and had cost her a sovereign. "You'll be right," her informant had told her. "Plenty of time to find the right one before the next sailing."

"Next sailing?" Eliza hadn't understood, even though the man had told her that children like Claire were being taken to be sold. "Especially now the navy's stopped them taking people from Africa. They been hit hard by that, these last few years. Need to find a source of income elsewhere."

"They've been taken as slaves?" Eliza had felt sick.

"Yes. And no. Some of them, the little 'uns, they'll go to families." He tapped the side of his nose and winked at her. "Not saying they will be sons and daughters of them families, if you get my drift, though some might be lucky. Others will be trained up to work.

But it'll be a damned—er, dashed sight easier than the older children and the women'll have it." He refused to elaborate on that, though Eliza could guess.

"That's appalling," she whispered. Her stomach churned and her head spun at the idea of it. "Doesn't the law stop it?"

He grinned, showing a mouth of missing and blackened teeth. "They can't find a few barrels of brandy brought in by simple fishermen. What makes you think they'll get the better of professionals like we're talking about?"

"But—"

"Look, miss, take it from me. The militia and the Watch round here, well, they can't find their arses with a chair seat. Begging your pardon for my vulgarity, but it's true. And, if I'm honest, I'm not sure they'd want to find this lot, even if they could. Interfering with some men's business can be injurious to one's health."

"It's not right," she stated.

The man looked around, checking nobody else had heard her. "It is what it is, miss. My advice to you, find your niece, get her out and get home. Then forget all about it."

Eliza wasn't sure she would be able to do that. Oh, yes, she would search for Claire, and she would certainly get the girl to safety as soon as she could. But she didn't think she could simply abandon all the others to their fates.

"Where are the people kept?" she asked him.

He shook his head. "No idea. I don't want to know, neither. What I've already said could get me killed." It had taken three more sovereigns before he revealed that the kidnapped people were not kept in Rye. "Too dangerous, here, see?" he said. "Revenue men are everywhere around here. They got men stationed all over: Rye, Hastings, on to Brighton to the west, round the Kentish coast to the east, then north up to the mouth of the Thames. Now, the Gentlemen," he used the nickname given by locals to the smugglers, "they can generally sneak a cargo or two past them, if the goods can be moved quick-like. But something as big as this…" He pulled a face.

"So where would they be, if not here?"

The man shrugged his shoulders and looked around, uneasily. They sat just inside the porch of the church, sheltering from the bullying wind and hiding from prying eyes. He leaned forward to satisfy himself nobody was near enough to hear their conversation.

"Well, see," he said, at last, "it has to be somewhere that's a little inland from here. Away from the scrutiny of them that keep the beaches under surveillance. But not so far inland that they can't get to the sea quickly, if they need to."

That sent panic through her. What if they loaded Claire onto a ship before Eliza could find her?

"They won't." He gave her a smile she suspected was meant to make her feel better. "They can't. Not right now. There's no sailings to the Americas in the winter months, see? Nor to India, or any other far-flung places, neither. Not till after the spring storms have come and gone. Too dangerous, see? Can't risk the ship going down with all them people on it."

"At least they have enough conscience to worry about the loss of lives," she said, relieved.

He scoffed. "Loss of lives? Loss of profit, more like. Every single one of these people is worth about a hundred pounds to them. They don't want to lose that to the winter weather, do they?"

The picture he painted was bleak. It made Eliza's heart heavy, and it sat like a stone in her chest. She wanted to cry for everyone who'd been taken, especially the children, who must be so confused and frightened. She silently prayed she would find Claire in time, and then be shown a way to destroy the whole enterprise.

"Now, I'm going on hearsay, mind," said the man. He looked up at the sky outside the porch. It had changed from a pastel grey to an angry indigo, threatening to dump rain, or even snow, on the ancient churchyard. Though he wore a thick woolen smock, he shivered, and Eliza realized how little protection his clothes gave him. Unlike her own warm coat over an equally warm dress, and stout boots. He would, no doubt, appreciate finishing their business. She suspected that, if he'd talked with anyone but a clergyman's daughter, he would have met them in the local tavern, where he could sit beside a roaring fire and consume beer and a hot meat pie while he talked.

"I can't swear to it, you understand," he continued, stressing his information was 'hearsay.' "I'd never get involved in such evil shenanigans, myself. But, you know, I keep my eyes and ears open, and I hear and see more'n you'd think."

Eliza nodded, acknowledging his words. "What did you see and hear?"

The coins in his pocket jingled as he pulled out his hand and rested it, palm up, on his knee. Eliza handed him another sovereign. His fingers closed around it and his fist disappeared back into his pocket, where it clinked against the other coins. "Rotherton," he said.

"Rotherton?" She thought for a moment, seeing in her mind's eye the map of Sussex she had studied before coming here. "Little town to the north of Lewes?"

"Aye. But it's more than a town. It's a whole district. Got to be coming up for a dozen villages and hamlets. Some nice estates that way, too. Now, I'm not saying it's definite. I don't *know*, if you see what I mean. But I heard what I heard, and that's where you should start your search. But I will say this, and I'm confident about it. That list there," he pointed at the paper he'd given her, "that's your key. A church in the area is where you should concentrate your efforts."

A week later, she dressed in widow's weeds and gave herself a false name before renting the cottage in Rotherton High Street and setting out to get to know the area, especially its places of worship.

How could a small rural district sustain so many churches? As well as Anglican churches—one in every single village and two in Rotherton itself, there were also several Roman Catholic buildings, a smattering of Baptist churches, a Quaker meetinghouse, a Methodist church, and one place of worship where she wasn't quite sure what denomination they followed. Also, some of the larger estates had private churches on their land, and the tinier hamlets boasted chapels-of-ease, small meeting houses for when the weather made travelling to a proper church too difficult.

Even so, she'd thought it would be a relatively simple job, over quickly. She had reckoned without locked buildings and condescending churchmen, many of whom preferred to spend their weekdays hunting and fishing, socializing with their wealthier parishioners, and, occasionally, visiting the sick and the dying. They did not want to give time and effort to a widow with no fortune or connections. Consequently, in just over four months, she had made little progress and was conscious that summer and the resumption of sailings, approached.

Eliza knew, because she listened carefully, that the long sea voyages had not fully resumed yet. The weather may have been better than it had been for the last two years, but it was still squally, with heavier than average rain. There had been flooding along the coast, and farmers and fishermen alike were filled with prophecies of doom and gloom. But the inclement weather could not go on forever, and sooner or later those ships would sail. Knowing that added urgency to her task.

She would love to get into one of the three churches that the Reverend Mr. Burgess presided over, but he, a cleric who seemed genuinely to care for his flock, was always busy. If he wasn't working on his sermon, he was visiting the sick or going to the almshouses to administer to the elderly poor. He seemed to be from home on most days. Which was admirable, if frustrating.

It would be pointless to ask Prudence to unlock the buildings. Prudence would never leave her alone. The curate's sister had chosen Eliza as her particular friend, and it was certain she would want to stay with her. Why, had she not introduced Eliza as her "Bosom Bow"—or "Belle" as Prudence had insisted on calling it—to Mr. Finch just yesterday?

Thinking of Mr. Finch brought his image to mind. She could not deny she felt a liking for the gentleman. More than a liking, if truth be told, although she couldn't have said why. True, he was very handsome. His eyes, more grey than blue, sparkled in a way that drew people to him, suggesting as they did both humor and intelligence, and his honey-blond hair complemented perfectly the light golden tan of his face. That tan was, she suspected, a legacy of time spent in the Peninsula, fighting Napoleon Bonaparte. She had seen similar color on the faces of other veterans of that war.

But it was more than his looks. Mr. Finch had a charm that many people lacked. There was an ease of acquaintance about him that people found endearing, and Eliza was not immune to it. It was a pity he was so far in debt, for it was the one flaw in him that could not be overcome, the one thing Society would find unforgivable. That he was a creature of Society, she made no doubt. Indeed, if not for his debts, she suspected, he would never have left London at all. He probably missed it greatly, and the fact that he had not yet returned told her he must be deep in trouble, financially.

Not that his lack of funds had any impact on her. She was, to all intents and purposes, a clergy widow with an interest in old churches. Even if she hadn't been masquerading as such, Mr. Finch would never have been for her. Not only was he a rogue, completely unsuitable for a clergyman's daughter, but he was also the son of a lord. He might not have a title himself, but he did have expectations, and she did not fulfill them. Which didn't mean she couldn't enjoy his company in the meantime. They had been introduced and so could converse, and they would probably attend the same places over the next few weeks.

But casual acquaintance was all that could be between them. When Mr. Finch finally had the funds he needed, he would leave. And when that happened, Eliza promised herself, she would not miss him. Not in the least.

Her cheeks flamed, making her uncomfortable, and she spent a minute examining the list of churches without actually seeing it. Which was an absurd thing to do, as she had already decided which one she would look at before she left home.

"Hadlow," she said, giving herself the order to move forward.

She passed through the village of Crompton Hadlow, hurrying past the curate's cottage and praying that Prudence would not see her and come to join her. Even though she felt guilty for the lack of charity in her thoughts, her prayer was answered and it was a relieved Eliza that came through to the far side of the village moments later.

She reached the edge of the Hadlow estate and scrambled through a large opening where the perimeter wall had disintegrated, then took a shortcut across the overgrown and unkempt park land. The cocksfoot grass was up to her knees and deposited tiny white seeds over her skirts as she brushed past it. The length of the grass kept the soil moist, and her boots sank slightly into it. Here and there were patches of red clover-blanket, breaking up the tall plants and giving the park a ragged appearance. Almost hidden in the grass she saw the lacy white flowers of cow parsley, as well as purple fog grass, and the pretty colors of meadow foxtail. Here and there was the bright yellow of cowslip and the brilliant white of oxeye daisies, the spiky pink flowers of ragged robin and the delicate pink-white of lady's smock. Birds chirped, their cheerful calls making the place seem friendly, and the grasses whispered as the strengthening breeze caressed them.

The church, or what was left of it, was in keeping with the rest of the park. Nature and the elements, it seemed, had taken it over, which confirmed it was disused, ignored, and forgotten.

Would that not make it perfect for people to hide evidence of their nefarious deeds? Eliza prayed so. It filled her with hope, although that was tempered by a profound sadness at the way the building had been allowed to fall into disrepair. In times gone by, people had gathered here, worshipped and prayed, met with their neighbors, celebrated good times and condoled each other in the bad. Their whole lives had been punctuated by what went on here, and now it was forgotten, ready to follow to the grave those who had loved it.

She shivered and looked up. Since she had set out from her home that morning, the blue sky with its pretty white clouds had changed and was now the color of old linen. Eliza did not think rain was imminent, but it was enough of a possibility that she wanted to complete this task and return home as quickly as she could.

Shoulders squared, she walked through the tower, checking the rough walls for any sign of a crevice big enough to hold incriminating evidence, although, she acknowledged, she didn't really know what that evidence might be. She looked for a place where someone might hide a document, or a letter, written instructions, or even a bill of sale.

The very idea of the latter pertaining to children, or to any human being for that matter, churned her stomach and she felt hot bile in the back of her throat. Eleven years ago, when she was just fifteen years old, she had rejoiced to hear that the trade in humans from Africa was to be made illegal. Since then she had written copious letters in support of Mr. Wilberforce and his efforts to see slavery outlawed completely in all British colonies. She'd been passionate about the rights of enslaved men and women to be free and to choose for themselves the lives they wished to lead. And all the time, she—and, she assumed, other abolitionists—had failed to notice the alternative trade going on right here in Britain. The poor and the vulnerable had been snatched by the dozens, and if Claire had not been taken, who knew how much longer Eliza would have remained in ignorance of it?

She found nothing in the tower but damp mold that stained the tips of her gloves, so she moved on to the nave. Although more open to the elements, the ruined nave was drier and cleaner than the tower, and much lighter, making it easier to search. There was, however, nothing there, either. She walked across the floor, back and forth several times, looking for a sign that someone had dug into it recently, and she checked the gaps between crumbling stones until she was satisfied she had missed nothing. Then she headed into the main church building.

Once inside, she didn't know where to start. The pews perhaps, or the pulpit, the lectern and the makeshift altar? There were no Bibles or prayer books that she could see; they'd presumably been taken away for safekeeping. No plate, either. A ragged curtain was drawn back from the sticky door, probably once used to keep out the draught and make the worshippers a little more comfortable at prayer, although nothing could truly take away the chill of a stone-built church.

She checked each pew, lifted each kneeler and checked it for signs it had been ripped and re-sewn. None of them had been tampered with. She examined the memorial to the first Viscount Hadlow, and the one celebrating the clergy who had officiated here over the years. The candlesticks, the base of the Cross, the walls. She found two elderly vases, their insides dark with dried vegetation, and a rusting watering pot. She checked the hem of the curtain. There was nothing here to be found.

On a heavy sigh of defeat, she turned to leave and gave a squeal of alarm to see the man standing in the doorway, shoulder resting on the door jamb, his arms folded and one leg crossed nonchalantly over the other.

Chapter Five

The widowed Mrs. Rawlins certainly took her interest in church architecture seriously, thought Freddy as he stood in the doorway, watching her make a close inspection of every inch of the little building. Or perhaps it was the history of the place which prompted her careful study of the kneelers.

When he'd realized it was she whom he had seen going into the church, he'd relaxed somewhat, only to tense again when he saw just how intensively she searched. He'd stood still and tried to figure out what she hoped to find.

Now she'd had a moment to realize who he was, her panic subsided. She put her hand to her chest and gave an embarrassed grin, her voice breathy when she said, "Mr. Finch. You startled me."

He stood up straight and gave her a perfunctory bow. "My apologies. It was not my intention." Although, in fairness to her, he had been standing behind her, not making any noise or otherwise drawing attention to himself, so it was hardly surprising she was alarmed to see him.

Stepping fully into the church, he scraped his boot heel on the stone floor. The frictional ring echoed in the tiny space. "It's strange to find this building here, is it not?" he asked. "Churches are usually surrounded by the homes of their congregants, not put in the middle of nowhere."

"I believe this one was originally built for Lord Hadlow's estate workers."

"A long way from where they live, though. For some of his tenants and workers, it would have been closer to travel to Crompton Hadlow rather than use this church."

She shrugged her shoulders and looked around, as if she could see the surrounding land through the church walls. "Mayhap there were homes here when the church was built. Things do change. For whatever reason, people move. New houses are built and old ones disappear."

"Leaving the church to stand alone." He sauntered along the central aisle, looking around and trying to work out for himself what she might have been searching for. It couldn't be the gold. Not only did he doubt she knew about it, since few people did, but she had looked in places it would be impossible to have hidden it. Whatever she sought, it was something small, and easily concealed.

"Finding a church on its own, without a nearby settlement, is not an unusual sight in the English countryside," she pointed out.

"Yes," he agreed. "But most of them are remnants of the Black Death. This place," he waved a hand to indicate the building, "wasn't built until two hundred years after that."

Freddy thought he saw a new gleam of respect in her eyes. Why that should please him, he couldn't say. He'd spent a long time, and not a little effort, cultivating the persona of a devil-may-care rake who had never done anything useful in his life and who certainly would never have paid heed to his history tutor. Yet the thought that this woman might perceive him as goose-witted was…regrettable. He wanted her to know he wasn't stupid, needed her to see he had hidden depths.

Confused and discomfited by the way she made him feel, he tried to overcome it by challenging her. He turned quickly, fixed her with a too-steely stare, and spoke in a tone that was harsher than he intended. "Why are you here, Mrs. Rawlins?"

She raised her eyebrows and blinked at him. He looked away, made a show of studying the memorial to the first viscount.

"I heard about this church. I wished to see it."

He glanced at her, then looked around the church, from its plain ceiling to the stone floor, from the wooden pews, stark against the whitewashed walls, to the altar table and its ancient, battered metalware. He knew he looked skeptical at her claim. Hoped he did, anyway. He wanted—needed—to make her as uneasy as she made him. So she would tell him the truth. No other reason. What other reason could there be?

The silence stretched to more than half a minute. Her smile, which had been bright, faltered. She looked away, cleared her throat, then looked back and held his gaze with an air of defiance.

"I believe I told you, visiting churches is an interest of mine." Her eyes flickered down to the left before immediately staring back at him. Freddy intensified his own gaze, trying to trap hers, wanting it to make her more forthcoming with the truth.

It didn't work. "Indeed," she continued, her voice taking on a sing-song lilt and her smile brightening again, "one might almost call it an obsession of mine. Don't you find the architecture of sacred buildings fascinating? Are you not drawn to the history? The monuments and memorials," she gestured at the viscount's plaque, "the lists and records." She pointed at the names of the incumbents through the ages. "All the stories these stones could tell. Dozens, nay, hundreds of people must have worshiped here in the past. People with lives and loves, joys and sorrows, worries. Are you not in the least bit curious as to what has happened here in the times before we came?"

Now it was his turn to shrug and try to look nonchalant. "I am sorry to say the idea has never occurred to me, Perhaps I am lacking in imagination…" *Though I have no trouble imagining spending time with you.* The wayward thought ambushed him and he pushed it back, telling himself this was neither the time nor the place. He had a job to do, and he should concentrate on it.

"Lacking imagination? You?" She chuckled, soft and low. A buzz went through him at the sound. He wanted to shake it away. It took everything he had to stand still. She continued, "I should be astonished to discover that was true, Mr. Finch."

He frowned. *What was that supposed to mean?* She could not possibly have known the direction of his thoughts. Was she baiting him? He swallowed hard and moved the conversation onto what, he hoped, would be safer ground.

"I would have thought any records to be found pertaining to this place would have been ruined years ago. It must be damp in here."

"Or moved somewhere else for safekeeping," she argued. "A much more likely scenario, for if there had been damage to records and artifacts left here, we should surely have found at least some trace of them. Fragments of paper, perhaps, or shards of pottery. There is nothing."

She had him there. He smiled wryly at her. Her lips twitched in the faintest of returns. Then she inclined her head. "However, I am sorry to have intruded. I should have asked permission before I made my way onto the estate. In my defense, it was difficult to know to whom I should apply, with the new Lord Hadlow yet to arrive…" Her eyes widened and her mouth formed a perfect O. "How insensitive of me. I am sincerely sorry. You are still mourning your friend. Please, forgive me."

He held up a hand. "There is nothing to forgive, dear lady. We are, none of us, immortal, and life must go on. As for permission to be here—consider yourself permitted, at least until the new viscount arrives to countermand my decision."

"You act for the previous Lord Hadlow?"

Freddy shrugged his shoulders. "I dare say I will do as well as anybody. We were friends. True friends, that is, not…" He stopped himself before he could sneer contempt at the companions Bertie had surrounded himself with in the last years of his life, people who encouraged him to gamble his fortune into their hands, who drank his brandy cellars dry and plied him with women who robbed him blind, and the Lord knew what else.

"You knew him a long time, I think," she said, her tone rich with understanding.

He swallowed and nodded, surprised at the emotion her question invoked. The adult Bertie had annoyed and frustrated him. Freddy had wanted to shake him until his teeth rattled and commonsense was forced into his brain. More than once, he'd been tempted to knock him flat.

He'd resolved, many times, to walk away and have nothing more to do with him. And yet, now he was gone… Tears burned the back of Freddy's eyes and a lump in his throat, hard as a peach stone, threatened to choke him.

"Since we were eleven," he answered her. "We were at school together. Met on our first day." Freddy had been a sullen, angry boy who knew all too well that, as the spare second son, he was not considered of much use. His father lavished his time and attention on his older brother and left Freddy very much to his own devices.

Bertie was already the eighth Viscount Hadlow by then, but he'd fared no better than Freddy when it came to love and attention. His guardian saw him as a burden, while the trustees of his estate thought him a means to profit themselves. He was lonely and shy, and ripe for plucking by the bullies and sharps that populated any boys' school. Freddy had seen Bertie being victimized on that first day and, ever one to push against an injustice, he'd knocked the bully down, loosening two of the boy's teeth in the process. From that moment until they reached adulthood, nobody picked on Bertie if Freddy was near, and the two were firm friends.

"You have my condolences," said Mrs. Rawlins, bringing Freddy back to the present.

He nodded, curtly. "Please, feel free to look around," he said, moving to the wall near the pulpit. "The memorial here is fine, don't you think? And the pulpit is beautifully carved." He waved his hand, as if to point it out.

What was he doing? Telling her she could stay here was one thing. He'd already ascertained the gold was not here, so there was no danger of her stumbling onto it.

Nor, unless he missed his guess, was whatever she sought. He longed to ask her what it was, but he didn't think she would tell him, and he didn't have the time to delve into her mystery, when he had a big enough one of his own. But he wasn't just giving her permission to stay. He was actively working to make sure she did, and, apparently, he was intent on staying here with her.

Nonplussed, he moved to the altar. Looking anywhere but at her, he studied the wall behind it, let his eyes rove over the whitewashed stonework to the pulpit, then back, and to the lectern on the other side. To the crack in the plaster behind it.

No. Not a crack. It was too straight and even. Now that his eye had focused on it, he saw where the vertical line met a horizontal, and then, two feet away, another vertical. A door!

He strode over to it, ran his fingers over the cracks, then over the panel between them until he found a small indentation, slightly larger than the circumference of his forefinger.

"What have you found?" she asked from behind him. Her voice was no more than a whisper, and she was so close, he fancied her breath moved the hair at the nape of his neck. He closed his eyes for a moment and pulled himself together.

"I think it is a door." He looked around. In the corner, flush against the wall, was a ball-shaped object with a metal rod protruding from one side. He picked it up, showed it to her, then fed the rod into the hole on the panel. The ball became a doorknob, and suddenly, the door was more than obvious.

There was a moment of hesitation as he realized what he had just done. If the gold was hidden behind this door, she would see it. He would then have to explain his mission to her and hope he could trust her. He believed he could. Mrs. Rawlins was a lady, through and through. If she gave her word, he did not doubt she would keep it. On top of which, she was the daughter and widow of clergymen. That alone meant she would fully understand the concept of confidentiality.

But then, Miss Burgess should understand that, too, and Freddy knew instinctively that he would never trust her with anything he wished kept secret.

"Aren't you going to open it?" she asked.

He glanced back at her and realized he had no choice. Slowly, he turned the knob.

The door was swollen and stiff in its frame. He had to tug hard to budge it. When it did come free, the force made him stagger backward and he heard the rustle of her skirts as she hurriedly stepped back to avoid colliding with him. Not that he would have minded.

The thought came in that instant between action and rationality. For a moment he pictured being near enough to feel the warmth of her, to hear the steady cadence of her soft breaths, and smell the intoxicating floral perfume of her soap. In his imagination she reached out and touched him to steady him, and her hands shot hot flames of desire through him. He fought the image down.

"I do beg your pardon," he said, his voice thick and deep.

"No matter," she replied. She sounded as if nothing had happened. And why should she not? Nothing had happened, except in his head. He cleared his throat and pulled the door fully open.

The room beyond was lit by a narrow window, its glass wavy and distorted, affording a level of privacy that must have been needed when the church was in use, for this was the vestry, and the clergyman using it on a Sunday morning would not have enjoyed the idea that somebody outside might watch him robing.

As well as a tall cupboard for his robes and a small wooden table and chair set under the window, there was a bookcase, now empty, and beside it a small chest, the kind one put papers into for safekeeping. In the corner near this was a piscina, the little basin used to pour away holy water once it had been used. On a shelf to one side of the piscina Freddy saw a cruet, a ciborium and a paten, all fashioned in highly decorated ceramic, the glaze on them crazed with age. Beside them was a small bottle, half full of what looked like discolored oil. In the center of the room was a larger table that took up most of the space, its top pitted from years of use. Several chairs surrounded it, most pushed under the table, though some were pulled out and sat skew-whiff, as if waiting for their occupiers to return to them. On the table were half a dozen candleholders, and a lamp.

Eliza frowned at the large table, which seemed out of place. "Would the parish committee have met in this church?" she asked, her voice soft as if the question were aimed at herself.

Freddy would not have thought so. The vestries of many an Anglican parish church were used to conduct local government business, but this was not the parish church. It was a private chapel, and, therefore, nothing to do with the area's governance.

He shrugged. "Who can say what they used the place for?" Eliza made a noise of acquiescence and they both turned from the table in tacit agreement that its reason for being here was unimportant.

The walls of the vestry were smooth plaster, once white but now greying. There were a few pits and gouges where something, probably furniture, had bashed or scraped against them, but nothing deep or large enough to suggest an opening or a way out to somewhere else, and no indication of a hidden cupboard or compartment.

"Not the most beautiful room I have ever seen," he murmured.

Eliza chuckled, quietly. "I doubt it was meant to be beautiful." She walked around slowly, her heels clicking against the floor. "Practical. That's what I would call it." She nodded, as if agreeing with herself. "Everything within a church tends to be practical, if you think about it. Even the artwork is not merely decoration, for it tells the stories of the Bible for those who cannot read."

Freddy frowned. The lady was speaking, yet saying nothing. Something had made her nervous. But what? Could it be him? The fact that she found herself here, alone and unchaperoned, with him? Was it because he had a reputation as a rake and he frightened her, or would she feel the same about being alone with any man? Even Silas Burgess might upset the sensibilities of a delicate female in such circumstances.

Although "delicate" was not the first word that came to mind when he contemplated Mrs. Rawlins. She was strong and sensible, battered by life's storms and yet still standing. Those were not words he would have used to describe a woman of delicate sensibility.

Then again, her sensibilities might have nothing to do with it at all. She was, after all, a widow, not some frightened debutante. As such, she would be better able to weather any squall set off by gossiping tongues. Besides, being discovered here with him was unlikely, so deep in the confines of Bertie's—er, the new Lord Hadlow's private estate. She must know that, so what had her so on edge?

She had been looking for something, he thought. She had stopped abruptly, guilt plain on her face even as she tried to look innocent, after he had startled her. Whatever she sought, it had to be something small and easy to secrete, considering the places she had searched. Briefly, he wondered what it could be. Not the gold he sought, for that could not possibly have been hidden in the kneelers, or in many of the other places she had looked. A gold fob watch, perhaps. Or a diary. A piece of jewelry lost after an indiscretion.

Surreptitiously, he took in her appearance. Slender, yet with tantalizing curves, she would make any man dream of indiscretions. But that delectable figure was encased in deep black, in the most buttoned-up, modest clothes in the whole of Sussex. Her hair was pulled taut and confined ruthlessly inside her bonnet, her spine straight, her hands clasped demurely at her waist. If this lady had ever had an indiscretion in her life, Freddy was an elephant. Indeed, she gave off such an air of innocence he could hardly imagine her having been married, even to a straightlaced clergyman. The very thought of her committing carnal acts was so shocking, it made his lips twitch.

Her eyes narrowed and she studied him, skeptically. "Are you laughing at me, Mr. Finch?"

His eyes widened. "God forbid I should do any such…" He flinched and raised his eyes heavenward. "Sorry," he said. She shook her head as if in despair, but he saw the tiny smile play over her mouth. She lowered her head, hiding behind the brim of her bonnet. It seemed as if the room had dimmed a little.

More nonsensical, poetic thoughts! He was turning into a sap. Freddy cleared his throat, straightened his shoulders, and pointed at the chest. "Mayhap the historical records you seek are in there."

She nodded, but she made no attempt to move toward it. For a moment, they stood there, still as statues, gazing at each other.

Finally, he took a deep breath. "Shall we look?"

Eliza turned to the chest and gave it all her attention.

The sole of his boot scraped on the floor as he moved to the chest, which he picked up and hefted onto the large table. It was heavier than he had expected, far too heavy for documents, or even the weighty tomes in which births, marriages, and deaths were recorded.

Could it hold the gold? It was a lot smaller than he had envisioned but, he realized with a start, nobody had actually told him how much gold he sought. It could be a mountain of the stuff, or just a couple of bags. A chest this size could easily hold enough for a king's ransom.

Or an emperor's.

It didn't rattle when he moved it. That meant nothing. Coins would rattle, but gold bars would not. If it was the gold, though, he did not wish to open it in front of her. Although he did not truly believe Mrs. Rawlins would rush out to spread the information to all who would listen, Fremont would not thank Freddy for letting her know what they were about, if he didn't have to.

So he tried to look as if he struggled to open the lid, and it would not budge for him. After a moment, he stopped pretending. There was no need to, because the lid truly was sealed to the box.

"It is locked tight," he said, trying to sound more

chagrined than relieved.

"I can see." She did not sound as disappointed as he might have expected her to be.

He glanced at her, wondering about her matter-of-fact reaction. "Do you think it may be important?" He cringed, and quickly added, "I thought you, being familiar with churches, might have some idea?"

"I don't," she replied. "It could be anything: worthless paper, or valuable information. Copies of old sermons, or the vicar's laundry list."

"Do you wish to see inside it?"

"Of course I wish to see inside it," she answered, and a bright smile lit her face. "But I dare say it can wait. There is plenty of time to open that chest later."

Freddy folded his arms across the lid of the chest and leaned into them. "You, Mrs. Rawlins, are a very unusual woman. Most females of my acquaintance would be at my shoulder now, encouraging me, if not downright commanding me, to try to pick the lock or, if that didn't work, to have at it with an axe."

Mrs. Rawlins raised her eyebrow, though he could not tell if she was surprised, or if she disapproved. He rather thought the latter, when she said, "Patience is a virtue, Mr. Finch."

"One they sadly lack." The thought struck him that patience was not the only virtue most of them had learned to live without, but he kept that observation to himself. She probably already thought he was beyond the pale, considering he had been rusticating here for some weeks. There was no need to prove to her that she was correct. Instead, he looked down at the chest again and said the first thing that came to his head. "Are you sure you would not wish me to attempt to open it now? I can give a bit more effort to it."

What was he doing? He did not want to open the chest, not in front of Mrs. Rawlins, or anybody else, for that matter. If it contained the gold, witnesses would complicate things enormously. Yet here he was, offering to do just that.

In his mind's eye, he saw his father, sneering at him. "Not all parts of your anatomy are meant for thinking with, boy. Until you learn that, nothing you do will be a success." It galled Freddy that he was proving the old man right.

Mrs. Rawlins stared down at the chest. She caught the left-hand side of her bottom lip beneath her top teeth. The temptation to open the box was clearly very great for her. Just as the temptation to take that abused lip and smooth it with his thumb before kissing it better was almost too much for him. He wondered what it would taste like. The mint of her tooth powder, perhaps, the flowers in her soap, and the chocolate she had undoubtedly drunk at breakfast. All combined with the special something that was uniquely her. Freddy shook his head, clearing it of the damning thoughts, and forced his mind back to where it should be.

He had just offered to open this chest for a woman he barely knew. If she said yes, he would have no alternative but to do so and take the consequences. What if it contained the gold and she wished to share it with him? The character he had portrayed for the last few weeks, the devil-may-care, rakish rogue, would need and want the money. How would he persuade her that it was not theirs to share, yet still keep his secrets?

Suddenly, he was struck by something he had not considered before. What if she knew this chest contained the gold, because she was part of the plot? What if she thought, by dint of his greed, she could recruit him to the cause?

The idea that she might be one of the traitors sickened him. He wanted to push it from his mind, dismiss it as absurd, but how could he? The woman was a stranger to him. He had met her just yesterday, at Adam's wedding. For all he knew, that delightful, innocent face could hide the darkest heart and the most villainous soul in all England.

Lord, he hoped not! He would give his eyeteeth for his suspicions to be wrong.

Seconds passed. She was clearly torn between wanting to open the box and knowing she should not do so. Finally, she raised her gaze to his face, smiled ruefully at him, and shook her head. "It is not ours to break open," she said. She looked wistfully at the chest once more. "Perhaps, once the new viscount arrives, he will have the key. Perhaps, if we ask him very nicely, he might even allow us a glimpse inside."

Freddy hid his relief behind the most nonchalant shrug he could manage. "As you wish."

"Oh, not as I wish," she replied. "But it is as it must be." She took one more longing look at the chest. "Besides, look at the huge flakes of rust on those hinges. If you try to open that lid, they will come away onto your clothes, and the stain they make will never come out. I would not wish to be responsible for explaining to your man why your coat needs replacing." She gave him a mischievous smile. "Or, worse, if you should cut yourself whilst opening it, and some of that rust found its way into the wound and into your blood… I certainly do not wish to be blamed for your demise."

Freddy looked more closely at the hinges. She was right. They were rusting badly. This chest had not been opened for a very long time. Therefore, it did not contain his gold.

But did it contain the documents she purported to be so passionate about? If the history of the church was what she truly sought, wouldn't she have leaped at the chance to see inside? Especially when he considered the thorough search she'd made of the church before she realized he was with her.

Not that he thought the historic records were actually what she was looking for. Had they been, she would hardly have looked in the kneelers and under the pews for them. The most likely place to keep such ledgers was on bookshelves and in cupboards. Having discovered the contents of the shelves and cupboards had been removed, one might surmise the records had been taken too, and were no longer within the church building. Yet she had continued to search. So what was it that Mrs. Rawlins truly expected to find here?

He was so lost in his thoughts that her voice startled him and he jumped visibly.

"I apologize," she said. "I did not mean to…" She moved her hand, gesturing what she could not voice. "I merely tried to bid you good day."

"Good day?" To his own ears, he sounded bewildered, and not a little stupid.

She grinned. "Would you rather I wished you a bad one?" His commonsense roused itself then, in time for him to give her a raised-eyebrow look. It made her chuckle. "I need to return home, sir. I have things to do."

"Of course. Thank you for your company."

She inclined her head in acknowledgement and he

answered with a slight bow. As she turned to leave, Freddy felt torn. Part of him wanted her to leave so he could open that dratted chest and make absolutely sure it contained nothing of interest to him. The other part of him clamored to stop her, not ready for this impromptu meeting to end.

He stood, legs apart, hands clasped behind his back, more so he would not reach out and try to touch her than because he was at ease with the situation. She turned and took a step away from him.

Freddy was uncertain about what happened next. Either she tripped over something or she put down her foot awkwardly, twisting her ankle. Whichever it was, she started to fall, her arms out instinctively in front of her to take the brunt of it when she hit the floor.

His own actions were equally instinctive, and quicker than he would have believed possible even for a trained soldier in far better shape than people gave him credit for. In the blink of an eye, he stepped forward and put his arms around her waist, keeping her upright at the same time as twisting her around, so that when she came against him it was chest to chest, her soft breasts against the hardness of his own body.

He could feel her heart, beating madly. It reminded him of a bird he had once held in his hand. He would not have hurt it, but the bird hadn't known that and terror quickened its heart until the beats melded into one rough tremor, the same tremor he felt in her now.

This close, he could see clearly the tiny shards of silver and navy buried in the light blue of her eyes, every one of the dark lashes that surrounded them, every single freckle on her nose. Her hair was... Had he thought it merely brown? It was so much more than brown. It was honey and sunshine, chestnuts and autumn leaves, hidden in silk-soft doeskin. He yearned to touch it, caress it, to take off her bonnet, steal her pins, and feel it cascading, unfettered, over his hands and down across her shoulders. Would it reach her waist? Would it, when set free, hang straight and heavy, or would it curl and wave and bounce, joyously unruly and full of life?

He smelled the flowers on her warm skin, the fresh air on her coat, mingled with the cold, dry dustiness of the church on her gloved fingers, and the nervousness shallowing her breaths. Her lips parted, slightly. It was an unconscious action, but, oh! so seductively inviting.

Slowly, not wanting to spook her, he lowered his head until their lips touched, the barest brush of warm flesh on warm flesh. Her eyelids lowered and he kissed her again, more firmly this time. Her lips were soft and full, their warmth tempered by the cool air. He drew his tongue along the seam of them and she opened, letting him in. His tongue danced with hers, savoring the feel of her. She tasted not of chocolate, as he had imagined, but tea, mingled with the fruity sweetness of the jam she'd eaten with her breakfast, the soft, fresh mint of her tooth powder, and something else, something uniquely—indefinably—her.

Her hands moved up, over his chest. Even through the layers of his clothes and her gloves, he felt the scorch of her touch, the jump of his nipples as her fingers moved over them. His thighs hardened and his trousers tightened, a sense of urgency growing within him that he hadn't felt since he was a green boy. She wrapped her arms around his shoulders, holding him in place, anchoring him.

It was a kiss that could easily become so much more.

All he had to do was give in to it, let it take him over. He could let his hands stroke her back until her spine arched, pushing her corc against his, while she made little mewling sounds of pleasure, before moving slowly, softly up to caress her throat. As she melted into him, he could nibble her neck, where her pulse beat hard and fast, before undoing the buttons on her spencer, pushing it out of the way so his hands could smooth their way down, over her arms to her waist. His fingers would span her tiny form for a moment before moving up to the underside of her breast. He would take a moment to weigh it in the cup of his hand before he took her nipple between his finger and thumb, stroking it through the fabric of her gown, drawing it to a peak before releasing it, admiring it, taking in the color and the shape of it before lowering his head and tasting it…

Outside the opaque window a crow cawed loudly. The rough sound jarred on the quiet midday air. Startled, she gasped and pulled back, sharply. Freddy released her, though it took everything within him not to reach for her once more.

She took a step back. Her cheeks were flushed, a hot pink that made her freckles stand up and her eyes shine. Her breasts, still safely within the confines of her still-buttoned coat, rose and fell, rose and fell, heavy and fast, and there was a shocked, confused look on her face that was probably mirrored in his own.

Suddenly awkward, Freddy looked away, studying the piscina as if his life depended on it. What on earth did he think he was doing? In a church, no less! And with this woman! This was not the type of woman one kissed wantonly and indulged in—whatever he'd been about to indulge in. True, some widows might be more willing to take part in a dalliance than would a virginal girl, although Freddy did not think Mrs. Rawlins was one of them. The shock and shame on her face now, the discomfort she clearly felt, told him so, and he was the most dastardly blackguard for even thinking such a thing of her.

"I should go." Her voice was shaky and breathless. Her face, though, gave nothing away, and he could not tell if she was breathless because the kiss had affected her as profoundly as it had him, or if she was shocked, and perhaps a little frightened by it. He prayed it was not the latter. The last thing he would ever want to do was frighten her.

He swallowed, nodded, stared at the air above her head, afraid to meet her eyes. "It is getting late," he said.

"Yes."

"Almost the end of the day."

"My cook will expect me soon. For my dinner." She smiled, shyly. "I dare not be late and keep her food standing."

"She is exacting?"

"She considers herself an artist, and has cultivated an artist's temperament."

He smiled at her soft humor. "One should never show disrespect to the work of an artist."

"No. One should not."

She stepped back further from him. The air around him chilled at her loss. "Good day to you, Mr. Finch," she said, and she all but ran from the church. Freddy swiveled on his heel and followed her outside.

The sun hung low now. It would be dark soon. Already the trees were silhouettes against the sky, which was the luminous blue-white of evening, the few tiny white clouds edged with a golden pink blush. The grass of the meadow seemed greener in the sharp, enhancing light. In the village, people would be lighting candles, pushing back the dusk that invaded their homes, and stoking evening fires that sent wisps of smoke up chimneys to smudge the perfect sky. Workers would be making their way home from fields and shops, their steps quickened by the delicious smells of a dozen meals cooking in the houses they passed. Some, particularly those without wives and mothers to cook for them, would head for the Golden Goose for a pot of ale and a bowl of the landlord's stew. Even in villages as small as Crompton Hadlow and Rotherton the streets would be busy. A lady like Mrs. Rawlins should not have to make her way through those streets alone.

"I will accompany you to your home," he said.

"It is not necessary. Please don't trouble yourself."

"It is no trouble."

"Nevertheless…" She bowed her head at him and walked briskly back through the field toward wherever she had entered the estate.

"Nevertheless." He repeated her word, softly. She was probably right. The streets of the villages, though busy, were not really a threat to her. She had probably walked them, unaccompanied, a hundred times before. Nobody would think less of her for doing so tonight. Although they might look twice to see the respectable widow walking with the wastrel friend of the recently deceased wastrel viscount.

For the first time, the reputation Freddy had cultivated galled him.

He walked back across the fields to Hadlow Hall. He would make certain it was locked before heading back to Lord Rotherton's home and whatever delightful repast the earl's cook had created. The thought made him smile. David, Lord Rotherton, was the kind of man who liked plain food without frilly sauces and complicated touches. He would no more hire an artistic cook for his kitchen than he would try to fly. Unless Freddy missed his guess, he thought Mrs. Rawlins would prefer plain foods too. Although he could see her employing a cook who created works of art, if that cook needed the job badly. Then, every evening, she would bravely work her way through a dinner with a name she could not pronounce, rather than hurt the servant's feelings. She still had that eager innocence about her that tinted the world a rose pink and made everybody as important as she was.

Freddy stopped dead. The widowed Mrs. Rawlins had an air of complete and untried innocence, which was quite at odds with her status. He understood the soft heart of a mistress who liked her servants to be as happy as she was, but there was more to it than that. The woman did not kiss like somebody who had been married. She did not behave as if she had ever known a man. Why, if he didn't know better, he would have said she was not a widow at all but an innocent miss, and that the kiss he had given her today was her very first.

He shook his head at that absurdity. Of course it hadn't been her first kiss. That was merely wishful thinking on his part. She had been married. And yet… He frowned and continued walking as he pondered over it.

Perhaps marriage to a clergyman was not like marriage to other men. Mayhap it was more…chaste. Less…sensual.

The church, he knew, frowned on fornication, although not within the boundaries of marriage. But even within marriage, did the people of God look upon His gift of sex as a duty rather than a pleasure? Was it for procreation only, perhaps? Did they believe it was never supposed to be a joy?

"What a waste," he murmured. Especially for someone as delectable as Mrs. Rawlins.

Chapter Six

Eliza raced across the meadows and through the gap where the ancient dry stone wall had collapsed. She did not dare slow her pace or look back until she was once more on the public lane.

She had kissed Mr. Finch! And not in a chaste, sisterly way. She had kissed him in the most carnal, wanton fashion imaginable! What must he think of her?

But that kiss! She had never realized what kissing a man could be like. Before today, had she been asked what a kiss was, she would have said it was the meeting of two people at the lips, a token of their affection for each other. It had never occurred to her to think of the feelings that might be incurred, the strange, wonderful, unsettling desires that the kiss built within a person. It had been so totally unexpected, the way her heart had beaten so hard and fast, while her stomach swooped and swirled and her breasts tingled, so sensitized they chafed at the cotton of her shift and sent shafts of longing through her, down to that most secret part of her, where such an incredible, delicious ache had begun. She had wanted to move closer to him, to feel his body pressed to hers, giving her release. She had wanted him to stop, to give her a moment to breathe and think, and savor all that was happening, yet at the same time, she'd wanted the kiss to go on forever. She wished she could shout from the rooftops and tell everyone of this wondrous thing she had found. She wanted to keep it a secret so the world did not intrude.

He'd been warm. Vibrant. His heart beat in time with hers. His lips were firm, and there was the slightest rasp where the shadow of a beard had begun to grow on his chin and cheeks. His arms were strong around her, making her feel safe, secure, as if nothing bad could come anywhere near her while he was there.

"And therein lies the danger," she muttered, as she moved briskly through the village. Because the very last thing Mr. Finch should make her feel was safe. The man was a rake, a wastrel who had come here to avoid his creditors. Any woman fool enough to marry him would spend her life avoiding the duns and wondering where the next meal would come from. It was rumored that even his father had turned his back on him, throwing him out and cutting him off.

Coming as she did from a loving family, she found that hard to understand. She had always been certain of her parents' support. But then, she hadn't indulged in the sort of behavior it was whispered Mr. Finch had. The fact that he was still here in rural Sussex, avoiding London Society, gave credence to those tales: stories of loose women, copious amounts of alcohol, excessive gambling. He was, she had been told by gleeful gossips, up to his neck in debts. In short, not the kind of man Eliza was used to knowing.

And he had given her her very first kiss.

The lemon-yellow lights of the tavern spilled onto the pavement in Crompton Hadlow and gleamed in the dusk. It would be full dark before she reached her home. She had hoped to have finished her search of the Hadlow estate's chapel much earlier than this. She would have done so, had she been alone in there. Although, she was honest enough to admit, she did not regret Mr. Finch's company. She certainly did not regret the kiss. If that made her a wanton, so be it.

Her first kiss. And, very likely, her last, for suitors had never lined up to woo her the way they had her prettier sister. Charlotte and Eliza looked nothing alike, for where Eliza's hair was an insipid brown, Charlotte's blonde locks had always shone like spun gold, and Eliza's dull grey eyes became a lively blue in her sister's face. And where Eliza was resigned to a life of dutiful spinsterhood, moving from family member to family member according to their need, Charlotte's marriage to a successful businessman, Jonathan Russell, had been inevitable. Their love had been obvious from the moment they met, and losing him in the carriage accident had almost broken Charlotte. The one thing that had given her the strength to go on was Claire. If the child was not found, if Charlotte lost her, too…

She would be found. No other outcome was acceptable.

Eliza thought back to the day they had lost Claire. Eliza had arrived just two hours earlier, sent by their father to help her newly widowed sister get over her loss. She had not even unpacked her frugal belongings when the child and her nurse had been missed. They had gone for a walk, but had been expected to return for nuncheon, and to meet Aunt Eliza. At first it had been thought they had forgotten the time, and their absence was met with mild irritation, but as the day went on and the light began to fade, annoyance had changed to concern. The hue and cry had been sounded and the area searched. Everybody had come out to look for them.

The nurse's battered body had been found in a ditch. Charlotte had needed to be sedated. Her brother-in-law, Donald, had announced he would pay a ransom if the child was returned unharmed. That had led to two attempts to claim the money by chancers who were quickly found to have had nothing to do with Claire's disappearance.

"Poor little lamb," tutted the cook, when the latest attempt to claim the money turned out to be another fraud. "This house misses her so much."

"Aye," agreed the housekeeper. "And the mistress is, well, she's had far too much to deal with already." She shook her head and sipped her tea. "What will happen next?"

"We will find her, that's what," declared Eliza, who had taken to drinking tea with the upper servants at midday, since Charlotte was not in any fit state to bear anyone's company. She'd sent for the watch commander, who had been no help at all. He told them, in a most sanguine way, that Claire was the fourth child to disappear in a year, and there had been no trace of any of them.

It hadn't taken Eliza long to discover that, as well as the four children who were missing, several young women had disappeared too. Further enquiries revealed there were more missing women and children from surrounding towns, and possibly more from nearby cities. With the number of people crowded into a city and the itinerant lifestyles of many of them, it hadn't been easy to verify these last ones. More, until Claire, all the missing persons had been from the lower classes, so their disappearances had not garnered much attention, nor warranted investigation. The watch commander had even admitted, somewhat sheepishly, that he and his colleagues had suspected the children of having been, as he put it, "done away with by their parents."

"Happens all too often to the poor little beggars," he said, with a shake of his head and an exhortation to "excuse his French." He added, quickly, that he knew a fine lady like Mrs. Russell wouldn't do any such thing, so they could be assured the authorities would leave no stone unturned in their search for her little mite.

Alas, Claire had not emerged from under any of those turned stones. Which was why Eliza, frustrated at their lack of progress, had begun her own investigation, and followed a trail that led her here, to Rotherton.

The church in the area is where you should concentrate your efforts. Her informant's words repeated in her head, over and over.

"But which church?" she muttered, crossly. "And why do there have to be so many? For pity's sake! Almost everyone in the area could have their own place of worship all to themselves." She sighed, glanced skyward and sent up a silent apology to the Lord. It felt vaguely blasphemous to be so disparaging about His houses. Although he would surely agree that so many buildings to search was clearly a hindrance to her task, when time was very much of the essence. "A little help to move in the right direction, Lord?" she asked, silently.

It would be easier if she knew what she was looking for. In a perfect world, of course, she would walk into the correct church and find Claire and the others hiding behind the altar table, tired and hungry but no worse for wear, their captors absent for long enough that Eliza could free them and lead them to safety. But, this being less than a perfect world, she knew it wouldn't be that easy. And given that most of the churches were in use on a Sunday, it was extremely doubtful that kidnapped children would be left lying around in plain sight for any Tom, Dick, or Francis to trip over them.

Therefore, she decided, she was looking for information on where they might be found. Ledgers perhaps, detailing the names and ages of the stolen children, and where they were being shipped to. Maybe even a bill of sale for them. Whatever it was might be small enough to hide inside a disused chalice or tucked between books on a shelf, or it might be large enough to fill a chest like the one they had found today.

Thinking of the chest made Eliza think of Mr. Finch again. She wondered why he had been at the church. Clearly, the place had not been used for worship in a long time, and even if it had, Mr. Finch did not strike her as the kind of man who would spend time there for a Sunday service, let alone someone who would go there for quiet contemplation. So why had he been there?

She stopped dead as a dreadful thought came to her. What if Mr. Finch was one of the wicked people taking the children? Her informant had told her that each child who reached their destination could be sold for a hundred pounds, and it was no secret that Freddy Finch had no visible means of income. Yet his clothes were good quality and expensive, and she knew he kept a horse, for she'd seen him riding it several times. Could he have stayed in the area to wait for the money he would make when the sailings to America began again?

Eliza shuddered. He was a personable man, with an easy charm and beguiling sense of humor, and she did not want to think him capable of such villainy. But what if he was?

The thought made her feel nauseous, and she stood for a moment, her fingers pressed against her lips. Her throat shivered and her skin was clammy, and she welcomed the cool night breeze on her cheeks.

To one side, the Church of Saint Simon and Saint Jude was a silhouette against the darkening sky. Like many of the churches in this part of Sussex, it was Norman in origin, its stone walls thick and steady, held in place by thick buttresses, although there was evidence that more had been added to the building in later years, the stones laid differently and, in places, replaced by brickwork. A steeple stood proud at one end, a weathervane perched on top, moving lazily in the evening breeze. The grounds were dotted with headstones, most of them old. Some leaned drunkenly, while a few looked ready to fall over completely. Grass grew tall around the stones and it waved gently, rustling as the wind passed through it. A path wound its way from the rundown lych-gate to the church door.

To the other side of her was the curate's cottage, where Prudence and her brother lived. She saw a light shining through one of the windows of their home and willed away the nausea, so that she would be ready to move on. She did not wish to stand here for too long, for if Prudence saw her there, she would invite her in, in a way Eliza would find difficult to refuse without being rude. Prudence would want to know why Eliza was out this late at night, too, and that was not something Eliza wished to share with the curate's sister.

She took a step forward, then stopped again, and looked around. She had heard something, though she could not say what. She cocked her head and listened, hoping to hear it again so she could identify it. It had been brief and muffled, but she thought it had sounded like a child, crying.

A minute passed. Two. Then there was a rustling, whooshing as the grass was disturbed, followed by the crack of a broken twig and the ring of boot heels on the path. Eliza jumped and let out a startled, "Oh!" as a huge man came around the side of the church and into view. He wore a laborer's jerkin and breeches, with dark stockings and heavy shoes, and his head was covered by a floppy brimmed hat. His lower face was hidden behind a bushy beard. In his right hand, he carried a shovel in a casual, non-threatening way.

"Beg pardon, mum," he said, and he nodded his head in a curt bow. "Didn't mean to startle you." His voice was a low rumble, more of a growl.

"Seth? Are you there?" Prudence's voice called out over the crisp evening air. The big man, whom Eliza presumed was Seth, grimaced and muttered something unintelligible. Although it was ill-mannered of him to show his feelings in that way, especially about the person Eliza suspected was his employer, she couldn't help but silently agree. She didn't wish to talk to Prudence tonight either.

The lady in question materialized from the other side of the darkened church building. She stepped around a buttress and picked her way between headstones to the lych-gate where Seth and Eliza both waited for her. She was dressed in her usual dark colors, so that only her face was clearly visible, and she walked briskly, taking shallow steps that made her look busy and purposeful.

"There you are. I was just looking for you. Have you…" She spotted Eliza and her face, which had seemed stern and imperious, softened into a smile.

"Eliza, dearest. Are you here to see me?"

"I was just…" Eliza indicated with her hand that she had come along the street.

"It is late for a social call, but—why don't you stay for dinner?"

"Oh, no, I—"

"Seth," Prudence changed both the subject and the person to whom she spoke before Eliza could finish her sentence. "Did you finish digging Mr. Johnson's grave?"

"Yes, mum."

"The cesspool needs working on as well. It's backing up. Could you do it as a matter of some urgency?"

Eliza raised an eyebrow, her mind conjuring a rather unedifying picture of the cesspit.

"Yes, mum. First thing in the morning."

"Very well. You may go now."

Seth bowed and lumbered away along the lane. Prudence watched him go, her arm slipping through the crook of Eliza's elbow, anchoring her. "He's a good man," she said in a tone that suggested she was imparting a confidence. "But he has no initiative. I suppose one cannot expect miracles from his class, but it does mean one has to be vigilant. He needs to be told what to do, and he needs his work checked. And Silas is so heavenly bent that he would let the man do a shoddy job rather than find fault with him, so it falls to me."

"Your brother is lucky to have you."

Prudence smiled, pleased. "If only he knew that. Now, what brings you to me at this hour? I do hope it's not an emergency."

"No. I—I was walking through the village and your sexton startled me, that is all."

"We can't have him doing that. I will speak to him."

"It wasn't his fault. I was woolgathering. Didn't hear him approach."

Prudence shook her head and gave Eliza the sort of look one would give a naughty child. "You should take pains to avoid that, my dear Eliza. For, as Ecclesiastes will remind you, in the multitude of dreams, there are also divers vanities."

Eliza's smile was brief. "You are right."

"Were you coming to me?"

"I was going home."

Something passed over Prudence's face but it was gone too quickly for Eliza to interpret it. It might have been disappointment that Eliza was not coming to her. Or it may have been relief. Eliza knew from experience that a clergy family treasured the rare evenings when there were no guests at the table.

The next moment, Prudence gave one of her thin smiles. "Why on earth were you out at this time of day?"

"I was exploring a church." Eliza smiled. "I was enjoying myself far too much, and I allowed time to carry away without me." *Aided by a very handsome rake who should probably never have been there in the first place.*

"One cannot be admonished for spending time in the Lord's house." Prudence smiled. "Although, I would counsel you to get home now, before the evening air gives you a chill. Perhaps you can come for tea tomorrow? I would love to hear what you found in your church."

Eliza opened her mouth to answer, then closed it as she heard the sound once more. It most definitely did sound like a child crying.

"What was that?"

Prudence looked blankly at her.

"I heard somebody crying."

"Did you?" Prudence looked around as if searching for the unhappy person.

"It seemed to come from the church." Eliza looked over at the church building, which was in complete darkness.

"There's nobody in the church," Prudence assured her. "Perhaps you heard a fox bark."

Eliza shook her head. "It didn't sound like a fox barking. It sounded like a child."

Prudence frowned. "The church should be locked. Silas keeps the key with him. He is from home at the moment, so nobody should be in there." She moved through the lych-gate and along the path to the church door. "Hello? Is anybody there?"

Silence.

"If you are there, come out."

Silence.

"Who is there?" Prudence pushed against the door. It didn't open. She rattled the huge metal handle, bashing it against the thick wood of the door. "It is still locked," she told Eliza. "There is no other door that could be open. And if there were somebody in there, I would have expected at least a sliver of light. Are you sure it couldn't have been a fox you heard?"

Eliza shrugged and shivered. "Possibly." Something about the situation made her very uneasy.

The two women walked away. Eliza looked back over her shoulder, but saw and heard nothing further. She declined Prudence's offer of a calming cup of tea, and they took their leave of each other. As full darkness fell,

Eliza hurried home. She wasn't sorry to reach her own front door.

****

Freddy locked Hadlow Hall and started down the pockmarked drive to go back to Rotherton Hall, then stopped and turned, looking thoughtfully in the direction of the disused church. Now the delectable Mrs. Rawlins had gone, he could open the chest without fear of discovery. He didn't expect it to contain the gold, but he needed to be able to tell Fremont he had left nothing to chance.

The temperature had dropped considerably now and there was a definite nip in the air. It might be May, but he wouldn't be surprised if there was a frost overnight. It made him think of his old nurse, a woman steeped in the culture of the countryside. He smiled as he thought of one of her sayings. *Ne'er cast a clout till May be out.*

Being a small boy and too clever for his own good, he'd seized on the advice given. "If I can't take my clothes off before June, that means I can't have a bath until June."

She'd clipped his ear and told him he was too tricky by half, and it would all end in tears for him. He chuckled to himself as he wondered what she would say if she could see him now. "Pleased I'm entering a church, eh, Nanny? Though not so pleased with my reasons, I'll warrant."

He felt the sting of a phantom clip across the top of his earlobe and heard her tell him there was no hope for him.

"I'll do better, Nanny," he whispered to the only person who had ever made him feel welcome and wanted in his childhood home.

Inside the church, he lit an ancient candle stub and took it into the vestry. Shadows filled the corners of the small room, turning the everyday furniture into grotesque creatures. The candlelight bounced off the window, painting the glass yellow and hiding whatever, or whoever, might be outside. He looked around, warily, then clicked his tongue, impatient with himself. "You are as lily-livered as an old maid," he murmured. "Do you think a ghost will jump out at you?"

He started at a sudden scratching noise, followed by a soft pitter-patter. From the corner of his eye he saw the field mouse scuttle across the floor. He rolled his eyes and grinned at his absurdity.

"The chest," he commanded himself, and bent down to examine the box once more.

It was the work of a few moments to remove the lock and push up the lid. It creaked, the old wood and dry, seized hinges combining to object to the unaccustomed movement. The noise sounded melancholy in its unwillingness.

"Now I'm talking about a box as though it were sentient." He shook his head and held up his candle so he could see inside.

There was a priest's vestments, carefully folded and wrapped in linen, which also contained sprigs of lavender. The plant had long dried, the flowers transformed into dried flakes and seeds, but the perfume lingered. He carefully laid the vestments on the table.

Under the vestments was another cloth, again wrapped for preservation. This cloth was white, long and narrow, with intricate patterns in Broderie Anglaise all along its length. An altar cloth, then. His guess was reinforced when he saw the faint pink ring left by the wine on the bottom of a chalice.

The chalice was in the chest, alongside a small silver plate and two carafes, presumably one for water, the other for wine. There was a small amount of wine dried to a stain in the bottom of one of the carafes, its color, once a deep, shining burgundy, now a rancid, muddy brown, and it smelled like old vinegar. Freddy wrinkled his nose in distaste.

At the bottom of the chest were three thick ledgers on top of an assortment of other books: prayer books, and a heavy ancient Bible, the text of which he could barely read. A long black chain was attached to one side of the Bible, with a sturdy lock on the free end which, presumably, had attached it to the lectern at one time. He lifted the Bible from the chest with some difficulty and held the book in his hands for a moment, appreciating its quality. He had heard of these chained Bibles, of course. Who hadn't? But he had never thought he would see one for himself. Carefully, he put it on the table.

Underneath where the Bible had been, he found a child's primer with beautifully drawn pictures of Jesus and his disciples, depicting His infancy in the manger, some of His miracles, and His time on the cross. The colors in the picture were as vibrant and fresh as if they had been painted yesterday, although Freddy could tell from the book's style that it predated Bertie, and very probably the viscount before him. It was, without doubt, valuable, both in monetary terms and in what it could reveal of its place in history.

It was also exactly what Mrs. Rawlins had said she was seeking. He grinned at the thought, for he knew very well she had lied about that. Still, this primer, and the other contents of the chest were things she must take an interest in, if she did not want to be called out for her untruths. Freddy would take the primer to her tomorrow, and offer to accompany her when she returned here to see the rest of the things. So that he could watch her and, hopefully, gain some insight into her true purpose. That was his sole reason for wanting to come with her. It was not an excuse to spend time with her, *per se*. That possibility didn't interest him in the slightest. He simply wished to satisfy his curiosity, and clear the mystery surrounding her.

Refusing to think any more on that subject, Freddy put everything but the primer back into the chest and relocked it to keep the things safe. Then he put the primer in his pocket and headed out of the church and into the night.

Chapter Seven

The following morning, Eliza sat in her parlor eating her breakfast of toast and jam, and savoring a cup of tea, the one luxury she allowed herself to indulge in. A small fire played in the grate, snapping and cracking at the logs her maid had put on there, though the sun shone in a flawless sky, highlighting the many shades of green that made up her garden. Here and there, flowers peeped shyly, their colors tiny splashes of paint on the green and brown, a promise of a heady summer vista. She wondered whether she should tell her staff to refrain from lighting the fire now the spring was making its presence known, but hesitated to do so. Not lighting unnecessary fires would save money, and she certainly didn't have it to waste. On the other hand, it had been welcoming when she came in last night, and had quickly scared off not only the chill of the evening but the shiver in her soul, which had lingered after she'd heard that horrid little cry outside Saint Simon and Saint Jude's church in Crompton Hadlow.

Thoughts of the cry had kept her awake well into the night. It had sounded so like a child, and yet the church had been fully in darkness and locked tight. She and Prudence had rattled the doors hard, so if someone had been trapped inside, surely they would have cried out to them. Not only that, but the sexton had seemed to hear nothing untoward either. Perhaps it was just as Prudence had suggested, an animal calling out to its mate, or a cat marking its territory. She knew from experience that a cat could sound like a human. It might be worth another visit today, in daylight, just to put her mind at rest, although she could not think the child abductors would be brazen enough to store the children inside a church that was not only in regular use but sat right next door to a clergyman's home.

As she finished her tea, there was a knock on the front door. Eliza's heart sank. The people in Rotherton were friendly and welcoming, and ordinarily she would welcome calls from neighbors, just like anybody else. But while she was in this town she had a job to do, and time was of the essence. She had already lost a couple of hours of searching time this morning, since her restless night meant that when she'd finally slept, she woke late. If the callers stayed for too long…

A muffled voice sounded in the hall. Eliza frowned. It was a man's voice. She did not have gentlemen callers. She had no reason to have them. So who on earth could it be?

Her first thought was of Mr. Finch. She had seen him yesterday and he showed an interest in her purported study of the church. Had he decided to amuse himself by accompanying her to other churches? Lord, she hoped not, but it was just the kind of thing a bored man might do, especially if he was a rake, and the person he hoped to help was a young widow.

She stiffened at the thought. She would have to let him know, in a way that left him certain, that she was not interested in a dalliance. Then, hopefully, he would turn his attentions elsewhere and leave her to her search.

On the other hand, she thought, biting her lip

guiltily, she could well be maligning him. It may not even be him in her hallway, and if it was, his intentions might be quite honorable. She had no right to assume the worst of the man when she had no evidence to support her case. Just because he had a reputation… And because he had kissed her…

Being honest with herself, she must confess the kiss had not been unwelcome. Nor had it been one-sided, for she had kissed him back, with enthusiasm. More, she did not regret it in the slightest. It had been one of the most enjoyable moments of her life and she was not such a hypocrite as to say otherwise.

Which did not mean it would happen again. Oh, no. On the contrary, she would ensure that it didn't. That one kiss had been a solitary moment in time. It would never be repeated.

The door opened and the maid bobbed a curtsy, took a deep breath, and announced, importantly, "Mr. Finch, H'Esquire, to see you, madam." She then stood aside to allow the gentleman into the room.

Her first impression was that he was much larger than she remembered him being just yesterday. He seemed to fill her tiny parlor, taking up an inordinate amount of space. His coat of navy superfine fitted him perfectly, emphasizing the breadth of his shoulders. He wore it over a waistcoat of cerulean satin, and crisp linen so white it shone. His buckskin breeches showed off his long legs and the powerful muscles in his thighs. He must have borrowed Lord Rotherton's valet, because the shine on his boots was of a caliber that only a professional could have achieved.

Not that Eliza had any business noticing a man's boots. Or his thighs. Or anything else about his form. She lowered her eyes and took a deep breath, suddenly feeling there was not enough air in the room.

His eyes sparkled with humor as he gave her a perfectly respectable bow. She responded with a curtsy while the maid said she would fetch more tea, and left the room. She closed the door tight behind her, then opened it again with a "Sorry, madam," and positioned it just so. Her footsteps disappeared along the corridor and Mr. Finch watched the door as if he could see her through it.

"She is very eager to do her job."

"I have no complaints."

"Neither have I. She made me feel very important. If she does that for all your visitors, I am surprised there isn't a queue at the front door. Although, I should, in all honesty, point out that I am not a 'H'Esquire.' I own no land."

"Noted." Eliza smiled, his humor infectious. "Won't you sit down, sir?"

He sat at the table across from her, and declined a slice of toast. Even sitting, he seemed larger than life. For the first time since moving in, Eliza felt her parlor was too small. She swallowed, thinking she should make conversation with him but unable to come up with a single topic.

"I hoped to catch you before you left on your daily constitutional," he said, cheerily. "I have something to show you." He reached into his pocket and pulled out a small book with an aged and battered cover and handed it to her. As she took it, their fingers brushed and a sudden heat shot through her hand and into her arm. She jolted, and almost dropped the book. He withdrew his own hand as if he had been burned, and sat back in his chair, staring into the fire as if flames were the most fascinating phenomena he had ever seen. Eliza felt her color rise. She cleared her throat.

Thankfully, the maid entered with the fresh tea tray, giving them both time to recover.

"What is it?" Eliza asked when the maid had gone again. *Stupid question, Eliza. You could just look at it and see.*

"I found it in the chest. The one in the church."

"You got it open?" *Another stupid question. He didn't pull it out through the keyhole.*

To hide her embarrassment, she dipped her head and made a show of examining the book. It was a beautiful primer for children, depicting stories of Jesus' life. The pictures were crisp and bright, the text fresh, although written in a font that had not been in use for at least fifty years.

"It's beautiful," she breathed, turning the pages with reverent care.

"I thought you'd like it." He grinned. "I could hardly wait to show it to you. There are other things in the chest which might interest you, too."

"Oh?"

"I couldn't get everything in my pockets, so I left them there." He chuckled, letting her know he was teasing her. "If you would like to see them, we could go today. I'd like to know what you make of them, to be honest."

Eliza's heart sank. She had already established there was nothing in the little church that would help her find Claire, and she was eager to move on and continue looking somewhere else. However, she couldn't say that aloud. She needed to maintain her story, which meant she must be excited by his find, and eager to see it for herself. So, praying there would still be time to go on to a new search afterward, she smiled brightly and said, "I'll fetch my pelisse."

****

Freddy swallowed his guilt. He should be out doing the job for which Fremont paid him, searching for the gold. He knew it was not in the chapel on the Hadlow estate, which meant he had no real reason to return there. He ought to move on. Instead, he felt a strange compulsion to accompany Mrs. Rawlins to see the contents of the chest. He wanted to watch her, to see her reaction to the artifacts he'd uncovered.

Of course, he didn't think for a moment they were what she truly wanted. He only wanted to see her with them so he could catch her out, and thereby learn the true nature of her search, discover if it had some bearing on his investigation. Truly, that was his sole motivation. And so he would keep telling himself.

He had to admit, though, she had been very convincing in her excitement and admiration of the primer. If he didn't know better, he would have thought the book was the Holy Grail to her, the thing she had truly wished to find. For a moment, he had questioned his own instincts. Perhaps he had read the situation wrongly, and she truly was interested in the history of the churches. But then, there had been the slightest of hesitations when he mentioned returning to the church to see the chest, reinforcing his suspicions. He would watch her, closely. It was all he could do at this time. And it wasn't exactly the most onerous job he'd ever had. Today, she wore a dove-grey dress that fitted her perfectly, the bodice modest, just hinting at the full curves of her breasts. It didn't leach the color from her face as the black of full mourning had done, and her complexion was a pretty peaches-and-cream, which made the blue of her eyes sparkle. Her hair shone, the myriad colors of spring and fall catching the light, making him regret they must go out, for upon leaving the house she would wear a bonnet, and he hated to see all that glory hidden.

What was the matter with him? Spring and fall? Peaches and cream? Hidden glory? If Adam—or any of his friends, for that matter—knew he'd used such phrases, even in the privacy of his thoughts, he would never live it down. He'd be the laughingstock of the *ton*. He cleared his throat and vowed to remain sensible and businesslike from now on, as he followed her from the house and walked beside her along the road.

The day was a pretty one, the sun warming as they walked toward the Hadlow estate. Trees were in bud, and already the first crops were sprouting in the fields. The ground didn't seem as waterlogged as it had been for the last two years when the summers had been abnormally short and filled with rain, wind, and cold. All over the country, crops had failed in those years, driving landowners to ruin and pushing up prices beyond the reach of many. Thousands of the poorest had died of starvation, and those who survived were thin and haggard. Freddy sincerely hoped this year's summer would be temperate, and give both the land and the people chance to recover.

Thoughts of universal hardship were far too disheartening, so instead Freddy made small talk, encouraging Mrs. Rawlins to talk about her family. Hers had, it seemed, been a happy childhood, with parents who loved each other and cared deeply for their children. Her father, especially, must have had a profoundly positive effect on her because, several times, she spoke of him as if he were still alive. She also spoke fondly of her two brothers, both of whom had become clergymen, and of her sister, also a widow, living in Leicestershire.

"Was your sister married to a cleric too?" he asked. Part of him thought it touching that the whole family seemed centered on their faith and service to God. The other, more cynical part wondered how they could stomach such a surfeit of religious righteousness. Freddy's uncle had been a vicar, and having known him, he was firmly of the opinion that one clergyman in the family was more than enough.

"No," Mrs. Rawlins answered him. "My sister married a man of business. He and his family had a number of enterprises in and around Leicester. Alas, he was killed in a coaching accident a year ago. Charlotte, my sister, was gravely injured. She has not walked since, although we pray constantly that, eventually, she will make a full recovery."

"I am sorry to hear of her woes," he said. "It must be difficult for a young woman to find herself constrained physically, unable to do all she did before. Are there children of the marriage?"

Mrs. Rawlins bit her lip and seemed reluctant to answer, and Freddy felt guilty. He had clearly touched a nerve with his last question. It occurred to him, then, that if both husband and wife were in the coach when it met with an accident, the children might also have been there. Had those little ones perished, along with their father?

"Forgive me. I shouldn't pry," he said. She made no attempt to answer, which left him feeling awkward. He cleared his throat. "And your husband?" he asked, in an attempt to restart the amicable conversation.

"My husband?" She looked perplexed for a moment, then nodded and smiled. "Oh, yes. My husband. What about him?"

"Did he have a large family?"

She shook her head. "Nobody. He left nobody. Except me, of course."

There was another moment of silence. She looked around at the countryside as they strolled through it. The lane they travelled was uneven, the middle of the road raised, with ruts either side where dozens of carts had worn the surface down over the years. To either side the lane was bordered by dry stone walls and occasional hedges, with here and there a tree that hugged the wall and let its branches reach out across the road. Beyond the walls were fields, some pasture dotted with cows and sheep, calves and lambs at their sides. Other fields were filled with young crops.

"Did you assist him in his work?"

She blinked, clearly having lost the thread of their conversation. "Assist him…? Why, yes. Yes, I did," she said, her smile too bright.

Freddy nodded and pretended her demeanor was as it should be. "I have heard it said that a clergyman's greatest asset in his work—after God, of course—is a compassionate woman at his side."

Mrs. Rawlins nodded. "The family of a vicar does work alongside him, that is true." She took a deep breath. "And what of you, sir? Do you have family still living?"

He had the distinct feeling she asked as a means of changing the subject. So, the lady did not wish to discuss her husband? Had her marriage been an unhappy one?

Unable to ask her that, or to bring the conversation back round to her, Freddy answered her question, albeit reluctantly. "Most of them are still with us. Brother, father, mother, grandparents—we are a fairly long-lived group of people."

"That must be comforting to know. If the entire family is long-lived, your own chances of reaching a great age must increase."

Freddy laughed. "One would hope so. Although, I have always made it my business to flout the rules and do the opposite, so perhaps it isn't as comforting as you might think."

"An out-and-out rebel, are you?" Her lips twitched.

"Dyed in the wool."

"Why would that be?"

The question startled him and he realized he had never before thought about it. He had always accepted that he was as he was, and that was that. Now, for the first time, he took a moment to ponder the question.

"I don't really know," he said, at last. "Partly, it must be that I am that way by nature. One doesn't go against one's character, surely?"

"One also doesn't rebel against things that make one happy." He had to acknowledge the truth in her words. "What made you unhappy?" Her voice was gentle, her interest in his answer clear and genuine. Freddy looked across the fields to the bruised blue of the Downs on the horizon, the white-blue of the distant sky shining above them. Then he glanced back at her.

If he had seen pity in her eyes, he would have changed the subject again. The last thing he needed, or wanted, was that. But she showed none. Instead, her eyes reflected interest and empathy, care for the boy he had been, and compassion for the man he had become. Before he realized he was going to say anything, he found himself telling her of his unhappy childhood as the spare son of an earl, useful only as a last resort should his older brother die or prove incapable of providing the next generation. There was, he thought now, something sordid about knowing he was really only of value to his family in the event of a tragedy.

He told her of the times he had longed to join his father and brother as the older man prepared the younger for his future. Freddy's efforts to join them had always been rebuffed, his interest scorned and his presence barely tolerated when it was allowed, so that it was a relief to go away to school.

His mother had had no more interest in him than his father had, caught up as she was in doing good works, chairing committees to help run orphanages and schools to give the poor opportunities to improve their lot, saving lost women, and teaching females from the slums how to be better mothers.

He scoffed at that. "She never took her own advice, of course. She had nursery nurses to do that."

Mrs. Rawlins said nothing, but she slipped her arm through his. The comfort in the small, innocent gesture was incredible. He felt the heavy rock pressing on his chest begin to lighten, even as the back of his eyes stung with tears he refused to shed.

"It must be awful to be so unhappy at home," she said. Her tone was one of contemplated understanding, which was a relief. It helped him to tamp down the sudden and disquieting self-pity. She continued, in that same even tone. "Even more so if everyone around you is content, and you are alone in your misery."

That made him scoff. "Oh, they weren't content. They were miserable, too. Another family trait." She frowned but said nothing, so he continued. "My mother and father tolerated each other long enough to produce the heir and spare that duty demanded, then went on to separate lives, avoiding each other unless that wasn't possible. I know he has mistresses; he makes no attempt to hide them. If my mother has lovers too, she is discreet enough that I know nothing of them."

"That is sad."

"But all too common."

"Is the continuation of the line and the protection of property really worth so much unhappiness?"

"They would say so. As would my brother. He married the woman whose land marches alongside my father's, and their marriage makes my parents relationship seem heavenly."

She gave him a considering look. "Is that why you have never married?"

The question took him by surprise. He opened his mouth to answer, closed it again, frowned, then spoke. "Do you know, I've never really thought about it. But now that I do, there may well be an element of truth in that."

They walked on in a companionable silence for a few minutes, and reached the outskirts of Crompton Hadlow. As they approached the first buildings of the hamlet, Mrs. Rawlins let go of Freddy's arm and moved away slightly, putting a more respectable distance between them. He missed her closeness immediately, the warmth of her hand on his arm. He wished he could take it back, let the world think what it may, but he knew he could not. He would leave here once he found the gold for Fremont, and the lady would have to stay and weather the gossip that would be inevitable from such behavior.

The fragility of a woman's reputation was highlighted when he heard hurried footsteps behind them and turned his head to see Miss Burgess rushing to catch them up. Her face was flushed with the exertion and she breathed heavily, indicating that running was not something she did as a rule.

She reached them and pushed between them, forcing him to step aside to let her in. He pursed his lips but said nothing.

"Eliza," she said, breathlessly. "How lovely to see you." She glanced at him, her mouth puckered in distaste. "And Mr. Finch."

"Prudence," returned Mrs. Rawlins.

Prudence. Freddy thought the name suited the curate's sister well. As "Eliza" suited Mrs. Rawlins. It was a sweet name, straightforward and honest, with its mixed connotations of regality and ordinariness.

"You are out for a walk," said Prudence. Freddy glanced at Mrs. Rawlins—Eliza. Her lips twitched slightly and he knew she shared his humor over the obviousness of the comment.

"I am," she replied, blandly.

"With Mr. Finch."

Once again, Prudence Burgess glanced at him. He wanted to tell her that her powers of deduction were second to none, and with observational skills like hers she should be working as a spy for Lord Fremont. He pressed his lips together and stayed silent.

"Where are you going?" she continued.

"Mr. Finch is going to show me the chapel on the Hadlow estate."

"Alone?" Prudence's voice was shrill with disapproval. She cleared her throat. "What I mean to say is, one cannot be too careful, you know." She lowered her voice slightly. "You can use hat pins as a weapon, if you need to."

Freddy bristled at the implied insult. What did she think he was going to do? He may have a reputation about town but, as far as he knew, nobody had ever accused him of dallying with women who didn't know, and live by, the rules of play. Something which, on their short acquaintance, he knew Eliza Rawlins did not. Nor was he so lax in his morals, nor so uncontrolled in his behavior, that he would importune a respectable lady, especially in a public place—and most especially in a church!

Although, he couldn't claim total innocence on that score. Had he not kissed Eliza just yesterday? Inside that selfsame church? It had been one of the best kisses he had ever had in his life, and he would jump at the chance to repeat it. To hold the lady's slender frame in his arms, smell the warm flowers of her perfume, feel her breasts rub against him with every breath she took…

Perhaps Prudence Burgess was right to be skeptical of her friend's safety after all. He took a deep breath, tamping down the fire his thoughts had kindled and looked to the two ladies. Prudence chattered on, oblivious to the offence she had caused. Eliza's cheeks were a soft peach-pink and her bottom lip was caught under her top teeth, her discomfort and embarrassment plain to see.

"Besides, a woman's reputation is, in itself, a fragile flower," Prudence said, putting her arm through the crook of Eliza's elbow. "It would matter not whether you had done anything to warrant your ruin, dearest, for we all know that the tongue is a sharp weapon that does not always have a care to speak only the truth."

A fleeting irritation passed over Eliza's face so quickly, Freddy almost missed it. Prudence, who was looking straight ahead, certainly did so.

"I know you for a virtuous woman," she continued, "with a price, as the good book says, far above rubies. Strength and honor are your clothing, but you must ensure you are always seen to wear them."

Eliza rolled her eyes. "Quite so."

Freddy wondered if he should come to her rescue, but decided that doing so might make things worse, and he should abide by another ancient quote, though probably not one found in the Bible: least said, soonest mended. A moment later, though, his resolve to stay quiet was shattered.

"You do not want it said of you that your feet go down to death, and your steps take hold on Hell, do you?" Prudence turned to Freddy with a look of disdain. "I'm sure you know, sir, that is a warning from the Book of Proverbs."

"Thank you," he answered, through gritted teeth.

"Proverbs warns of the consequences of immorality on several occasions, you know. For example, a woman that makes her husband ashamed is as rottenness in his bones."

"That may well be," said Freddy, quietly, "but neither that nor the other phrase applies to Mrs. Rawlins in any way. She, I am sure you will agree, is a crown to her husband." *See? I can quote the Bible too.*

Prudence looked taken aback; whether that was because a sinner like him knew biblical verses well enough to quote them, or because he'd had the temerity to admonish her when that clearly didn't happen often, he could not say. "It is not whether one is virtuous that is important to one's reputation," she said through lips so puckered and tight he wondered she could make the words come at all. "As I said before, it is whether you are seen to be virtuous. Which is why, if you are going to the church with this gentleman," she addressed Eliza, having given Freddy one last look of disdain, "I shall come with you and act as your chaperone."

Freddy grimaced at the thought of enduring the woman's company to the estate and back.

"There really is no need…" Eliza began.

"There is every need. It's what a real friend will do." Prudence tittered. "I know you would perform such a service for me, and I shall trade you like for like. No, I insist," she went on when Eliza made to object once more.

And that was that. They could not protest her presence too much, nor could they abort their outing, without giving rise to speculation. They had no choice but to continue, with the thoughtful Prudence ensuring Freddy didn't succumb to his baser instinct and ravish the delectable Eliza.

Freddy and Eliza stayed silent, but Prudence had no trouble filling the void. She spoke of her neighbors, the wickedness in the world and the need to guard against it, her brother's attention to his flock and their lack of gratitude for him, and the appalling lack of promotion the bishop had seen fit to give to "poor Silas." Eliza made noises of agreement, astonishment and outrage in all the right places. Freddy lost himself in his own thoughts, using the time in an attempt to decide where he could look next for Fremont's gold.

They reached the church in the meadow and Prudence studied it eagerly. "I have never been in here before," she said, running her hand over the ancient ruined walls of the nave. "Such a shame to see the Lord's house go to rack and ruin in this fashion." Freddy ignored her and pushed open the door to the intact chapel.

"These kneelers are still in such good condition," said Prudence, examining one of the bright-colored pads. "I shall have to see if we can use them at Saint Simon and St Jude's. We were thinking of asking the ladies of the parish to make some more, but if we can take these, they'll be free to do other things."

When Freddy opened the chest to show Eliza what was inside, Prudence's eyes grew as round and big as saucers, and her mouth formed a perfect O. For almost half a minute she was rendered speechless by the treasures she saw. Then she grabbed the chain Bible and pulled it, possessively, to her.

"It's an original Bible, from the time of Henry the Eighth," she whispered. "How wonderful." She pushed it under her arm and clamped it against her body while she reached in for the chalice. "I'll also take this and the plate," she said. "I should have brought a bag. Would have, if I had known."

Freddy and Eliza exchanged startled glances. "You cannot take those things," said Eliza, a lot more gently and politely than Freddy would have. "They aren't yours."

"I know that." Prudence looked affronted. "I wasn't—you didn't think I was taking them for myself?" She laughed, a sharp, brittle sound. "For the church, my dear. Not for me. I want to put them in a church that is in use, where everyone can see them."

"No. They must stay here," said Eliza, firmly but kindly.

"But..."

"Indeed, they must," agreed Freddy. "They belong to the new Viscount Hadlow."

"I'm certain he won't mind."

"You cannot know that. He may have other plans for them," said Freddy. He was conscious of a cheeky and mischievous demon on his shoulder, goading and guiding him. "All these things, the Bible in particular, are worth a lot of money at a time when the estate is heavily in debt. The sale of these items could put a big hole into that debt."

Eliza gave him a sidelong look, which told him she thought he was very naughty. It was all he could do not to laugh out loud in return.

"Sell them?" Prudence looked as though the shock would knock her over. "Sell God's Word?" She shuddered and paled. "Heathens and unbelievers! Do you not know, ye cannot serve God and Mammon."

"Ye can pay off your creditors, though." Freddy's patience was stretched almost to breaking point by now. "Does it not say, 'Owe no man anything'?"

"But—" Prudence clutched the book tighter to her.

"It belongs to the estate." He was gratified to hear that, despite his rising anger, his voice was still firm, but not cruel. He held out his hands and, with a moue of disappointment, she handed the book to him. He placed it, and everything else, including the primer from his pocket, back into the chest, which he shut and locked. He glanced up at Eliza, apology in his eyes that she would not be able to examine these things today. Her return smile was reassuring.

Prudence, however, looked ready to cry. Her fingers twitched as if she was fighting to stop herself snatching everything back. It made him think of yet another biblical quote, one he couldn't fully recall at the moment but which had something to do with coveting a neighbor's ass. Even as he locked the chest and secured it, he vowed to return as soon as he could to move it to a safer place.

"Shall we go?" Eliza asked and she took Prudence's arm, leading the reluctant woman away from the vestry, out of the church and back toward Crompton Hadlow.

When they reached the curate's cottage, Prudence was at pains to invite Elizabeth in for tea. Although Eliza made attempts to refuse, it became clear that Prudence was not willing to take no for an answer. It was also clear that the invitation did not extend to Freddy, so he bowed and told them he had to get back, for he had promised Lord Rotherton a game of billiards. As he walked away, guilt weighed him down that he had abandoned Eliza to the tender ministrations of the curate's sister, but he dismissed it.

"They are friends," he told himself. "She will be happy to share a cup of tea with her friend." He walked on a few paces. "She will only be there twenty minutes. That is all a social call is supposed to be. Half an hour at most." He squared his jaw and fought his conscience. "I could do nothing else," he muttered. "The woman was too insistent. And besides, I could not tarry any longer. I have other things to do, places to explore, people to talk with, chests of gold to find." He resisted the urge to look back over his shoulder as he walked away.

****

Eliza sat in the parlor of the curate's cottage at Crompton Hadlow, sipping tea and nibbling on a biscuit while Prudence talked at her. Every now and then, Eliza nodded agreement, or injected an, "Oh, my!" into the conversation to prove she was listening, albeit with only half an ear.

The parlor was tiny, its small floor space and low ceiling serving to make her feel enclosed and trapped. It didn't help that the windows were tiny and let in only a meagre amount of daylight, or that there was enough furniture in the room to comfortably fill a space three times as large. Dark wood occasional tables that matched a dark sideboard and a pianoforte vied for space alongside two chintz-covered sofas and three armchairs, as well as several smaller chairs with upholstered seats, wooden ladder backs, and spindly legs. The hearth was dark and cold, the mantelshelf above it cluttered with porcelain figurines of Jesus and his disciples, along with an impressive piece that depicted the three crosses at Calgary, each with a man nailed to it. The piece was disturbingly beautiful, compelling and horrifying at one and the same time.

"It is wonderful, is it not?" asked Prudence, when she saw Eliza glance at it for what must be the tenth time in five minutes. "It's a family heirloom. Our great-great-grandfather acquired it from a French emigre, a Huguenot, I believe. He said it had been in his family for over a hundred years, although we don't know that we believe him. Our father always said he thought it was made to adorn a church, not a house. We believe the Huguenot may have stolen it from a church as he fled the persecutions."

"It does seem more suited to a church," agreed Eliza.

"A French one, perhaps." Prudence's lip curled. "It wouldn't be in keeping with the churches around here."

That was true. The churches dotted across Rotherton, at least those Eliza had seen so far, were all staunchly Protestant, not only in their worship but in their style, too. As such, they lacked statues, ornate pictures and other adornments that would be commonplace in the Catholic churches of the continent. Personally, Eliza had no objection to such things. A church her father had presided over had had a large and ornate crucifix hanging from the wall, and focusing on it had helped Eliza to concentrate on worship when her mind tried to wander. Not that she thought Prudence would appreciate her saying so.

"And besides," Prudence carried on, "if we put it into the church, the people might start to believe it belongs here. It would be difficult to retrieve it when it is time to move on. We wouldn't want to lose it, would we?"

"No." Eliza sipped her tea.

"That Bible today was beautiful."

"Yes."

"Such a waste. Locked in a chest, only available to the likes of Mr. Finch."

Eliza took another bite of her biscuit.

"He must know it is valuable. I am astonished he hasn't already appropriated it for himself." Prudence nodded, agreeing with herself.

Eliza bristled, offended on Mr. Finch's behalf. "He is no thief."

Prudence raised a skeptical eyebrow. "Who knows what a man will stoop to when he has pressing gambling debts? 'Then goeth he, and taketh with himself seven other spirits more wicked than himself, and they enter in and dwell there, and the last state of that man is worse than the first.' No, Eliza, do not look at me so. I say nothing that isn't the truth. The man's gambling debts are, apparently, gargantuan. That is why he is in this area in the first place."

"You are not being fair."

"I am not being unfair, my dear," argued Prudence. "I speak the truth. He is here on what they call a 'repairing lease.'"

"Mayhap he is. But that does not mean—"

"Really, the man knows no shame. If he did, he would not show his face in public. He has, or rather, had, so much when others have so little. And he has been frivolous with it, to say the least."

Eliza sighed. Trying to argue was a pointless exercise, for Prudence was not listening.

"So many have what they do not deserve," continued Prudence, intoning as if she were delivering a sermon, and doing it so effectively that Eliza wondered, fleetingly, whether the lady wrote her brother's homilies for him. "Others," she continued, "do not have all they should have."

Eliza felt an almost overwhelming urge to defend Mr. Finch. Not only was he not here to defend himself, but she felt he was not as terrible as Prudence was making him sound. Yes, the man was a gambler, hiding from his creditors, but he was also honest. If he were not, he would have taken the church treasures for himself instead of showing them to Eliza today. He had had plenty of opportunity to do so.

He had also behaved like a gentleman in all his

dealings with her. True, he had kissed her, but she had wished him to do so. And the kiss, while not exactly what one might call chaste, had not been disrespectful or depraved. Eliza knew, from her father's work, there were men who would have pushed much farther, especially when they thought they were dealing with a widow, a woman of some experience. Freddy Finch had not behaved much like the rake he was labelled at all.

"If he wants to throw his money around," continued Prudence, bringing Eliza out of her reverie, "he should give it to those poor people who have done nothing to bring about their suffering. He should make their lives better for them by changing their circumstances."

Oh yes, the deserving poor. If Eliza had a penny for every time she heard people talk about the "deserving" poor, presumably as opposed to the "undeserving," she would have enough to help every poverty-stricken person in England. With a fixed smile that she knew did not reach her eyes, she said, "The poor are always with us, Prudence. Even Jesus said, 'Ye have the poor always with you.' If He could not rid the world of the scourge of poverty, I sincerely doubt Mr. Finch would be able to do so."

The look Prudence gave her was flat, a mixture of disappointment, impatience, and irritation. "He could try," she said. She took a drink of her tea, then put down the cup and saucer with a decided snap.

Eliza found herself wondering if she had been overly harsh in her own judgment. Prudence may have been critical of Mr. Finch, but her heart was in the right place, and she meant well. She had a desire to help the poor and the downtrodden, and it must be frustrating to see their needs unmet when others treated wealth in such a cavalier fashion. When she thought of it in that way, Eliza felt churlish for her offence at Prudence's opinion.

"These biscuits are wonderful," she said, in a cheery bid to change the subject of their conversation. "Do you think your cook would be willing to share the recipe?"

Chapter Eight

Freddy spent the next few days making his way around the area, trying to be unobtrusive while looking for something that seemed out of place, anything which could point him to the missing gold. Being a newcomer to Rotherton was an advantage, as he could claim to be exploring without raising suspicion, and if somebody should complain that he was where he should not be, he could say he was lost, apologize and move on.

Despite his efforts, he found nothing of interest, nothing to say the gold had ever been in near here. He knew the traitors hadn't had time to move it on to their French counterparts, but they had clearly hidden it well. So well, in fact, that he found himself wondering if the dratted chest actually ever existed in the first place. Each evening, the frustration of another fruitless day souring his mood, he found a tavern to indulge in a pint of ale and a plate of whatever the landlady had cooked for her customers. He soon discovered that not all of them were accomplished cooks, so that while some of his meals were delicious and satisfying, others were not. He forced his way through bowls of greasy lamb, and plates of beef so tough he could have made boots from it, and stews so lacking in ingredients they were more of a gruel. In each tavern, though, he made no complaint, but ate whatever was served, if not exactly with gusto, then certainly with a show of appreciation.

He always took a seat in a corner at the back of the room where he could observe the other customers without making it too obvious that was what he was doing. He ate his food slowly, and nursed his pint so it lasted all night, giving him an excuse to be there without having to become inebriated.

In Frantham, he was surprised to see the Reverend Mr. Burgess enter just as he was finishing his stew. The landlord greeted the curate like an old friend and handed him a tankard of beer with a head of deep froth. The curate grinned and took it, licked his lips, then drank half the beer in one go, wiping the froth from his lips with his fingers in a way that said he had enjoyed every drop. He shared a joke with two men who stood at the bar, greeted another group who sat at a nearby table, then saw Freddy, sitting in the corner, slowly chewing his last piece of meat.

Awkward embarrassment crossed the curate's face. He looked down at his tankard as if he was astonished to find it in his hand and wondered where it had come from. Then he glanced at the door, clearly contemplating leaving, before he realized that he had already been seen drinking, so there was no point in trying to hide it.

He crossed the room and smiled at Freddy. "Good evening, Mr. Finch. I haven't seen you in here before." He sounded as if he was trying to sound light, but didn't quite succeed.

"I haven't been in here before," answered Freddy.

The curate nodded and studied his beer for a moment. "I take my duties to my flock seriously," he said, quietly. "You know, meet them where they are."

"I see that." Freddy looked around the tiny tap room. The room was square and squat, its low ceiling making it seem even smaller than it truly was. A fire blazed in a hearth that took up the whole of one wall, its crackling logs giving off so much heat it was slightly uncomfortable. The chimney was in need of a cleaning—some of the smoke curled its way out of the fireplace, mixing with the fumes from the candles to give the room a foggy appearance that softened sharp edges and overbright colors and made everything seem friendlier. About a dozen men were crowded into the tiny space, most of them dressed in the smocks and wooden shoes of laborers. Their conversations had stopped momentarily when Freddy entered; no doubt they wondered why someone dressed like him was darkening the door of this establishment, but when he nodded greetings at them, ordered his fare and sat in a corner, they turned back to their friends and began to talk again.

Their conversations, just like the ones he'd heard in taverns in Crompton Hadlow last night, and in the hamlets of Millbrook and Rotherton Bellow on the evenings before that, were of little use to him. They laughed about incidents at work that were not funny to anyone who didn't work with them, extolled the virtues of various barmaids, and bemoaned the cost of food. In other words, the exact topics of conversation one might expect from a group of men at the end of a hard day. Which meant Freddy was no nearer to finding Fremont's gold than he had been when first tasked with recovering it.

"Why are you here?" asked Burgess. He sat at Freddy's table without asking if he might.

"I came in for a drink. And something to eat." Freddy lifted his tankard in salute, sipped at his ale and put it down again.

"Not the usual haunt for a man of your station." The curate lowered his voice so the other men wouldn't hear him so easily.

"I was out riding, and this place looked respectable." Freddy gave a nonchalant shrug.

They talked for a while about things that didn't matter, then Burgess finished his drink, smacked his lips in satisfaction, clapped his hands onto his knees, and stood. "Better be off, I suppose. Goodnight. Have a care riding home. The roads near here don't make for comfortable travel after dark."

Freddy fought to keep the frown from his face as he wondered if he'd just been issued a friendly caution or a veiled threat. The curate left and the landlord came to clear Freddy's plate away.

"More ale, sir?" he asked.

"No, thank you."

The landlord grinned. "Got to you, did he? With his Jesus bashing?"

"Does he do that a lot?"

The landlord waved his hand in a yes-and-no answer. "Enough to satisfy his bishop that he's doing his job, I expect. Not so much that I have to discourage him from coming in." He leaned in a little, conspiratorially. Freddy smelled stale beer and onions. "Likes a pint, does our clergyman. And why not? Long as he don't bring that 'atchet-faced sister of his." He chuckled, took the plate and moved away.

The next night, Freddy went into another small pub, in the hamlet of Mereham, ten miles from Rotherton. Here, he sat in the corner, ate the simple food, and nursed a pint of indifferent ale. Again, he heard nothing of value to him, and again, the curate came in. This time, Freddy leaned back into the shadows so he wouldn't be seen so easily.

For a while it worked. Burgess spoke with a small group of men. They lowered their voices so Freddy couldn't hear them, though they looked to be discussing a serious subject. He might have thought Burgess was ministering to his flock, except Mereham was not inside any of the parishes Burgess held. From what he knew of the Church of England, the vicar here would not take too kindly to a neighboring clergyman encroaching on his territory. Parishes were always guarded jealously. A cleric kept within his boundaries.

As the curate was leaving, he saw Freddy. He looked surprised for an instant, then masked it, said enough to him to be polite, and left.

Two evenings later, the curate came into the tap room at the Golden Goose in Rotherton. He saw Freddy and this time he frowned, disapprovingly, and made a beeline toward him.

"Why are you here?" He sounded as if Freddy's presence was a personal affront.

Freddy blinked, slowly. "Same reason most of the patrons are here, I should think," he replied. "Why are you here?"

Burgess swallowed, clearly uncomfortable. He stretched as if his neckcloth was too tight. "This is my flock. It is my duty to administer to them."

"You administer to them better than most." There was a moment's pause. Freddy took a sip of his beer. "Your address in church last Sunday was inspiring." Not that Freddy would know. He'd spent the time trying to think of new places to search for the gold, and hadn't heard a word.

"Thank you. That is gratifying. It is good you were in the church to hear. But, alas, if I confined my evangelism to Sunday services only, far too many would *not* hear. Certainly, many who need to hear would be left wanting."

"So you come in here."

"So I come in here. For did not our Lord say, 'They that be whole need not a physician, but they that are sick'?" He sat beside Freddy. The landlord brought him a tankard of ale. He thanked the man, and waited till he had gone again before he looked Freddy up and down, and said, "I begin to wonder if, sometimes, the sick are coming into the hospital but not faithfully taking the medicine."

Freddy smiled, wryly. "The medicine was given in large daily doses when I was a boy. I had a tutor who knew the Bible inside out and vowed that my brother and I would know it in the same manner."

Burgess nodded his understanding. "Holding a child's nose until they open their mouths, then forcing the spoon in, can have an adverse effect. A lifetime's disgust of that which is best for them." The look on the curate's face left Freddy wondering whether Burgess was still warning him of the dangers of Freddy's dissolute living, or whether he was speaking of himself.

"I have had but one pint of ale, sir."

"Some will say the smallest sip can give the devil a foothold."

They made eye contact and held it for a long moment before Freddy looked away and sipped at his drink again. "What the eye doesn't see, the heart does not grieve over." He drained the tankard and put it firmly on the table. "I must away, I'm afraid. I am promised to Mrs.

Potter's soiree this evening, and I don't want to be late."

Burgess smiled. "No, indeed. I believe you made quite the impression at her last event."

Freddy raised his eyebrows but didn't take umbrage. It was true that his arrival at the Potter's last soiree had been noteworthy, although Freddy had not been the guilty party. That role had been taken by his friend, Bertie, Lord Hadlow, who had already been well and truly foxed by the time they got there, and who had tripped over the threshold into the room, drawing attention to himself and his companions in a way that did not endear them to anybody present. Were it not for the fact that Freddy was now Lord Rotherton's guest, he doubted he would have been invited a second time.

He wondered who else would be there. Now that she'd gone from full to half mourning, perhaps Eliza would be invited. He smiled at the prospect. It was a week since their trip to see the treasures in the chapel, and it would be good to see her again. The thought made him smile.

Burgess cleared his throat and frowned at Freddy. Freddy blanked his expression as he realized the clergyman had misinterpreted the reason for his smile and was shaking his head at the idea that Freddy found Bertie's rude behavior funny.

"He was a character," he said, allowing Burgess to continue in his mistake, because it was better than him knowing the truth.

"Not an asset to his family name, though." Burgess sipped his drink. "Do you know when his successor will come?"

"I don't. The new Lord Hadlow is not known to me."

Burgess nodded. "He will come soon enough, I dare

say." He smiled and stood. "Enjoy the soiree," and he left the tavern.

****

Eliza was, indeed, at the Potters' home that evening, although at first Freddy did not see her. The place was crowded with the great and the good of the neighborhood, so much so, it was not immediately possible to know exactly who was there. As Lord Rotherton's houseguest, Freddy was made welcome, although his hostess could not completely hide her disdain for him, and he was under no illusion that he would not have been invited were it not for his friendship with the earl.

The daughter of the house was there, on one of her first forays into Society. Dark haired and doe-eyed, she looked like what she was, a schoolgirl dressed up in adult clothing. Not to Freddy's taste at all, although one might think he had a reputation for debauching innocents, considering the pains Mrs. Potter took to keep a distance between him and the girl. Freddy didn't take offence at this, since the woman had a duty to keep her daughter from the company of rakes and scoundrels, and the fact that she judged him to be one meant he was doing his job properly. It did amuse him, however, to have Rotherton introduce him to the girl, just to see the mother attempt to hide her horror.

"You are incorrigible," whispered Rotherton as they walked away, leaving the woman to fuss around her daughter, clearly relieved at the lucky escape she'd had.

"It's part of my charm," he replied.

He took a glass from the tray of a passing servant and looked around the room hopefully but saw no sign of Eliza. *Of course, she may not be coming tonight at all.*

He had surmised that she was ready to rejoin Society and take part in events such as this, but he might have been mistaken. Or, she may not even have been invited. She was, after all, merely the widow of a clergyman. Mrs. Potter had set her sights far higher than that.

About an hour into the evening, he was involved in a lively and lighthearted discussion on whether Johnson's new Ladies Walking Machine was a seemly mode of transport for young and unmarried ladies, when he felt a strange shifting of the air around him. The hairs on the back of his neck stood to attention, and his spine tingled. He had to make a conscious effort not to shake his shoulders to alleviate it. Perplexed, and a little nonplussed, he looked around and saw Eliza, standing a mere four feet from him, listening to the conversation.

"The machine sounds intriguing," she said when the group acknowledged her.

"Positively decadent," argued Mr. Potter, with a shake of his head. "Shouldn't want my daughter using one."

"Apparently, like all velocipedes, it can double the speed a person walks at, compared to walking without it," said Rotherton. The humor in his voice told Freddy he was being provocative.

"To what purpose?" asked Mr. Potter. "Why does a lady, or anyone for that matter, need to move faster?"

Freddy took a step back and left them to their debate. He smiled at Eliza, who smiled back. "Are you enjoying the evening?" he asked, then struggled not to roll his eyes. Was that truly the best thing he could think of to say to her?

"Very much." There was a moment's awkward silence before she continued, "I understand some of the guests will entertain us later."

"Miss Potter has been invited to sing to us, I believe."

Eliza glanced over to the young woman, who looked as if she would rather be elsewhere. "She seems to view the prospect with dread."

He followed her gaze. "I'm sure she will be all right. If her voice is sweet, she will have to grow accustomed to it before she has her Season. And her voice will be sweet, for if it were not, her mother would not have put her forward for this performance."

"Are you always so cynical?"

"Only when it's warranted. How goes your search?" She looked up sharply at him, her eyes fearful. *Interesting*. "For church historical records," he clarified.

Her smile was one of relief. "Slowly," she told him.

Freddy wanted to ask what she really looked for. He wanted to hear the truth on her lips, to learn her secrets, and then to spend more time with her in the quiet isolation of underused buildings, helping her to unearth whatever it was she sought. Her floral scent would sweeten the musty air of those churches, and her presence would fill the space, leaving an indelible print there. They would work closely, so closely he would feel the warmth of her body, see the shine in her hair and the peachiness of her skin, the rise and fall of her breasts as her breathing quickened…

He cleared his throat and lifted his chin, pulling on the persona of disinterested male like a well-worn cloak. For he must be disinterested. Not only was he on a quest of his own, and duty bound to give it all his attention, but if he had the time to devote to a dalliance, it would not be with this woman. She was a vicar's widow, for goodness' sake! Of all the women here, she was the least likely to welcome an affair. A woman of virtue, whose reputation he should do nothing to sully. In fact, he should not be seen so much in her company. He should take his leave of her, leave her to socialize with others, and move away.

It took all he had within him to do so.

For the rest of the evening, Freddy was only vaguely aware of the other people in the room. They spoke to him. He answered. He couldn't tell what any of them had said. He shared jokes with other gentlemen, but didn't recall what was so funny. Ladies flirted and he answered in kind, but two minutes later, he could not recall their names. Older men talked of hunting, shooting, and fishing, and offered him the chance to fish their streams and shoot their birds. He remembered none of them. There was nothing to remember. Nothing, save the beautiful woman nearby, her dark curls framing her beautiful face, the dove grey of her half-mourning gown enhancing her elegant figure and the soft colors of her complexion. He made a conscious effort to move away from her, to engage with others properly, to try to hide the obsession for her that grew within him.

That he failed to do that was made clear in the carriage on the way home. Rotherton studied him, his eyes glinting in the dark. Eventually, he said, "Mrs. Rawlins."

"Excuse me?"

"What is happening between you and Mrs. Rawlins?"

Freddy felt his face heat, and he was glad the darkness of the carriage hid his color. "Nothing. I find her pleasant and friendly. Nothing more."

Rotherton stared at him for several seconds before he answered, "Good. Because it would pain me to know a guest of mine had caused trouble for a respectable widow who rents a cottage from me."

"Causing trouble for her is the farthest thing from my mind." Freddy knew he sounded defensive. He could not say if that was because of guilt or insult.

"Yet all too easy to achieve."

"See here—"

"No. You see here. It is the way of the world. A woman must be careful of her reputation in a way we men do not have to be. Once lost, it can never be recovered."

Freddy spoke through gritted teeth. "I have no intention of ruining the lady."

"And yet…" Rotherton sighed. "You will leave here when your job is done, Finch. She will stay. Whatever happens between you—even if nothing actually happens, but people perceive that it may have—it will be she who faces censure."

Freddy pursed his lips against a retort and stared out the window. All he could see was the night, and a small blur of road and grass verge, lit by the carriage lamp. He was angry at Rotherton for the warning, but at the same time, he should have expected it. The earl had a duty to deliver it. Freddy was a man who was supposedly known for his dalliances with widows. Although surely people could see this widow was a far cry from the ladies with whom his name had been linked in London? Then again, he thought bitterly, he could hardly complain if people judged him by what they'd heard. Not when he'd been at pains to encourage those very tales.

Rotherton sighed again. "It cannot be easy, living

down such a reputation. Tell me—I am curious. Whose idea was it to saddle you with such a character? Yours? Or Fremont's?"

Freddy frowned but did not answer.

"No matter," continued Rotherton. "Just complete whatever task he's given you, and try not to cause too much scandal while you are doing it. Remember, as your host, I will be tarred with the same brush. I'd rather not be."

"I will be careful." Part of Freddy was annoyed at being warned over what was, in the general scheme of things, quite innocuous behavior. Another part of him was grateful that there was someone willing to defend Eliza. And he was happy to know that, no matter what the world thought of him, at least one man didn't believe him to be the rogue he was made out to be.

He had gone along willingly with Fremont's plans for him, had worked to portray himself as feckless and immoral. But occasionally, the disguise was wearisome. When he started working for Fremont, he'd been enthusiastic, keen to save Britain from her enemies, ready to take on the world. It was important work, and he was proud to do it.

It was still important work. He was still proud of it. But he was also tired. Tired and jaded. Perhaps it was time to rethink his career, step aside and leave the work to someone who still had the passion for it.

But then, was it a loss of passion for his duty? Or was he simply feeling the disappointment of being unable to court the lovely Eliza in the way he would have liked? If he were not here on government business, not wearing his disguise as a rake… Well, then he would not be here at all. And surely, in the balance of things, it was better to have been here and met the delectable widow, even if he could take their association nowhere, than never to have made her acquaintance at all?

One thing was clear: he needed to stop obsessing about her and get his mind back on the true task. He changed the subject abruptly. "Where, in this vicinity, might nefarious people hide something they didn't want discovered?"

Rotherton thought for a moment. "Am I permitted to know what it is you seek?"

Freddy hesitated. He wasn't at liberty to give details.

"No matter," continued the earl. "Though dimensions might help. It will have a bearing on the hiding places that can be considered plausible. Are we talking of something small like a trinket, or as big as a trunk?"

That much Freddy could answer. "More trunk than trinket."

"Let me see." Rotherton thought for a moment. "There's Marshy Meadow, I suppose, although if anything was there, I dare say Ned Fellowes would have seen it."

"Ned Fellowes?"

"Feral boy. Not quite the full shilling, if you get my meaning, but for all that, he has a certain…" He searched for a word, moving his hand through the air as if grasping for it, "…nous that more able people often lack. I believe he lives in the Marshy Meadow area. In a cave, if what I have been told is true. Not a lot gets past him."

"Should I question him?"

Rotherton laughed. "No. Waste of time. If it comes to it, I'll see what I can discover from him for you. Now where else? There's Wetherby Grange. It's an old house near Crompton Hadlow. Hasn't been lived in for years." He thought for a moment longer. "Give me tonight to think about it. I will likely have a couple more ideas for you by breakfast."

Freddy thanked him. He would search the places Rotherton suggested, and any others that came up. And from now on, he would concentrate all his attentions on the task he was here for, and leave the widowed Eliza—Mrs. Rawlins!—alone.

Chapter Nine

May turned into June and Freddy was no nearer finding Fremont's gold. He had travelled the district, looking in likely places and unlikely, ruining several coats and pairs of boots in damp, dark caves, on the rubble of decrepit follies, or in abandoned houses. He had searched stables and outbuildings, pretended an interest in horticulture to explain his presence in a private garden, and been warned off by two different gamekeepers when they found him in their employers' woods. Knowing the farrier had been among the traitors arrested, he searched Rotherton forge, which currently stood empty and cold, waiting for a new man to take it over. Rotherton gave him a list of suggestions and he checked each one, but he found nothing.

Sometimes, while he was out and about, he saw Eliza. He knew she was searching too, though for what, he couldn't tell. Whatever it was, she didn't trust him enough to tell him about it, and whenever he probed, she insisted she was interested in the architecture and history of the churches. More than once, he found himself loitering near those churches, and though he told himself he was merely doing his job, he also had to admit to a certain delight if their paths crossed, and disappointment when they did not.

At other times, too, he caught himself looking for her. As he walked through the town's High Street, he looked out for her. If he attended social events in the evenings, he kept one eye on the door so he would not miss her arrival. In church on Sunday mornings, he glanced frequently over to her pew, reassuring himself that she was there. He spoke to her, but not intimately, as they had done on their walks. In deference to Lord Rotherton and the warning he had given, he would do nothing inappropriate, nothing that might jeopardize her reputation. Nothing that might lead to another kiss.

Sometimes, when he was alone, he mused about the kiss they had shared in the church on the Hadlow estate. When he brought it to mind, he could feel the soft warmth of her lips against his, her fingers stroking the back of his neck and shoulders inexpertly, but eagerly. He remembered the press of her body against his, their closeness setting him aflame. The very thought of it was enough to make his body react, leaving him awkward and uncomfortable, and grasping at something else—anything else—to occupy him. The trouble was, no other subject fascinated him the way that she did, and before long, no matter how he tried, she would be back in his thoughts, and the whole thing would start again.

Another person he had begun to know better was Ned Fellowes. Rotherton had described the boy as feral, which he was, and "not quite the full shilling." Freddy had his doubts about that. The boy was different to other people, it was true. He couldn't speak, read, or write, but Freddy thought he was far from the simpleton people assumed him to be. There was, as Rotherton had indicated, a certain knowingness about him, as if he had fathomed all the secrets to be had. If only he could impart them.

Late on a fine Friday in the second week of June,

Freddy walked through the countryside between two of the smaller hamlets in the area. It had been yet another day of fruitless searching, and he was feeling a fair measure of self-pity at the lack of progress.

The sun was high and hot. It was one of those glorious days, all too rare over the last couple of years, when the sky was a flawless blue, with not a single cloud to break it. The air was sweet with the perfume of the hedgerows and the comforting buzz of bees, and the fields and woods around him were myriad shades of greens, browns, and yellows. The sun warmed his face and scorched his back through the heavy wool of his coat, until every footstep seemed harder to take. Finally, he hopped over a wooden style into a field where cows and sheep grazed peacefully. He took off his coat and spread it on the ground like a blanket, feeling the relief of removing it as he sat down on it and leaned back against the dry-stone wall, adjusting his position until he was comfortable against the uneven stones. He loosened his cravat, then set to, eating one of the two bread rolls with cheese that Rotherton's cook had provided this morning. He finished his feast with a huge, red apple and a couple of nips of brandy from his flask, then sat back, tilted his head so the sun warmed his cheeks, closed his eyes and dozed.

A shadow passed over him. Even with his eyes closed, he noticed the change in the light, and it brought him to full alertness in an instant. His eyes snapped open and he jerked upright and found Ned Fellowes leaning over him, reaching for the second bread roll.

The boy jumped back but he wasn't quick enough. Freddy grabbed his forearm and held him tightly, though not tight enough to hurt him. The boy pulled and squirmed and growled low in his throat. He was an excellent mimic. If Freddy couldn't see it was him who made the noise, he would have looked for a fearsome dog.

"I'm not going to hurt you, Ned," he said, in the voice he would use on a skittish horse. "You want the bread and cheese, it's yours."

The boy stopped struggling and looked at Freddy, his head cocked to one side, eyes filled with suspicion.

"Sit and eat," encouraged Freddy. He let go of Ned's arm. In a flash, Ned grabbed the food, then moved back out of reach. Freddy made no attempt to touch him again. Ned looked around, satisfying himself this was not a trap or an ambush, then sat on the grass six feet from Freddy, his long, skinny legs crossed in front of him. He unwrapped the bread and what was left of the cheese and ate it with gusto.

"Good?" Freddy asked. Ned grinned and crowed like a cockerel. "I don't have a drink for you, I'm afraid," continued Freddy. He did not think it was a good idea to give Ned any brandy. Ned shrugged, indicating the lack of a drink didn't matter, and took another bite.

They sat for some time, enjoying the warm day. Freddy made small talk. The one-sided conversation was a test of his social skills, although Ned did respond sometimes, with a look, or a sound, or a gesture, all of which clearly conveyed what he wanted to say.

"If only you could speak," said Freddy at last. "I bet you know all the answers to my questions."

Ned shrugged, nonchalantly.

"You would know where to look, wouldn't you?"

Ned cocked his head to the side, a puzzled frown on his face.

Freddy chuckled softly. "You haven't seen a chest of gold by any chance, have you?"

Ned moved to kneel, put his hands together in an attitude of prayer and raised his eyes to the sky, a pious expression on his face.

"I suppose I could try praying," Freddy said. He smiled at the idea. It was the last thing he would do, and the last thing he had expected Ned to suggest.

Ned frowned and shook his head. He made a sound like coins chinking together and Freddy marveled. How did a lad who couldn't speak make all these wonderful noises? Then Ned stopped the noise and put his hands together again.

Freddy had a sudden epiphany, realizing what Ned was trying to tell him. "It's in a church?" Ned nodded. "You are certain?" Ned nodded, again. "I wonder... I don't suppose you know which church?" Although how Ned would convey that information without speaking, Freddy had no idea. "Could you take me to it?"

The boy growled.

Freddy assumed that meant no. "Please?"

The growl got louder, more menacing.

"I need to find it, and I'm running out of time." He hoped he could appeal to Ned's sense of duty. "It's for the good of our country."

A moment later, he concluded Ned didn't have any sense of duty to the country, because he sprang to his feet and darted away across the grass at an impressive speed Freddy could never hope to match.

"I'll just look for myself then," muttered Freddy and he stood, brushed the crumbs from his shirt and waistcoat, retied his cravat, and put on his coat.

Over the next few days, he made a list of all the

churches within reasonable distance of Hadlow Hall and was amazed at how many there were. England had never struck him as a particularly religious country. The only time most people of his acquaintance went willingly to church was to see someone hatched, matched, or dispatched. Many of them attended Sunday services, but more out of a sense of obligation than a desire to be there. Yet there was at least one place of worship in every hamlet and village, two or three in the bigger towns. The Hadlow estate was not the only private property to have a consecrated building on it, either, and that was without taking into account large houses that might have chapels within, for the sole use of the families who lived there.

Many of the smaller churches had fallen into disuse, the hamlets they served too sparsely populated to warrant a weekly service with their own dedicated vicar. The people who lived in those places now made their ways to other churches in bigger villages. It was these abandoned churches he checked first, reasoning that a building that wasn't used would be better for storing secrets than one with a constant flow of foot traffic.

None of them yielded anything more than dust, grime and cobwebs. He didn't even see any sign of Eliza as he explored them, which left him disappointed, even though he told himself he knew she wasn't truly interested in the old buildings. Besides, she had been searching for far longer than he had. She'd probably already looked in these places.

After another week, he was running out of buildings to search, and had seen no trace of the gold, or anything else that might have been hidden illicitly. There was no sign of smuggling activity, either, which suggested one of three things: the recent smashing of the treasonous smuggling ring had put a stop to all activity in the area; the remaining smugglers were lying low until the authorities had lost all interest; or the smugglers had found somewhere else to hide their contraband. Freddy knew which one he would put his wager on.

Now, it was the third Thursday of June, and his options were diminishing rapidly. The only buildings left to search were churches that were in regular use, where it was unlikely anything would be hidden at all. Still, he had to look.

Which is why he walked along the narrow pathway from the lych-gate to the church porch of Saint Simon and Saint Jude's Church in Crompton Hadlow. It was another warm day, when the sun was strong in a deep blue sky dotted with white clouds that promised no rain. A light breeze kissed his cheek. The bright leaves on bushes and trees waved gently as he passed, and flowers nodded their heads at him agreeably. Newer tombstones in the churchyard stood tall, unblemished, the names carved proudly onto them, easy to read. Older stones leaned and stooped, their age-darkened surfaces spotted with lichen, the words obscured by time and the elements. Grass grew around the oldest stones, although the newer graves were tended well. A yew tree grew by the dry-stone wall that surrounded the churchyard, its branches cut neatly into shape.

The church itself was tiny, a true village church. Made of stone, dark with age and exposure to the elements, it had a short spire, on top of which sat a weathervane. A clock face was attached on the three sides Freddy saw as he approached. The church had a slate roof and plain glass windows that were too high for him to see through. The door was oak, thick and sturdy and black with age.

He strode up to this door and rattled the huge ring handle. It did not budge. He tried turning the ring the opposite way and pushing hard, but the door stayed fast. The church was clearly locked. He grimaced but was not overly surprised. It wasn't the first church he'd encountered that had been shut up tight. Considering the value of plate and tapestries inside some of these buildings, he supposed it was not to be wondered at, although it was sad that the faithful believer could not go into God's house whenever he wanted.

Freddy had managed to gain entry into other locked churches, and he had no doubt he would find a way into this one. With that in mind, he walked along the building's side, looking for an entrance. Halfway, he stopped, convinced he'd heard something. He had no idea what it was because, to his shame, he had not been giving his surroundings his full attention, but he did know it was a sound that did not belong.

For a moment, he stood, listening. Birds chirruped their songs in the nearby trees, and a seagull mewled. Leaves swished and rattled on the breeze. There was nothing else.

He looked around, saw nothing untoward, and shrugged mentally. Whatever it was had gone. He pulled his watch from his fob pocket and checked the time against the clock faces on the spire. Twenty past two. He took a step forward, then stopped when he heard the noise again.

A child's cry. Distant, muffled. Distressed. It didn't come from inside the church building, that much he could tell, although he had trouble pinpointing its direction accurately. It sounded as if it came from the graveyard. More than that, it sounded as if it came from a grave near to the church wall. A shiver ran down his spine and the hairs on his neck stood to attention. Freddy swallowed, hard, and fought the urge to hurry away from here.

He was being stupid. He knew very well there was no such thing as ghosts. The shudder of fear was brought on simply by the idea of being alone in a graveyard, coupled with the leftover effect of childhood nights, sitting in the school dorm after lights out, each boy trying to terrify his friends with stories of supernatural happenings.

The tales his friends had told might be fantasy, but the cry he could hear now was very real. Since he refused to believe in spirits, there had to be another explanation. With some trepidation, he approached the grave.

It was well tended, outlined by a chain barrier that prevented people from walking on it. Inside the chain was a rectangular concrete slab on which was written the name of a woman who had died in the last century. There was a surround of pebbles between the grave and the grass of the cemetery.

The cry stopped as he approached. Freddy leaned over the grave, but could see nothing out of the ordinary.

"Can I help you?" The gruff voice startled him. He straightened and took a step back, his heart racing. He turned and saw the sexton watching him from a few feet away. Freddy smiled, partly in an effort to charm the man, partly in relief that the voice belonged to someone who was flesh and blood, and alive.

"I thought I heard something," said Freddy, feeling foolish as he voiced his concern. The man was going to think he was dicked in the nob. Or drunk. Or both.

The sexton nodded. He did not seem surprised. "We get that a lot," he said, and he grinned. His teeth were mottled brown and black along with the ivory white, and there were several gaps. "It isn't a ghost," he assured Freddy. "No ghoulies to jump out at you here. Reverend and his sister wouldn't allow it."

"I—never thought…" answered Freddy, although he knew he had.

"Some science behind it, but don't ask me what it is. All I know is, it can be downright creepy when the wind blows in the right way."

The explanation made a lot more sense than hauntings did. Freddy cleared his throat. "I was hoping to get into the church. Have a look around. Can you help me?"

The sexton shook his head. "I don't have the key. You need to speak to the reverend about that."

That struck Freddy as off. "You don't have a key? How do you do your job?" Surely the man must have access to the church to care for it.

"I tend to the churchyard," the man said. "Don't very often need to go inside. If there's something ever needs doing in there, the reverend will come and tell me. He lets me in at that time." He frowned at Freddy. "Why?"

The man's question put Freddy on the back foot, neatly turning the interrogation on its head. He supposed his questions might seem odd to a man who saw nothing unusual in the arrangement and would wonder why a visitor questioned it.

"No reason," said Freddy. "Thank you for your time." He glanced back at the chain surrounding the grave once more. The crying sound had stopped. He nodded a goodbye at the sexton and walked away toward the rear of the church.

As he turned the corner, he almost collided with Eliza and her friend Prudence Burgess. The ladies startled backward, and Prudence gave a tiny yelp of alarm, raising her hands defensively and spilling some of the flowers that filled the small Sussex trug she carried. Freddy stepped back, mumbled an apology, then bent to pick up the blooms she had dropped.

"I do beg your pardon," he said as he handed the flowers to her. She seemed nonplussed, and concentrated on placing them just so in her trug. Beside her, Eliza watched. Today, she wore a plain dress the color of a summer midnight, and a dove grey spencer that matched her bonnet, around which was a wide ribbon in the same dark blue as her dress and gloves. There was a healthy rose glow in her cheeks, and her eyes sparkled with life and vigor. She smiled and bobbed a curtsy at him. He bowed in return.

"What do you here, sir?" asked Prudence. Her voice seemed somewhat sharp, which drew his attention. He saw Eliza glance at her friend as well, her surprise evident.

Prudence kept her steady gaze on Freddy as she waited for him to answer her.

What was he doing there? He could hardly tell the ladies that he was prowling around the building looking for an unauthorized point of entry, so he smiled and lied, and hoped it sounded more convincing to them than it did to him.

"Lord Rotherton tells me that walking in the fresh air is good for my constitution," he said in his most insouciant tone. "Of course, he may have been bamming me, but I felt I needed to try it before I gainsaid him."

"Admirable of you," said Eliza, "to have walked so far from your host's home, in the pursuit of scientific inquiry."

He gave her a sardonic bow. "If a job is worth doing, it is worth doing well."

"And your conclusion?"

He paused, grinned, and said, "That my feet ache."

Eliza chuckled.

Prudence frowned. "You have come quite a distance from Lord Rotherton's home," she said. "If you are not used to such walking, your feet will hurt."

"Quite so." From the corner of his eye, he saw Eliza look away across the churchyard. He imagined she was as amused as he was by her friend's earnest answer.

"What brought you here?" Prudence repeated.

"To Crompton Hadlow? It is a charming village."

"To the churchyard?" She looked suspicious, as if she expected him to say he planned to rob the graves, or some such heinous act. He stiffened, insulted. He had cultivated the image of a rake, not that of a body snatcher.

"I find the church fascinating," he told her, his voice even, betraying no sign of the annoyance he felt. "You can tell so much about people by looking at their church."

"You can?" Prudence's eyes widened. So did Eliza's, but her expression was more one of disbelief than interest.

"Yes, you can. For instance, if it is well kept and tidy, maintained with love, then they will be a people for whom faith is important, a people whose pastoral leaders are conscientious in their care for their flock."

Eliza coughed. "Excuse me," she murmured.

"Well, of course," Prudence agreed with Freddy. "For is it not written, take heed therefore, to feed the Church of God, which He has purchased with His own blood?"

"Having met your brother and yourself, I know that you will take such a commandment very seriously," he went on.

Prudence smiled, pleased. Eliza turned away and took great interest in a nearby headstone.

"There is nothing more pleasing to the eye than a properly kept church," continued Freddy. "It does one's heart good. Even a sinner such as myself may benefit from the sight of it."

Eliza looked at him over her shoulder. He did not dare to look back at her. Prudence made mention of another Bible verse, one he did not know.

"I wonder," he said, ignoring her quotation, "could I be permitted to see inside the church? I was, of course, in there for Bertie's—I mean, Lord Hadlow's—funeral, but that was hardly an occasion to wonder at the beauty of the church and its furnishings, was it?" He narrowed his eyes, trying to look pensive. "I do seem to recall, though, is there not a list of past rectors on the wall? I was astounded to see it went back to the year 1070!"

"Yes," said Prudence. "Yes, it does."

"Only imagine," he said. "The first named man on that list served William the Conqueror!"

With that comment, he lost her. Prudence's smile disappeared and she pursed her lips. "No," she corrected him frostily, "he did not. He served God." She shifted the trug so it was in front of her, like a shield. "My friend and I are going to take tea in the cottage, so I will bid you good day…"

Freddy smiled at her, wracking his brains for a way to retrieve the ground he had lost. "Perhaps I may look in the church while you have your tea with Mrs. Rawlins? I will, of course, return the key to you directly."

Prudence straightened her shoulders. "There, I could not help you. You would have to ask my brother. He keeps the key." Her brow wrinkled as she thought. "He was from home earlier, but he may have returned by now. Why don't you come and see him?"

The last thing Freddy wanted was for the curate to shadow him as he looked around the church. "I wouldn't wish to bother him," he said.

"I know he would welcome your interest. The angels are not the only beings who findeth joy over one sinner that repenteth." With that, Prudence shifted the trug into the crook of her left arm, and put her right hand onto his sleeve. "I insist, sir. Come and take tea with us, and speak with my brother."

Alarmed at the trap he had just wandered into, Freddy looked over his shoulder at Eliza, silently pleading for her help. Her expression told him he would get no assistance there. She clearly thought he had brought this on himself and, he had to concede, she was right. Sometimes he was too clever for his own good.

Prudence led them across the churchyard and through a side gate in the wall.

"I can come back another day," Freddy tried, desperately.

"I wouldn't hear of it," said Prudence. "It would distress me, and anger my brother, were somebody to be led by God to the church because they are clearly seeking salvation, only to find that we did not aid them in their search."

Behind him, he thought he heard Eliza laugh, softly. He was glad someone was enjoying themselves.

A few steps from the side gate and they were at the curate's cottage, with its shiplap walls and sash windows. It was larger than most of the houses in the village, but not by much. The garden was well tended, a mixture of vegetable plants and flowers, with a small herb patch near the kitchen door.

"I am sure you won't mind coming in through the back door, will you, Mr. Finch?" asked Prudence. "It is quite a way round to go to the High Street where the front door is, and we don't really stand on ceremony here."

"This will be fine," he replied.

"I do apologize for the smallness of our home," she continued. "Of course, you will be wondering why a man of my brother's status is required to live in such mean accommodation. He really ought to have the vicarage in Rotherton, which is much more suited to our needs. Alas, Lord Rotherton had already let it to Lord Leonard and his family before we arrived."

She led her guests into a parlor. Although the window was large and south-facing, the light it allowed into the room seemed to be soaked up by the sheer amount of things that were in there. There was a large table and two occasional ones, all made in fashionable zebra wood, and several highly polished wooden chairs, their seats upholstered in plush blue velvet, which matched the heavy curtains and the chaise longue in front of the fireplace. A large sideboard and an overstuffed bookcase also took up space, along with a square piano, the lid closed over its keys. Every available surface was covered with ornaments and knick-knacks in a hodgepodge of styles, ranging from a Chinese dragon in silver gilt and an Egyptian-inspired cat carved in wood to Meissen figurines of commedia dell'arte characters, as well as shepherds and shepherdesses. There were china flowers, china dogs, and a very ornate clock on the mantel shelf, beside a huge and rather discomfiting crucifixion scene, made in the Sèvres style. The walls of the room were covered in paintings, most of them small, but well made. They depicted landscapes, seascapes, dogs and horses, and there were two miniature silhouettes, which Freddy guessed were of Prudence and her brother. The effect of the cluttered room was to overwhelm the visitor and leave them disoriented. Certainly, that was how Freddy felt as Prudence urged him to sit while she rang for tea.

A young woman came running into the parlor, her apron slightly askew, her unruly hair trying to escape her cap. She bobbed a tiny curtsy.

"Tea please, Mildred," said Prudence, and she waved her hand, imperiously. "And be so good as to tell Mr. Burgess that he has a guest." She smiled at Freddy.

Mildred bobbed again. "Beg pardon, mum," she said. "Mr. Burgess isn't at home today. He went out after breakfast. Said he'd be back for dinner."

"Bother!" Prudence apologized to Freddy for her brother's absence. He answered that it was of no consequence, and he could always return another time. He stood to leave, and she looked at him, askance. "You will stay for tea, surely, sir?"

"Well, I…"

"I absolutely insist."

Freddy glanced at Eliza, who looked wonderfully innocent. He sat down again.

For the next half hour, he and Eliza sat, drinking

weak and tepid tea, eating biscuits, and listening to Prudence tell them about the work of her brother and what he had planned for his parishioners.

"Of course, we don't expect to be here to see our efforts reach fruition," she said with a smile. "Once the bishop is apprised of all Silas has done, he will be promoted and given a bigger parish."

"Well deserved, I am sure," Freddy answered.

"Not that promotion is the reason for his works, of course. We think it our Christian duty to improve the lives of the less fortunate. As I'm sure you do too, do you not, Eliza?"

Eliza smiled and agreed politely. Freddy noted Prudence did not ask him. Surreptitiously, he checked the time on the mantel clock, and lamented how slowly the minutes seemed to pass.

Finally, though, the tea was drunk, the biscuits eaten, and the half hour deemed a polite length of time for a visit had passed. Freddy stood to take his leave. Eliza also got to her feet. "I must go, too," she said, and she thanked Prudence, not only for the tea, but for showing her the interesting tombs in the churchyard. "Would you mind if I walked with you as far as Rotherton, Mr. Finch?"

Freddy schooled his face to remain impassive, but inside, his spirit leapt for joy at the prospect. "I would be honored, Mrs. Rawlins," he said.

They took their leave and walked away, two feet of space between them as they strolled from the cottage, along Crompton Hadlow's High Street, and out of Prudence's sight. Only when he was sure the curate's sister could no longer see them did he move closer to Eliza.

As they walked, they made small talk, speaking lightly and saying little. He savored the feeling of being with her, glancing at her often, admiring the golden glow of her skin, which was a legacy of her hours walking in fresh air and sunshine. He followed the curve of her cheek and noted the brightness in her eyes. A breeze blew, pushing her skirts against her, outlining the slender curves of her waist and hips, and the length of her legs. He looked away and pretended he had not seen.

Soon they approached her cottage and the pleasant interlude came to an end. It was, he felt, far *too* soon. Surely, the distance between Crompton Hadlow and Rotherton was not so short?

"Thank you for your company," she said, and she turned to her door.

Desperate for a few more seconds with her, he cast about for something to say, to delay her departure. "Do you go to the Bells' home for dinner tomorrow?" he asked, then kicked himself, for if she had not been invited…

"Yes," she replied. He breathed a small and quiet relief, then struggled not to grimace when she added, "the Burgesses have offered to bring me in their vehicle."

Nothing is perfect, he told himself. Aloud, he said he looked forward to seeing her there.

As he walked away, he smiled. He had achieved nothing for Lord Fremont today, and his attempts at searching yet another church had been thwarted, but he had spent time with Eliza, and to his mind, that counted the day as a success. He prayed he would sit with her tomorrow at Mrs. Bell's table. For intelligent conversation, of course. Nothing more. What more could there be?

Chapter Ten

The Bells' dinner party was what in London would be considered a small and intimate affair, although here in the country it was more of an event, the party of twenty containing most members of the local Society. As well as Mr. and Mrs. Bell themselves, there was their daughter, Amelia, and her husband-to-be, Josh Summersby, and her younger sister, Miss Julia Bell, who was placed beside Lord Rotherton. The earl had expected that, as he had told Freddy on their way here.

"Now that the oldest daughter has caught herself the heir to an earldom," Rotherton had said, flicking imaginary lint from his coat, "the Bells will want nothing less for their second daughter. She is considered the prettier of the two." He'd smiled, ruefully. "Alas, she—or her parents, at least, are chasing the wrong man. I am not in the market for a wife, and I doubt Julia Bell would snare my interest if I were." She was, he had said, a charming girl, but too young and innocent, and not to his taste at all.

"You will be good practice for her for when she is out," answered Freddy, which made Rotherton laugh.

Freddy himself was placed next to Eliza, which suited him perfectly, although he suspected it had been done because of his reputation as a wastrel, and a desire to keep a distance between him and the younger, more innocent ladies in the party, for as well as Julia, there were others who were not yet out, all of them present with their parents.

They sat down to a sumptuous meal, beginning with vermicelli soup, followed by fish, which was, in turn, followed by a fillet of veal, served with fried artichoke bottoms, cauliflower *a la flamond*, julienned carrots, and duchesse potatoes. Then came apricot tartlets, their pastry as light as air, raspberry puffs, and apple-and-berry pie topped with finely whipped cream. The whole was washed down with both red and white wines of the finest quality.

To Eliza's other side, Freddy was dismayed to see Mrs. Bell had placed Silas Burgess. The hostess made it clear she thought the widow and the clergyman would make a good match, and she wanted to be able to claim the credit of it. Personally, Freddy thought such a pairing would be disastrous. Silas seemed personable, and he certainly wasn't as keen to quote Biblical verses as his more pious sister, but he was nowhere near enough for a woman like Eliza Rawlins. She needed someone whose conversation was not only intelligent enough to stretch her, but good humored too, with plenty of laughter, and which included a variety of topics, not just sermons and Scripture. Were she to marry Silas, the poor woman would be bored to death within a week.

Which was not to say she would be any happier with Freddy, of course. As attracted as he was to her, he held no illusions that she would thrive with him. She was a clergyman's widow, used to quiet living and good works. She would not want even to contemplate becoming part of the *ton*. Besides, he told himself, she was far too good for most of them. Himself included. More was the pity.

And where had those thoughts come from?

Freddy was not looking for a wife, and Eliza was not the sort of woman to whom a gentleman offered anything else. With no title to pass on, no family line to continue, Freddy had a great deal more freedom and choice than his older brother, whose duty to the earldom had been drilled into him since birth. As the spare, family pressures had not weighed Freddy down, and he liked it that way.

It wasn't that he couldn't afford to keep a wife; contrary to popular belief, he was not a poor man, and he had a small estate of his own, left to him by his great-uncle. But just because he could afford something didn't mean he wanted it. Marriage, a wife, children, these were not things Freddy had ever been drawn to, and just because Eliza Rawlins made him feel things he had never felt before, just because he thought of her incessantly, looked for her wherever he went, and listened for news of her in every gathering, well, that didn't mean he had changed his mind on settling down to marriage. The bucks of the *ton* called it leg-shackling for good reason. It wasn't a trap Freddy would walk into. Not willingly.

He was protesting too much. He knew it while being thankful the argument had been only in his head, so nobody else had any idea. He shook himself, took a bite of apple-and-berry pie, and listened to the conversation around the table to push away the unwelcome debate within himself.

The party was speaking of children, but it was not the usual joyous, boastful talk of proud parents extolling the virtues of their offspring. They were talking in far more somber tones, about the perils of childhood.

"I know all too well how easily a child can be lost," said Eliza, her smile sad. "And how devastating that is."

"You have lost a child?" asked Mrs. Bell, her face set in a mask of sympathy.

"A four-year-old."

"Oh, my dear," said Mrs. Bell, her hand to her chest, her voice breathy. "How awful for you."

Eliza shrugged, but it wasn't quite nonchalant. "It is, sadly, far too common an occurrence," she replied. "Every family who loses a child will be as devastated as I was."

"Your charity does you credit, dear Eliza." Prudence leaned forward across her place setting so she could see Eliza more clearly. "Alas, it is misplaced, for not everybody has your sensibilities. Some families are only too glad to reduce their load. Indeed, for the lower classes, ridding themselves of an extra mouth to feed may actually be a blessing in disguise."

Freddy's eyebrows shot up. Glancing around the suddenly silent table, he saw his was not the only expression of astonishment. Mrs. Bell looked appalled, her mouth opening and closing as if she wished to say something but had been rendered speechless.

"Oh, not the death of a child," clarified Prudence, and she tittered. "I am sure nobody would wish for that. But to relieve themselves of the latest baby, to give it to somebody else to rear. There are fewer mouths to feed then, and that makes many of their worries disappear."

"I cannot believe that." Amelia Bell shook her head emphatically. "No mother would want rid of her child, no matter how difficult it might be to make ends meet."

"The lower classes do not feel as we do," argued Prudence, "and they do not experience grief in the same way. They are often grateful if someone takes a child or two from their hands, for then life is easier for everyone."

"We are not talking of dead children, then?" asked Mrs. Bell, looking somewhat relieved.

"No," answered Prudence. "Hale and hearty children can often be rescued, and pressed into useful service and productive lives that might otherwise have been denied for them. In their new environment, they learn skills and work hard, and grow into decent people."

It seemed Freddy was not the only one who didn't know how to answer that, because the table was very quiet for well over a minute. One or two of the diners continued eating, the silverware clinking against their porcelain plates. Others looked around, each willing someone else to speak.

It was Eliza who broke the silence. Quietly, contemplatively, she said, "I would take such a child, if I could." There was an audible gasp, and she looked around at her fellow diners. "Not to put to work," she said. "To love. I miss the little girl I have lost so terribly, and I have all the love in my heart, with nobody to bestow it upon. If I could find another child to draw to myself, it would be such a wonderful thing." She smiled to herself. "A four-year-old, so I could see her grow."

Freddy was astounded. Was Eliza really suggesting she would take somebody else's child from them to keep for herself? He did not doubt her sincere wish to give such a child love and care, but that was by the by. Who did she think she was? Who did anybody think they were, that they should decide whether a child should be torn from its mother's arms or not?

He shook his head to clear it, just as Mrs. Potter, a buxom lady in a tight pink dress with a neckline far too low for her, said, "Children are hardly commodities to be bartered for in the open market."

At least there was one lady in the room who realized that.

"I didn't say…" began Eliza, just as Prudence spoke over her.

"Of course they are not," said the curate's sister. "But, unfortunately, so many people don't seem to realize that. And so many children are born into the most unfortunate circumstances, with parents who are…well, they are not like us. They see their children at best as a way of making money, by having them beg, or pick pockets, or other such things. At worst, they see them as a nuisance and put them out onto the streets to fend for themselves."

"I hardly think…" Eliza started to object, but Prudence went on.

"These children would benefit from removal, from being given to somebody better, somebody able to give them a good upbringing."

"Surely you are not suggesting that Mrs. Rawlins should take a base-born child from the stews and elevate it to a class it was never intended to be part of? That would be cruel in the extreme."

"Why would it?" asked Freddy. He had never thought of any such thing before, but the sneer in Mrs. Potter's voice angered him, momentarily distracting him from the disgust and disappointment he felt at the suggestion Eliza would steal somebody else's child for her own ends.

"They would not fit in," she answered him.

Her smug attitude goaded him to play devil's advocate. "If they were in their later childhood, already well formed in their character, I can understand you may be right. They would be out of their element and discomfited. But a small child of, say, four or five years is still unmolded. They would become that which they were taught to become by the surrounding environment. Regardless of their origins."

Eliza smiled at him. He felt ten feet tall for an instant, before he remembered that he was angry with her. Although, he had to admit, there was also some satisfaction for having put Mrs. Potter's argument to flight.

That lady, however, was not ready to turn tail and run. "Blood will out," she insisted. "You may take a child out of the slums. You cannot take the slums out of the child. So while I am all for taking them from inadequate parents and putting them with the respectable lower classes, where they can learn a trade, or how to be in service, the course Mrs. Rawlins proposes is not acceptable at all. To anybody."

Freddy pursed his lips and struggled not to say anything further. At this moment, he wanted to tell them all, in no uncertain terms, that it was not the place of any of them to decide who could be permitted to have a child, and who should be forbidden. How dare any of them judge somebody in this way? Why, he was willing to bet that not one of these women had raised their own children, but had handed them to nurses and nannies, tutors and governesses. If the children were lucky, they might see their parents for half an hour between supper and bedtime for a quick pat on the head and a "well done" for the day's accomplishments. Was that really a better upbringing for a child?

He could not speak to Eliza's circumstances, of course, since she was, technically, not of the *ton* and may well have been more involved in the raising of her own child than most ladies of his acquaintance. He felt deeply for the fact that she had lost her child. But that did not give her the right to take somebody else's, and so he would tell her as soon as he could.

Meanwhile, he kept his thoughts to himself and let the dinner party continue in its normal, polite trajectory.

However, the thoughts engendered by the conversation festered within him and his anger continued to simmer. When the ladies left the room and the men poured brandy and smoked cigars, he barely joined their conversation. His entire mind was taken up by what Eliza had said, and what he intended to say to her. He could hardly credit that the woman he thought he knew would voice such an opinion, and that led him to recount the conversation in his mind, wondering if she had really said what he had heard. She had expressed a wish for another child, but had she actually said she would take one from somebody else? She had not condemned Prudence, nor Mrs. Potter, for their thoughts on the matter. She had made no objection at all to their ideas.

The more he thought about it, the more confused and upset he became. He knew he could not resolve it in his own mind until he had spoken with her.

The chance to do so came when the gentlemen rejoined the ladies in Mrs. Bell's drawing room. He accepted a cup of tea from his hostess, then crossed the room to where Eliza sat, slightly apart from the noisy group of people laughing at their friends' *bon mots*.

"May I?" he asked, pointing to the seat beside her. She nodded and smiled at him. His pulse sped up and he wanted to push aside his anger, simply talk to her as they usually did, of little things that were pleasant and good-natured, and meant nothing. But if he did that now, his anger would return later, and it would grow. His mind would start to interpret her words, perhaps making them worse than they really were. So, he took a deep breath and tackled her.

"I was deeply disappointed earlier, when you intimated that you would happily take someone else's child to replace your lost daughter." He winced. He hadn't meant to put it quite so bluntly, but he found he couldn't help himself. He had held his thoughts and his anger inside himself for such a large part of the evening that he could hold them back no more.

She frowned. "I didn't say that, exactly," she answered.

"You inferred it."

"No such thing!" Her eyes flashed, and her lips narrowed. His criticism of her clearly stung.

"It certainly sounded like you did. It is clear that Miss Burgess feels able to judge other people's parenting skills and find them wanting but, to be honest, I expected that from her. I had not thought you of the same ilk."

She stiffened, put her teacup carefully on the occasional table beside her, then stared squarely at him. "You do not know me well enough to know my 'ilk,' Mr. Finch," she told him. Her voice was low and even, and full of ice.

"I do know you would like someone to give up their child for you. And then what? How would you raise the child? You have no husband anymore, no family to speak of, and no means of support that is worth very much."

Her expression hardened. "How dare you presume to lecture me, sir?" Her spine was as straight as a ramrod now, and her shoulders were braced. "You know nothing of me, of what I want or need, how I live, or any other pertinent fact. Yet you presume to sit here and act as judge and jury over me. You, sir, are the one who is being judgmental and unreasonable."

"The difference, Mrs. Rawlins, is that my judgment of you may result in hurt feelings. Nothing more. Your actions toward those you deem unworthy could have far-reaching and damaging consequences."

At that, she stood and looked down her nose at him. "Believe what you will. You have clearly made up your mind." She moved away and joined the ladies, leaving Freddy alone, still angry but now feeling that, somehow, he was the one in the wrong.

****

Eliza hardly slept that night. In the quiet darkness of her bedchamber, where there was nothing to distract her thoughts, she replayed her final conversation with Freddy over and over again. *She* had disappointed *him*? *He* thought *she* was judgmental and cruel? She went back over the whole evening and could not think how he could possibly have thought she would wish to forcibly separate a mother from a child, which, unless she mistook his meaning, was what he had accused her of wanting to do.

She had meant her comment to sow its seeds in the minds of anyone at the party who might know of the child-stealing ring. It was, of course, not a guaranteed route to finding Claire, but every possibility needed to be explored. From what she had learned so far, the people doing this were organized, and they had the means to move about the country, secretly removing children and young girls, then hide them somewhere safe until they could ship them to new lives in the Americas. To Eliza's way of thinking, that meant someone with money must be involved. If she could persuade whoever it was that she was someone with whom they could do business, they might offer her Claire. And once her niece was safe with her, she could approach the authorities and close the criminal enterprise completely.

She had clearly been convincing in her efforts, for Freddy Finch had believed her to be sincere. Which hurt. Of all the people sitting around that table tonight, the one she had not expected to fool had been him. She had believed he knew her better than that.

It hurt that he could think so ill of her, that he could judge her so harshly. She wished she could go to him and explain what she was truly about. But how could she? If she was to have any success at all, she had to keep her secret. If she told one person, then someone else might hear of it and everything could collapse into failure. Worse, she could endanger not only herself but the children and girls who were missing at this time.

Besides, when she truly thought about it, how did she know Freddy was innocent? He was a rake and a wastrel. Which did not make him a criminal, of course, but how could she know? He had been at Hadlow when the crimes had been committed there. He had been hailed a hero for his part in thwarting them, but what if he wasn't? What if, in reality, he was up to his chin in nefarious goings-on? What if he was, even now, part of the plot she was trying to uncover?

He was everywhere she went. He seemed to be exploring churches, too. What if he was really watching her, making sure she didn't find Claire?

Could he really be so wicked?

No! No, he could not. He just…could not. She threw back her blankets and swung out of bed. The floor was cold to her bare feet and the night air chilled her skin through her thin night rail. She pulled on her robe and fastened it tightly, then found her slippers before pacing her room as she thought about Freddy.

A rake. A wastrel. Devil-may-care. Or was he? The more time she had spent in his company, the more she had questioned his personality as portrayed to the world. She had had numerous conversations with him now, and the man she was coming to know was decent, kind and honorable. He was intelligent and well read. She would expect the son of an earl to be educated, of course, but she had met others who had had the benefit of expensive schooling and learned very little from it. Freddy Finch knew the Bible well enough to argue with Prudence, and he was well versed in Greek mythology too, as well as many other things.

Yet he hid all of this behind a disreputable mask. Did he want people to think badly of him? She could only assume that he did, although why that should be was beyond her.

Would a true rake have been disappointed to think she was selfish enough to take somebody else's child? Would a selfish wastrel have cared enough to call her out on it?

There was clearly more to Mr. Finch than met the eye.

Until she could fathom him, his behavior and his motives, she would keep her secret. Let him think what he may.

Chapter Eleven

The next morning, she was enjoying her breakfast when Prudence arrived. The maid quickly laid another place at the table and brought fresh tea and toast to the ladies.

"I came to seek you out as soon as I could," said Prudence, around a bite of toast slathered with butter and jam. "I need to say something to you, and I don't believe I should wait."

Eliza held her breath. Could this possibly be about what had been said last night? Did Prudence know something about the missing children and their whereabouts?

That did not seem likely. She could not imagine a God-fearing woman like Prudence Burgess having any part in so heinous an activity. But, then again, Prudence may have heard a rumor…

More likely, she was going to follow Freddy and scold Eliza for what she had said. Although, unlike him, Prudence had expressed support for the idea of removing children from bad parents, so a scolding from her now would be somewhat hypocritical.

What the curate's sister wanted to say turned out to be nothing to do with the children, and everything to do with Freddy Finch.

"We are, I hope, friends now," she said. "And friends do have a duty to point out when one is taking a path that leads to concern. It has concerned me greatly to see you so much in the company of Mr. Finch over these last weeks. I have noticed, and you may be sure I am not alone in this, that you have been walking with him through the countryside, visiting buildings and spending time together inside them, without benefit of a chaperone."

Eliza felt her cheeks heat. She could not defend herself from the admonishment, because what Prudence said was true. Although, nothing improper had taken place—unless one counted the kisses he had bestowed upon her, and she could not bring herself to regret those, nor to think them wrong, no matter how much they might scandalize her neighbors, for they had been wonderful, leaving her floating on air, wanting more.

Which was probably not what she should be thinking at this moment, while Prudence cautioned her for it.

"A good name is rather to be chosen than great riches," she said now, quoting the Bible. "And again, 'Who can find a virtuous woman? For her price is far above rubies.' One would not wish to devalue oneself for the likes of that man."

Eliza blinked. *Devalue oneself?*

"I realize, of course, that you will have behaved in a proper manner throughout, and that if he had tried to take liberties, you would have stopped him and distanced yourself from him immediately. But, alas, reputation is balanced not solely on what we do, but on how we are perceived."

"I hardly think a walk in the daylight—"

"It is, of course, a fact that a widow has a certain freedom which would be denied a young, unmarried girl, and thus, scandal is not so readily attached to her. But it is still best to err on the side of caution, and spending time with that man is hardly that. He is, after all, a rake."

Eliza sighed. She was tired of people judging her and finding her wanting. Or, in this case, wanton. She smiled sweetly at Prudence, who poured herself a cup of tea. "Thank you for your concern."

Prudence put down the teapot and picked up the milk jug. "It is what friends are for."

"Quite. Although, I should tell you, Mister Finch has not behaved toward me in any way I would not wish him to." That was the truth, although she felt guilty that it suggested more innocence than she could perhaps claim.

"Well, of course he hasn't. He is experienced enough to know that you would never allow it, and he is not so foolish to chance his arm where it will not benefit him. But people talk, even when there is nothing to say. And, it must be conceded, the man is a lamentable character. Without actually doing anything wrong, he could cause irreparable harm to you." She stirred sugar into her tea. "I speak as a friend who would spare you such a fate."

"Thank you. Your concerns are noted, and I will consider them."

Prudence grinned, then sipped her tea. "You need something to do with your time."

"I have something to do." Eliza frowned.

"I meant something worthwhile. Looking at churches and examining their histories is all very well and good, but it is hardly on the list of occupations for a woman of good birth, is it? It brings the risk of being thought a bluestocking." She laughed, and Eliza made a halfhearted attempt to laugh with her. "No. I had in mind something far more edifying. I wondered if you," she pointed her cup at Eliza and looked inordinately pleased with herself, "would care to join my brother and me in our work amongst the poor and needy."

Eliza's heart sank. She would, of course, always be happy to help those who needed it, but, at this point, it was the last thing she could spend time doing. With every day that passed, the weather grew warmer and more stable, and the date of the ship's departure grew nearer. She needed to use every moment she had to find Claire before it was too late.

"I would, of course, be honored to join you," she said. "But I hope you will forgive a little self-indulgence. I do so love the churches, and I wish to continue studying them. Church buildings and church history meant so much to Mr. Rawlins." Beneath the table she crossed her fingers and prayed that the lie might be forgiven, since it was in a good cause. "I would honor him by completing my study."

Prudence grimaced. "As you wish," she said. "Although, there cannot be too many churches in this area that you have not studied by now."

Eliza shrugged. "I haven't been inside Saint Simon and Saint Jude's yet. Perhaps I might do that today?"

"Alas, the church is locked, and Silas is not home. He keeps the key, so we cannot gain access."

"What a pity." Eliza sipped at her own cooling tea. She was beginning to think that Prudence and Silas did not wish her to enter Saint Simon and Saint Jude's church, although she could not think, for the life of her, why that would be. Did they think she would try to run off with the silver?

"I cannot think why you are so interested, though."

Prudence frowned, thoughtfully. "It is but a simple country church, no different to hundreds of others."

"They all have their unique features." Eliza went on, before Prudence had a chance to realize how inane she sounded. "From home quite a lot, isn't he?"

"He is a busy man."

"As all good clergymen are."

Prudence nodded agreement and helped herself to a piece of pound cake and a wedge of cheese.

"Does he visit all his parishioners?" asked Eliza. "Or only those with known needs?"

Prudence covered her face with her hand so that she could speak with her mouth full. "Visiting his parishioners does take much of his time. But today, that is not what he is doing. Although he is on the Lord's business. It so happens he has travelled to Rye to visit a friend who, we hear, is at death's door."

"He is a good man," said Eliza, though her mind raced, and her heartbeat sped up. Silas Burgess had gone to Rye? Rye, where Eliza had met with the informative sailor, who had told her to look to the church in the Rotherton area?

Could she have been going about her search in the wrong way? Had the man not meant the church building, but its people? Was the Reverend Mr. Burgess somehow involved in the transporting of stolen children?

She could hardly think it. Silas did not seem sinister and villainous in any way, and she could not imagine him doing such things as stealing children.

Which had to be the most stupid thought she could possibly have had. If villains could be seen for what they were, they would be easy to spot, and nobody would ever fall prey to them.

Although, a man of the cloth… Silas Burgess was a bit of a bore when he gave his sermon, but he was not the only clergyman so affected, and he had given no indication that he would ever act contrary to his calling. True, he wasn't as pious as his sister, but then, that wasn't necessarily a bad thing. Too much piety could alienate his flock. A cleric had to be a man of the people, as well as a man of God.

"There was something else I wished to speak with you about." Prudence wiped her napkin daintily over her lips, then stared Eliza fully in the eye. Eliza raised an eyebrow, uncertain where this conversation would head next, as Prudence took a deep breath. "I want you to know I fully understand your desire to mother a child. Your own was ripped from your arms too soon, and you still have the need to nurture."

"Thank you." Eliza swallowed her guilt. "I realize my thoughts may have shocked some people, but—"

"Nonsense! They were moved by your heartfelt words. Only someone with no heart at all could not have been." She hesitated, before carrying on. "In our work, Silas and I do sometimes come across children whose parents can no longer look after them. Perhaps they are orphans, or their parents' income has disappeared, or, well, a hundred different things can happen to a family. The people caring for those unfortunate children are eager to see them given to homes where they may be better cared for and given a better start in life." She reached over and grabbed Eliza's hand as she emphasized, "It is all aboveboard, of course. The parents agree to the arrangements, so there is no hint of wrongdoing."

"I would expect nothing else," Eliza assured her, and

she meant it. She knew only too well that people in desperate straits often turned to the church to take children they could no longer care for.

"Such a child would, as Mrs. Potter rightly said, be unsuited to life in the *ton*, but then, you, like me, are not really part of that world, are you? I can see no impediment to a child being brought up by a respectable widow of impeccable reputation. So, I am suggesting you leave it with us, and we will see what we can do for you."

Oh, no! This was terrible. Eliza did not doubt the sincerity of Prudence's offer, but it was the last thing she wanted her friend to do. She could not, in good conscience, take a child from a family who genuinely wanted to hand their little girl over, not when her only reason for speaking of adoption was to entice the smugglers and find Claire. As Freddy had rightly pointed out, she had not the means to look after such a child for herself. It had to be Claire or nobody. To that end, she had been as specific in her requirements as she had dared to be, in the hope that the only child the villains could offer her was the one they had stolen from her sister. It had never occurred to her to think Prudence, or anybody else, might find another child for her.

Yet if she rejected the offer, as she must, she would cause suspicion and anger, perhaps even accusations of ingratitude, which could lead to much unpleasantness.

Of course, she might confide in Prudence, tell her what she was really trying to do, so that the curate's sister would better understand her actions. But she was strangely loath to do that. If she took Prudence into her confidence now, she would have to admit she had been lying to the woman for months, even about who she truly was. Eliza did not think Prudence would be understanding about that. She did not strike Eliza as the sort of person who would say the ends justified the means.

Then there was her attitude to the removal of children from those she deemed bad parents. Whilst Eliza did not think for a moment that Prudence Burgess would countenance the abduction and theft of children, she would probably have some sympathy for the motives of those doing such work. She might even believe Claire's removal from her mother's home was understandable, given how frail Charlotte had been since her husband's death.

As well as which, Prudence spoke to so many people. She would not mean to gossip, but if she were to let slip a morsel of information, why, the smugglers, fully warned, could spirit Claire away to somewhere Eliza would never find her.

No, she would keep her confidence to herself. Even if that meant that Prudence thought her odd, eccentric, and ungrateful.

Distracted as she was by her thoughts, Eliza could not have said what else they talked of during Prudence's visit. She hoped she hadn't been too vague or given Prudence any reason to think ill of her. The woman's heart was in the right place. It wasn't her fault Eliza was here under false colors. Praying that Prudence would not find a suitable child for her before this whole sorry mess was put to rights, Eliza was relieved when her friend left to visit others in need of her attentions.

Upset by the way the morning call had gone, and worried about unintended consequences, Eliza felt the need to get out of her cottage and be in the fresh air. She did not have the strength to continue her investigation today. So, instead, she asked for a small picnic lunch to be made for her, and she set off, ready to enjoy the delights of the countryside surrounding Rotherton.

It was a pretty day, not over-warm but not cold either. The sky was a powdery blue, thin trails of white cloud covering it in places, the way gauze covered the main skirt of a gown. Trees were in full leaf, painting the scene a thousand shades of green. Here and there, flowers added splashes of color: reds and oranges, lilacs and whites, and wheat grew in the fields, the once green shoots now turning to the yellow brown of harvest readiness. Birds sang in the bushes, and a magpie chattered, while seagulls scolded every creature they came across. A deer crossed the lane in front of her and pushed through the hedgerow into the field. She stopped and waited, knowing where there was one, there would be others. Her patience was rewarded when half a dozen more deer crossed in front of her. She smiled at the quiet dignity in their elegant walk and gave a small prayer of thanks for their calming presence.

After about half an hour of walking, she left the road and followed a path through woodland until she came to a glade beside a stream. It giggled cheerily over rocks, and clacked pebbles on the water's edge, its merry sounds raising her spirits. This was a perfect place to stop, she thought, with the trees to shield her from the sun's glare, and peaceful nature all around her. She took the small blanket from the top of the picnic basket and spread it on the grass, then settled herself onto it. A small fish leaped out of the water and dived back in, with a tiny splash. It made her smile.

She pulled out the first of the ham rolls her maid had

packed for her, then stopped when she heard a soft yap behind her. It sounded like a puppy, and not a very old one at that. She turned her head, surprised, wondering what such a young animal would be doing out here in the woods. This spot was not close to any houses, nor to any farms, and she could not believe the mother would let a pup venture so far from safety.

All became clear when the leaves rustled and Ned Fellowes stepped into the glade, a big grin on his face, showing the gaps where he had lost teeth, and the discolored, crooked mess of those that were left. He gave another puppy-like yap, then sat down beside her, crossing his long legs and resting his elbows on his knees. He looked from her to the bread and ham in her hand, and back. His eyes were big and round, and irresistible with longing.

"Hungry, Ned?" she asked. Ned's grin widened. She chuckled and handed him her roll. He wasted no time devouring it.

"You are a panhandler, Ned Fellowes," came Freddy's voice from the trees, startling Eliza. An instant later he, too, joined her. "Don't listen to him if he tells you he is starving," Freddy warned her. "I happen to know he had sausage, egg, and gammon only a couple of hours ago."

Ned's yap turned into a playful growl.

"Don't give me that, Mister Fellowes. You know I'm speaking the truth. I saw Rotherton's cook serve you a big plate of it." Freddy turned to Eliza. "It was piled to the rafters. And he made very short work of it." He gave Ned a look that was meant to be stern, but the light tone of his voice and the twitch of his lips took the sting from his words.

Ned's return grin was mischievous. The boy rammed the last of the bread into his mouth, stood and saluted Eliza with something that was halfway between a deep bow and a curtsy, then ran back into the woods and out of sight. Freddy watched him go, his eyes twinkling with humor.

"Incorrigible rogue," he said, and he shook his head as if in despair.

"He certainly looked hungry," answered Eliza.

"He always does. I've never known anybody like him. And I'm not even sure where he puts all the food he eats. He never seems to grow any fatter, although he devours enough to keep the whole of England well nourished."

"A slight exaggeration, perhaps?" Eliza tucked her feet under her.

"No matter how much he eats, he still remains skin and bone."

"I shouldn't worry. One day, mayhap, it will all catch up to him of a sudden and he will split at the seams."

"An edifying image. May I?" Freddy gestured that he wished to sit beside her.

Eliza nodded and concentrated on choosing something to eat from her basket as he lowered himself to the ground. She offered him food, which he declined, saying he had not long had breakfast.

"I know, I know, I ate late." He laughed, holding his hands up in mock surrender. "I got up late. I am a lazy, good-for-nothing, slug-a-bed."

"I did not say so," she pointed out primly, but the smile fighting its way to her lips betrayed the fact that she was not scolding him in earnest.

"You would have had every right." His own smile faded. "As you had the right to call me judgmental last evening. No, no," he insisted when she opened her mouth to argue with him, "I was rude and ungentlemanlike, and, yes, judgmental. I should not have been."

"I can see my comments might have led you to believe—"

"They did not. Or they would not have, had I not been narrow-minded and…and…"

"Judgmental?" They both laughed.

"All the way home," he told her, "and for most of the night, our conversation preyed on me. I found myself remembering what you had said and learning to be more accurate in my hearing of it. For when I stopped and examined your words, I saw the wrongness within me. You expressed a wish that it was possible for you to have a child. At no time did you say you would take another mother's baby, even if the chance arose."

"No, but I—"

"That was never your intention, was it?"

"It was not. But I can—"

"I can only apologize for jumping to conclusions about your meaning. It was unforgivable of me to do so, and worse to admonish you for your perceived fault in a public setting."

"Nobody heard."

"No thanks to me."

"Please, think no more of it. You owe no apology. My words were ambiguous. They must have been, for you were not the only one to interpret them as you did."

"Prudence Burgess?" She nodded, and he went on, "but then, Miss Burgess already agrees with the idea of separating children from their parents, so she was bound to understand you in that manner." He shook his head. "Do you think she would have taken the good Lord from his mother Mary, and placed Him with a married couple, had she been in Bethlehem?"

Eliza laughed. "It is true, not every Christian has the same sensibilities."

"Thank God." The laughter left his eyes and he studied Eliza for a long moment. "I believe your Christian sensibilities are softer than those of your friend, am I right? You hate the sin, but not the sinner."

"I endeavor to do that, yes."

"Which is why you tolerate me."

She gave him a sidelong look. "I am of the opinion, Mr. Finch, that your sins are not as many, nor as condemning, as you would have people believe."

He looked at her sharply. His laugh a moment later sounded forced. "Steady on," he said. "Are you trying to ruin my reputation?"

"No. But I think you are." There was a moment of silence before she added, "You are a man of hidden depths and more than a few secrets, are you not, Mr. Finch?"

"Freddy. Mr. Finch sounds so formal and unfriendly."

"You are avoiding the question. Freddy."

"We all have secrets, Eliza."

She bowed her head slightly, in acknowledgement of the truth of that.

"What are yours?"

Eliza gave him a startled look, then made a show of looking down into her picnic basket, murmuring that she hoped Cook had put in one of her most excellent cakes. He reached out and touched her arm, to stop her search.

The warmth of him seemed to envelop her, and a jolt of electricity went through her, making her jump.

She raised her head, slowly, lifting her gaze until it met his. His eyes were hooded, the desire within them obvious. His lips parted, and his breathing shallowed. His hair flopped onto his forehead. This close, she smelled his cologne, mingling with the scent of damp grass and woodland flowers. The stream gurgled an encouragement, and the breeze in the leaves whispered sweet nothings at them. Eliza's heartbeat quickened and her stomach did a funny kind of flip inside her, while lower, between her legs, ached in a strange, not unpleasant way. Everything seemed heightened. The colors were sharper, the light brighter. Sounds were clearer. The breeze caressed her skin. She could see every individual lash around his eyes, every shadowed hair already growing beneath his shaved chin.

She leaned forward, toward him. Or perhaps he leaned toward her. She could no longer tell.

The first kiss was soft, tentative, a barely-there caress, but it fired every nerve within her, making her ache for more. Her lips tingled and her eyes fluttered shut, of their own volition. He tasted of mint toothpowder, fresh air, and that indefinable something she knew was him alone. His lips were warm against hers, and there was a roughness on his chin where stubble had already formed. He made a soft noise in his throat, something between a growl and a groan, and deepened the kiss, pressing harder against her, firm, commanding, irresistible. His tongue pressed at the seam of her lips and she opened, letting him in, feeling the delicious slide of his tongue against hers. Her nipples stood to attention, rubbing against the lawn of her shift, and aching all the way through to the very core of her. She wanted to press against him, to make his touch firmer, and end the torment. She wanted to go on forever, until it drove her mad. Between her legs felt suddenly warm and wet and heavy, and she squirmed, needing release, uncertain where it would come from.

His arms wrapped around her and he edged her back, laying her down on the blanket, stretching the length of his body beside hers, his fingers playing with wisps of her hair that had escaped her bonnet. The ribbons loosened, the bonnet disappeared. She felt the freedom as, one by one, he took the pins from her hair, slowly, carefully, reverently. And all the time, his lips were on hers, kissing, stroking, nibbling. She made a tiny sound and arched her back, pressing herself closer to him, pushing her lips into his. There was relief as the last pins were taken and long hanks of hair fell free around her, fanning out across the blanket. He took some of her hair in his hand and rubbed his fingers through it.

"Beautiful," he whispered.

Her heartbeat raced and her breathing shallowed, and she heard a soft little moaning mewl. It took a moment before she realized it came from her. She reached up, touched his shoulder, her gloveless fingers reveling in the feel of the fine, soft wool of his coat, the smooth linen of his shirt, the rough warmth of the skin at his neck, the cool silk of his hair.

His tongue continued to slide along the length of hers, igniting fires within her that she had no hope of dousing. Her hips undulated and her back arched more, pleading for something, she knew not what. All she knew was that it was more important than life itself.

His hands moving over her were agonizingly slow.

He caressed her face, her jaw, her neck, each stroke of his fingers sending her higher, closer to madness. Her breasts were heavy, and her nipples ached, while a million butterflies took flight within her.

He pushed down the bodice of her dress and his fingers closed around her breast, kneading it, weighing it, before he took the nub of her nipple between finger and thumb and tweaked. She cried out and pushed herself further into him, wanting more. He smiled and his lips curved against her skin, as he tweaked her again. She felt her nipple grow and harden into a peak.

His lips left hers and she moaned, then gave a jolting cry as his mouth found her breast, suckling at her, setting her on fire. He blew where he had licked, his breath cool against her seared skin. She held his head, wanting to keep him there, wanting to feel his touch forever.

Her hips moved of their own volition, and her legs parted as a heavy wanting filled her core. Need rushed through her. She wanted to press herself against him, to feel him anchor her, to hold him close until she didn't know where she ended and he began. She wanted to fly away, soar through the summer sky. She needed it to stop, but she wanted it to carry on, forever.

His fingers found the hem of her dress and pushed it up her legs, deliciously, slowly, inch by excruciating inch, his fingers stroking her calves, her knees, her thighs. He reached the top of her stockings and she felt his fingertips, rough and calloused against her smoothness. And then he touched her at her most intimate part, and she shattered into a million pieces.

Chapter Twelve

Freddy barely touched Eliza before she came apart. She was so responsive, so full of passion. And yet, there was an innocence to her as well, a purity he had never sensed with any other woman. If he didn't know her to have been a wife and mother, he would have thought her untouched. She arched into him, pressing her hips against his hand, and there was an unpractisedness about her, as if she acted by instinct, as if she was doing this for the first time. He wondered at her husband. Surely even a clergyman could pleasure his wife and teach her the joy and wonder of the marriage act?

All thought of what had, or had not, gone before was suddenly swept away as she crested the wave and broke apart. Her hips bucked and her legs trembled, and her breath came in rapid, urgent pants that made him throb and harden more than he ever had before. High heat washed over him, fueling his own need, pushing him past the point of reason.

He fumbled with the fall of his trousers, feeling clumsy, overtaken by an urgency that had not gripped him since he was a green boy.

She lay still on the blanket, her legs parted, her skirt hitched to her waist. Her thighs above her stockings were soft and white, the juncture between them hidden beneath a mass of dark curls that glistened with her release. Her eyes were half closed and glazed, her lips parted, her breath shallow as she returned slowly to earth. She was everything he wanted, all that he needed.

His trousers opened and he sprang free, ready to take her. He rolled over her, cradling himself between her legs, the tip of him poised at the seam of her. He reached down between them and used his fingers to massage the nub of nerves in her center, bringing her back to the peak of madness before he thrust into her.

And then he stopped. Shock and horror replaced desire as he hit the barrier within her. She cried out, in pain, not in ecstasy, and he knew he had been lied to.

He moved away from her and sat up sharply, elbows resting on his raised knees. His desire was gone, leaving only the pain and frustration as his body urged him to finish what he'd started. He knew he could not, though for a moment, his mind was too clouded to reason why not.

Eliza Rawlins was a maid. She had never known a man. Which meant she had lied to him and to everybody else. A widow she might be, he supposed, although it would be a strange husband who could resist taking such a delectable wife to his bed. But she most certainly was not a mother.

As he sat there, trying to regain his composure and will his body to subside enough that he could redo his trousers, she seemed to come to and realize all was not well with him. She blinked and frowned at him.

"Freddy?" Her voice was filled with confusion.

"You lied to me." He sounded rusty, hurt. He hated that. He wanted her to hear his anger, his absolute fury, not this pathetic self-pity.

"What?" She sat up, never taking her eyes from him.

"You were a virgin."

She colored, deeply, and lowered her gaze. "I didn't know you could tell."

That enraged him. He sprang to his feet, re-buttoning his falls as quickly as he could. "Of course I could bloody tell," he shouted. "I'm not stupid!"

"I didn't—I meant—"

"I thought you were…" He bit off the words he was going to say. "What was your plan? To find some unsuspecting man and trick him so he had to marry you?"

"No! I—"

"Well, it worked. Though how happy you will be as Mrs. Frederick Finch is a matter for debate."

"I don't want to be Mrs. Frederick Finch," she retorted. "And certainly not through duress and obligation. If and when I marry, it will be for love, and nothing less."

"Love?" he laughed, bitterly. "Love is for schoolgirls and fools. And after what just happened here, there will be no 'marriage for love' in your future."

"I don't—"

"I may be known as a rake—"

"You are not—"

"But I am not an out-and-out blackguard. I do not despoil virgins. And now that I have done so, albeit unwittingly, I will not allow you to besmirch my honor as well."

"Your honor is intact. You have no reason—"

"You will marry me."

"I will do no such thing! You are being absurd."

"Absurd? Absurd? I've taken your maidenhead!"

"You took nothing. I gave it."

For a moment they stared at each other, both breathing heavily. Then he turned away and ran his hand through his hair as if to brush away all the anger and betrayal he felt. Briskly, she pulled her skirts down over her legs and tucked herself back into her bodice. He heard the angry swish of the material against her skin and, in his mind, saw pictures of her body beneath those clothes. He gritted his teeth and banished the images.

A few deep breaths later, he felt calm enough to speak. "Are you even a widow?"

"No."

He clenched his jaw, refused to say the angry words that sprang into his mind.

"I have never been married."

Freddy closed his eyes, the betrayal running deep.

"My name is Eliza Rolfe, and I am the daughter of the Reverend Mr. Jonas Rolfe, recently retired after serving his flock for more than thirty years."

Freddy glared at her. "You clearly have never had a child, either. So why say you had?"

"It seemed the only way to find a little girl who—"

He huffed angrily. "So you do want to steal someone else's child!"

"No!"

"Well, it is definitely not your own!"

"I am looking for a child who was stolen. I need to find her before it is too late."

He half turned and studied her, trying to ascertain the veracity of her words. She stared defiantly back at him. After a moment, he asked, "What child?" He was amazed at how calm his voice sounded, considering the anger still swirling within him.

"Claire is four years old, the brightest and most beautiful little girl. She is very much loved by all her family, but she was stolen from her mother earlier this year. We believe the key to recovering her safely is to be found here, in Rotherton. The district, that is, not just the town."

"Who is she to you?" He was thankful for the years serving Fremont, for that now helped him to focus on finding the facts, and enabled him to bury the emotions threatening to swamp him.

"She is my niece. Her mother is my sister, Charlotte." She went on to tell him of her sister's love match with Jonathan Russell.

"Jon was a solicitor," she explained. "He was also a silent partner in a business run by his brother, Donald. They were joint owners, though Donald ran the company while Jon and his partner built their practice." She sighed, heavily, and tucked her feet beneath her bottom. Freddy turned away; he didn't want to see her sitting there, looking delectable.

"About a year and a half ago," she went on, "the brothers had a falling out. I don't know what it was over, but they didn't speak again afterward. Charlotte was distressed by it. She has never enjoyed conflict. But despite her exhortations, there was no reconciliation between them."

Eliza reached into the picnic basket and rearranged its contents as she continued, "Then, ten months ago, the family—that is, Jon, Charlotte, and little Claire—were supposed to go on a trip. At the last minute, Claire came down with some childhood illness and couldn't go, but the trip could not be cancelled, and her parents went without her. On the way, there was a terrible accident. The coach overturned. Jon was killed outright, and Charlotte was badly injured. She had two broken legs, fractured ribs, a host of other injuries."

"While she lay in her sickroom, Donald came, demanding that he take Claire. Now that his brother was dead, he said, he would become Claire's guardian and she would live with him. Of course, Charlotte did not agree."

Freddy grimaced. "She must have had to fight to keep the child," he said. "A male guardian is usually preferred in such cases." It seemed absurd to him that the law would take a child from its own mother to place it with a man who was more distantly related, but that was the way of the world.

"That is true," agreed Eliza. "But Jon had, apparently, foreseen Donald's demands. In his will, he made his partner Claire's guardian, not Donald. That man was more than content to allow Claire to stay with her mother. Donald did not enjoy being gainsaid. He maintained that Charlotte's injuries meant she could not care for Claire properly, and he threatened to fight for custody of the child. So, even though Charlotte had servants to do what she could not, she sent for me to come and help her. She reasoned that a family member being on hand would be better than servants, if he carried out his threat."

"Where were you before she called for you?" Freddy's question was softly spoken.

"My father and I were staying with my brother, who is also a clergyman. I was keeping house for them but, since my brother was about to be married, I knew I would soon be somewhat surplus to requirements, so it was with some relief that I set off to be with Charlotte. However, just hours after I arrived, Claire disappeared."

"Disappeared?"

"Vanished. As if into the thin air. No sign of her,

whatsoever." She hunched her shoulders and tightened the hug of her arms around her knees, as if the memory sent a chill through her. "We looked everywhere. As did the local constabulary, and, to his credit, Donald, along with every member of his household and many of the workers at his manufactory. There was no sign of her."

"How on earth could that happen? I grant you, I know little about raising children but, from my own childhood, I don't recall being left alone and unsupervised long enough to be able to disappear for more than a few seconds. Not when I was very little, anyway." He grinned, sheepishly, as he remembered the times he and his brother had evaded their tutor who was, it had to be said, a singularly naive man. But by the time they were in his charge, they were older and more able to look after themselves. Also, they would have only escaped him to run off and spend time with friends, not to make a complete disappearance like the one Eliza described. "At your niece's age," he continued, "between our nursery maids, other servants and our parents, we were never alone for long enough to vanish."

"Neither was Claire," she answered. "My sister took comfort from that fact when the child first went missing. Wherever she was, Charlotte reasoned, she was with her nurse, who would comfort and care for her." Eliza sighed and the breath was ragged as emotion threatened to overcome her. "For a long time, she clung to the hope that the pair had taken a wrong turning on their walk and somehow got lost. Then, as the days passed, and that became more and more unlikely, there was a suspicion that the nurse might have abducted Claire. Even then, Charlotte said she knew the nurse would not hurt the child, so it was not as bad as it might have been."

"Presumably this nurse was not the culprit?"

Eliza shook her head and swallowed hard. "The poor woman was found in a ditch. She had been throttled. After that, Charlotte was beside herself. Because of her injuries, she was, of course, confined to bed, which made it worse."

She pursed her lips. "Then Donald tried to intervene again." Her voice was clipped, her anger at Claire's uncle evident. Freddy frowned. The man seemed insensitive and boorish to a fault, but surely even someone like that would know when to stay silent.

Eliza stared out across the landscape, although Freddy doubted she saw any of it as she lost herself in the oversetting memories. He wondered if she even remembered that he was here with her.

Tentatively, taking care not to move suddenly and startle her, he sat beside her and looked ahead too, as if he studied what she saw. The long grass around them danced, spreading the fresh, clean smell of its seed-laden stalks, mixing it with the soft perfume of a dozen meadow flowers, and the firmer, darker scent of the trees. The thin clouds traced patterns across the bright blue of the sky, their shadows rippling across the land. A squirrel scurried across the branches, stopped to check on his surroundings, then flicked his bushy red tail back and forth in warning, before moving on and out of sight. In the distance, a pigeon cooed incessantly, while other birds chirruped and trilled. Overhead, a seagull mewled, its lost, plaintive cry in keeping with the tone of their discussion.

Eliza shuddered, despite the heat of the day. "Once the nurse was found," she continued, "Donald decided they must be pragmatic. He was convinced, beyond the point of listening to any argument, that the same fate had befallen little Claire. He told Charlotte, and anyone else who would listen, that the child was dead."

Freddy shook his head. "That doesn't necessarily follow."

"I know."

"Why would the man say such a thing? Surely, like every other member of the family, he would want to hope against hope that she was alive and well."

Eliza shrugged her shoulders. "Who can fathom another person's thoughts? Perhaps he is one of those men who copes better by assuming the most pessimistic outcome of any situation, hoping that he will be pleasantly surprised when he is wrong, rather than vice versa."

"Perhaps." There were people, Freddy knew, who saw the worst in every situation.

"He wasn't content with voicing his opinion, though." Her jaw clenched. "He actually tried to have her legally declared dead."

"What? Why?"

She glanced at him. The angry spark in her eyes made Freddy shiver. He was glad that anger was directed at Donald, and not at him. He had a feeling the force of it would prove overwhelming, and a small part of him, a very tiny part, felt sorry for the man who had caused it.

"Money," she said. "Jon left his entire estate, other than Charlotte's widow's portion, to Claire. John's partner is named her trustee until she reaches the age of twenty-five, or until she marries a man of whom he approves. But, if she should die before either of those things occur, the estate reverts to Donald."

Freddy closed his eyes, and murmured, "Oh, Lord."

Eliza hugged her knees tighter. Freddy wanted to reassure her, to close the gap between them and wrap her in his embrace, but he knew that would be catastrophic for them both. His blood still fizzed in his veins after their lovemaking, and his compassion for her story warred with the anger he still felt at her deceit. Although, he had to admit, that anger had begun to dissipate as he learned more of her quest and the motive behind the lies.

"Thankfully," she continued, "once again, Donald did not get his way. The court granted an injunction against the declaration of Claire's death, and now it cannot happen until she has been missing for a minimum of seven years. Unless, of course, her body should turn up. They also struck down Donald's request to be made her trustee in place of Jon's partner."

That was, Freddy thought, a good decision. Donald did not sound as if he was the kind of man one could trust to act in anybody's interests but his own. Which begged the question: "What do you think happened to the child? Would her uncle be capable of engineering her disappearance?"

Eliza sighed, heavily. "I don't know. I'd like to say no, for who wishes to acknowledge that a family member could do such a thing to an innocent child?"

"The thought did cross your mind." It was not a question.

"I cannot deny it. Although, during our search for Claire, other facts came to light, facts that would seem to shift suspicion away from Donald."

"Such as?"

"We discovered she was not the only child to have gone missing from the area. She was the only child of her class, but her disappearance was by no means an isolated case. All the other children who disappeared were the offspring of laborers and factory workers and such."

"So of no interest whatsoever to the constabulary." It was a sad but true fact that those tasked with keeping the rule of law concerned themselves with the wealthy and well born and their comfort far more than they did with the rest of society.

"As well as that, the other children had disappeared over a number of years, so there had been no real cause for panic or alarm." Her smile was sad. "A lamentable state of affairs. I would like to think that even children in a workhouse orphanage would warrant some attention if large numbers of them began to vanish within a short period of time."

"A short period?"

She nodded.

"How long?"

"Five years. Perhaps six. During which roughly twenty children disappeared."

So, thought Freddy, just a few children in any one year. Enough to cause concern and grief for their family, enough for a localized and limited search, even, but not enough to panic the populace.

"There was little to connect the disappearances, either," Eliza continued. "They were both boys and girls, and they ranged in age from about three years old to fifteen. One young girl disappeared along with her baby brother, and it was concluded that she must be the child's true mother, despite the denials of her family. Two older girls were deemed to have run off with lovers, while another was said to have gone to London to seek her fortune. A young girl was found dead in a ditch, and a local boy hanged for her murder." She shook her head, sadly. "Considering that she, like Claire's nurse, was throttled, I wonder if he was truly guilty."

Freddy nodded, grimly. It wouldn't be the first time an innocent had gone to the gallows, and, no doubt, it wouldn't be the last.

"In some cases," Eliza went on, "where no trace of a child was found, the authorities decided a parent had sold the child for drinking money and tried to cover their tracks."

"Sadly, it does happen," he said.

She heaved a sigh. "I know. But…"

"I take it nobody saw a connection between the disappearances but you?"

Eliza nodded. "They dismissed me. Said I was weaving with straw and hoping for a silk dress."

"I can imagine." The authorities would not take kindly to anybody telling them they hadn't done their jobs properly. When the critic was a woman… "Given that you are here, I surmise you did not let their negativity deter you?"

Her back straightened and her chin came up, defiantly. "No, sir, I did not. Indeed, how could I? The more I looked at what I had uncovered, the more I was convinced of it. But nobody would listen, and the children stayed lost, and Claire…"

He heard the catch in her voice and struggled not to reach for her. The poor woman had endured so much, alone. He wanted to take her burdens from her, if only for a few moments.

Before he could act on that, Eliza scrambled to her feet and walked a few feet away, then stared out at the landscape once more. "Donald was…well, he was unreasonably angry with me for it."

"Why?" Surely the man should be grateful for any effort made on his niece's behalf.

"He told me to cease what he called my 'delusional insinuations.' He accused me of upsetting my sister, and his wife and mother, as well as causing unrest amongst his workers and other townspeople. He said if I did not stop this 'nonsense' he would see to it that I was made to stop."

Her voice deepened as she fought to keep the emotion under control. Something Freddy found difficult to do himself. This woman had been threatened for trying to do right by innocent children. His jaw tightened and his shoulders tensed. He wanted to find Donald Russell and show him how bullies should be dealt with. He wanted to ensure the man never even thought about threatening or insulting this woman ever again. How dare the blackguard be so cruelly dismissive? If he genuinely believed that Eliza's theories were wrong, he should have disproved them in a calm and rational manner, not simply thrown his weight around and tried to make her back down.

Clearly, she had not done so. But neither had she stayed to face his wrath. Instead, she had made her way to rural Sussex and begun her search again.

Why here?

He didn't realize he had asked aloud until she answered. "I followed a trail which did not go cold, as all the others had done. It led me to London, where I learned of more disappearances."

"London is a big city. People go missing there all the time."

She inclined her head in agreement. "I was careful

not to attach cases to the list until I was absolutely certain. That's when Miss Eliza Rolfe became Mrs. Rawlins. It seemed safer if people did not immediately connect me to Claire. And a married woman can go where a single lady cannot. I wanted to leave no stone unturned."

Freddy was impressed. She had powers of deduction to equal Fremont's finest, along with determination and courage, yet she was not reckless. She had kept her own safety in mind, even as she searched for her niece.

"The constables and the Watch in London were of little help. Although, in fairness to them, they were kept very busy with other things, such as keeping the peace and chasing burglars, and, for most of them, it is a part time position, to be fitted in whenever they are not working at their main jobs. On top of which, did you know that, by law, they cannot investigate a crime? They only have powers to arrest someone in a clear-cut case."

Freddy had known that. It was one of the promises made to reassure people that the constables would not pry into their lives and private business should they be affected by a crime.

"I was never so constrained," she said, with a wry smile. "Unlike them, I could, and did, investigate every piece of the puzzle. Doing so led me to Rye. And what I learned in Rye led me here."

She told him of the sailor she had met in Rye, the information he had been able to provide, the horrific idea that the children, and others, were being shipped abroad, and the rather vague clue that she concentrate her efforts on the church in the Rotherton area.

Her face fell and her shoulders slumped as she acknowledged her failure to discover more. "We are coming into full summer now," she said, "and the storms of winter have almost completely gone for another year. Ships are beginning to sail again, and it is only a matter of time before Claire, and others like her, are taken from England's shores and beyond my reach. I need to find her. Quickly."

"That explains your interest in church buildings."

She huffed a tiny laugh, then busied herself with putting the picnic paraphernalia back into the basket. "I think I am becoming an expert on the architecture of Sussex places of worship by now," she said. "Much good it has done me. I have searched through dozens of churches and chapels, and found not one shred of evidence of any nefarious goings on whatsoever."

Freddy thought for a moment. "If I may be so bold as to suggest, perhaps you should look at the problem from a different standpoint?"

Eliza frowned as she studied him. "Such as?"

"The church is more than a consecrated building. It is the people, too. And if the stones do not give up their secrets…"

"Look to the people of the church?" She smiled, sheepishly. "I did, for a brief time, wonder about that. Would you believe I suspected Mr. Burgess might be involved?" She laughed. "I can only imagine how absurd that would seem to anyone else."

"Why? Burgess is a human being before he is a cleric. He is as flawed and tainted by sin as the rest of us."

"True. But one can be a sinner without being utterly wicked and depraved. I do not seriously think Silas Burgess would steal children from their homes and ship them to the Americas."

"What made you suspect him in the first place?"

She blushed, clearly embarrassed. It made her eyes sparkle and her skin glow. Freddy wished he could hold the enticing color in his heart, to warm him on cold days in the future.

"His conveyance." Eliza explained, briefly, that the Reverend Mr. Burgess kept a pony and drove a cart of much greater quality than the average clergyman could afford. She had wondered, rather unkindly, she said, where he had found the funds to pay for it.

"Living beyond your obvious means is often a sign of ill-gotten gains," Freddy agreed.

"Or it is a sign of a generous benefactor."

"Ah." Freddy nodded his understanding.

"Besides, apart from an exceptionally comfortable conveyance, the Burgesses do not live high on the hog, do they? Truth to tell, I felt rather ashamed of myself for even harboring the thought that they may be less than saintly."

"What exactly were you hoping to find in your search?"

"I don't know. I didn't think I would find the children, of course. But perhaps a record of them having been here? An account listing them?"

"Doubtful you'd find anything like that. Written records can prove incriminating."

"Which is probably why, after months of searching, I have found nothing to lead me onward. The trail has gone cold, and unless I can make it warm again, Claire and any others who have been stolen recently will be on board a ship and out of the country—and out of my reach." She swallowed, hard, and for a moment he thought she would cry. She didn't. Instead, she took a deep breath, lifted her head, and pushed a determined look onto her face. "I will find her. I must."

Freddy's heart went out to her. Suddenly, he knew he must help her. Nothing else mattered but that she find the children she sought. Fremont's gold could wait. It was likely not going anywhere and would still be there to be found later, whereas the children could be spirited away at a moment's notice. Besides, who was to say that looking for one thing would not lead him to the other? Stranger things had happened.

"I'll help you look," he told her.

Her eyes widened in shock and she stared at him, clearly rendered speechless by his offer. A part of him was insulted by her surprise. Did she think he would stand by and watch children be stolen away? What kind of man did she think he was?

"That is very kind of you," she said at last.

"I don't think it is," he replied, and he heard the petulance in his voice. It did not make him proud. "It is no more than any other decent person would do."

She smiled. "Thank you. With the two of us working together, we are sure to find what we need to recover the children. Two heads are, as they say, better than one."

He nodded. They would find the children, restore her niece to Eliza's sister, and then marry. Even if she truly hadn't trapped him on purpose—and he was persuaded that she had not—he had ruined her and, regardless of his public reputation, he was gentleman enough to remedy that. For an instant, anger threatened to surface at the situation, but he quickly suppressed it. What was done was done. On top of which, he must share the blame. She hadn't forced him to try and tumble her here in the open air. He was equally responsible for his fate.

When he thought about it, that fate did not fill him with the dread he might have expected. The idea of being married to Eliza Rawlins—Rolfe!—did not send shivers along his spine or make his stomach churn. Those had been his responses to his last matrimonial close call, and he had been careful ever since not to endanger his bachelorhood. But when the bride would be Eliza, he could tolerate the thought of marriage. More than tolerate. He surprised himself when he realized he was actually happy with the idea. The pair of them rubbed along well as friends, and they were clearly attracted to each other. They stood a chance of a happy union.

Eliza pulled him from his contemplations as she began to list the places where she had looked already. It struck him that she had been thorough, travelling extensively throughout the area, finagling her way into many church buildings and, usually, contriving to rid herself of the person who had given her admittance. That could not have been easy. Most vicars, churchwardens, and the like, would be only too pleased to show an interested person the wonders of their church, keen to point out its history, or the eccentric quirks hidden within the building. That she had managed to spend so much time alone in these places was testimony to her determination to succeed.

"In short," she concluded her explanation, "the only places I haven't managed to search at all are St Denys' Church in Weninghope, which is a full day's journey from Rotherton and which would, therefore, require me to stay away for a night, mayhap even two, thereby drawing unwanted attention."

"I can see that would be difficult for you," Freddy

said. "Though it would be easy enough for me. People don't tend to question the perambulations of gentlemen in the way they do ladies."

"They might, however, question your desire to see inside a church."

He grinned. "I wouldn't worry about that if I were you. I can be persuasive."

"I'm sure you can." Her lips twitched and her eyes sparkled with humor. Then she cleared her throat and continued, "St Denys' at Weninghope is one I haven't managed to get to yet, as I say. Then there is St Mary's at Nettleton, and St Simon and St Jude's right here in Crompton Hadlow."

"I should have thought that one would have been first on your list." Had her friends the Burgesses not allowed her access? Or had she been unable to rid herself of them so she could search?

"Alas, no," she answered, with a look of weary exasperation. "Mr. Burgess keeps the key on his person. There doesn't seem to be a second key anywhere, and Mr. Burgess is so busy, and often away from home. There is no gaining entry."

Freddy was reminded of how he had looked along the side of that church, searching for another way in upon finding it locked. He hadn't found one, but then, he had been interrupted. It might serve him to return after dark, when nobody else was likely to be nearby. He could search properly and perhaps, find the path to the children.

Which he would do because it was the right thing. The joy he anticipated seeing on Eliza's face when he brought her niece to her had nothing to do with it at all.

"Is Weninghope truly a day's journey away?" he

asked, pushing aside all thoughts of Eliza's happiness and his part in creating it.

"It would be for me, for I would have to walk there. The stagecoach does not go near it."

He raised his eyebrows at her. Weninghope had to be at least fifteen miles from Rotherton. He would not expect a woman of the working classes to walk there, let alone a genteel vicar's daughter. "Could you not hire a pony and trap, then?"

She shook her head. "I don't drive. To hire a trap, I would need to hire a driver as well, and that would mean somebody would know where I had gone, and why. People, that is, the *wrong* people, might hear of it and wonder why I would travel so far just to look at a church." She chuckled. "There comes a point when an eccentric interest in church architecture becomes suspicious behavior, don't you think?"

"I could drive you there," he said. "I would be honored to do so."

"You would?" She smiled, and he thought the sun grew brighter. His Adam's apple pressed against his cravat, which was suddenly too tight. He swallowed hard. It didn't help.

"Yes, I would."

"Thank you. That would be wonderful."

"We will…" He cleared his throat to get rid of the sudden huskiness in his voice. "We'll go tomorrow if the weather is congenial. We can leave early, take a picnic nuncheon, get to Weninghope about two o'clock, search the church, and find an inn to have dinner before we come home again."

She blushed, and her cheeks turned a pretty shade of rose, somewhere between soft-pink and bright red. The color made her eyes glitter and her hair shine, and he wished he could see more of it.

"People will talk if we are gone for the whole day."

Let them talk. He knew better than to say that aloud, any more than he would remind her at this moment that she was now his fiancée in all but name. Instead, he used his most wicked grin, the one he had practiced for hours when he had first taken on the guise of rake. "If they talk, they will decide that I am courting you. Which is completely respectable and above board. I am a gentleman, and you are a gentleman's daughter, so there is nothing to wonder at there."

"Oh." Her blush deepened.

"Of course, the idea of you being pursued by me may worry your good friend Miss Burgess, but then again, I think we can weather that storm, don't you?"

Eliza nibbled at her bottom lip with her top teeth. It was an endearing movement, not least because it made him want to take the abused lip and kiss it until all evidence of the bite had gone.

"We would be doing her a favor," he continued, and Eliza frowned, puzzled. "I am of the opinion that Miss Burgess enjoys nothing more than worrying about her friends and neighbors. We can provide her with something to be anxious about." He grinned again. "It will also provide her other neighbors with respite, when she doesn't have time to spend worrying over them."

Eliza laughed. It was the most wonderful sound. If he was a poet, he would doubtless have compared it to silver bells, or a stream leaping playfully over rocks, or some other trite description. Thanking God he wasn't a poet, he just enjoyed the sound of it.

"You, sir, have a wicked tongue," she scolded him,

which sent his thoughts careening down another rabbit hole, as he imagined just how wicked his tongue could be, and the pleasure it could bring to her.

Dear God! If Eliza could read his thoughts at this minute, she would probably shoot him. He took a deep breath and tried to corral them. There would be plenty of time to indulge himself with that sort of thing once they were married and her reputation was safe.

He must have muttered something, because she frowned at him and asked, "Once we are married? What do you mean, sir?"

"Freddy," he corrected her. "I have asked you to call me Freddy, at least when we are in private."

"You said, and I quote, 'Once we are married.' Sir." She emphasized the word "sir."

He opened and closed his mouth, knowing he needed to say something but at a loss to know what it should be. The hardening in her eyes and the grim look on her face said she was not pleased with the way the conversation had turned.

"I have already made it plain that we will not marry." Her voice held a chill to rival a winter's morning. "There is no need for you to sacrifice yourself."

"I took your maidenhead—"

"You took nothing. I gave it."

"The consequences—"

"There will be no consequences. I don't intend to marry, so no future husband will need to be told I am, er, damaged goods. Plus, I am, supposedly, a widow. Nobody expects me to be…" She waved her hand in the air, as if trying to conjure the words she needed, before she gave up and moved on, that bright pink-red color deepening on her cheeks, making her face burn until he could feel the heat emanating from her. "We have no need to marry," she finished firmly.

Freddy opened his mouth to answer her, but she held up her hand to stop him.

"I must go home," she said. "Thank you for your company." She gathered up the picnic basket, pushed her hair into her bonnet and tied the ribbon under her chin, then started away from him.

Silently, Freddy cursed. Him and his big mouth! All had been going so well until he had let slip that he still intended to marry her. Now he felt as if he had taken one step nearer to her only to be repulsed and forced to take two steps back.

"I will come for you tomorrow at about ten," he said to her retreating back.

Her shoulders stiffened and she looked back at him. "I don't believe that is wise."

"We still need to look at the church at Weninghope."

"Nevertheless—"

"For Claire." It was a low blow, but he could think of nothing else that might change her mind.

Eliza nodded, curtly. "For Claire. And a picnic nuncheon. We won't need dinner in an inn."

Before he could answer her, she walked briskly away. He watched her go, his teeth gritted. If she thought he would give up that easily, she had another think coming.

Chapter Thirteen

As she walked home, Eliza played the time with Freddy over and over in her head. She had not expected to meet with him today. All she had thought to do today was to enjoy herself in the early summer sunshine and spend time with her thoughts, recounting all she had done so far in her search for Claire, hopeful that she might find some clue she had previously missed, and use it to work out where she should look next.

Unexpected it may have been, but she could not say her encounter with Freddy had been unwelcome. He was warm and friendly, and he had a way of putting a person at ease. They had been able to laugh and tease one another, and…

She had never experienced anything quite like his kiss, or what had followed. That had been wonderful! That feeling of flying, soaring away from herself, from everything around her, had been beyond anything she had ever experienced before.

Was that how it always was? No wonder families guarded their daughters so carefully and refused to let them have any unsupervised dealings with gentlemen. If the young ladies of the *ton* learned what they had been missing…

Eliza felt the color heat her cheeks as she walked briskly toward her home, the picnic basket swinging on her arm. She was grateful for the soft breeze cooling her, and she wondered, briefly, how believable it would be to blame that breeze and her brisk pace for the high color in her face, should she meet anyone she knew. She willed the blush away, thought of mundane things until, slowly, the hot prickle over her skin subsided.

What did not subside, though, was the feeling that had caused her to blush in the first place. The thought of what she had done today, of what she had allowed Freddy to do, was... Well, she didn't know quite what it was. There was no denying she had behaved like a wanton. She should be mortified, appalled at her own actions and ashamed of what he might think of her. But she wasn't any of those things. She did not regret the time spent in his arms. nor was she sorry for the things they had done. She certainly could not feel bad about the way he had made her feel.

There had been a moment of sharp pain when he entered her, but Eliza had not been worried by that, for Charlotte had told her it always hurt a woman the first time she made love. Of course, Charlotte hadn't told her the equally important fact that a man would be able to tell it was her first time. If she had known that, she might have done things differently. Perhaps she might have told him the truth before he discovered it for himself.

No. She knew she would not have done that. Eliza could not imagine having that conversation with Freddy Finch. And certainly not while they were in the middle of doing...*that*. Besides, she had not been capable of coherent thought at the time, much less able to find the words to tell him she...

Her cheeks heated again.

He had been so angry with her. Shocked, bewildered, betrayed. It hurt that he suspected she had deliberately set out to trap him, although she hoped he had seen the truth when she refused to marry him. Not that her refusal had deterred him, it seemed.

Eliza was unsure what had angered her when she had realized he still intended to marry her. Was it that he seemed angry and upset at the prospect? No woman wanted to feel her bridegroom was reluctant; it didn't bode well for a happy life after the ceremony. If he wasn't eager before the banns were read, how would he feel once things settled and they fell into their married routine?

Or was it that she was given no say in what was to happen? Freddy had decided they must wed, and he brooked no opposition. Eliza's wishes clearly did not matter.

That was nothing new, of course. All her life, Eliza had been subject to the commands of her father and, to a lesser extent, her brothers. If she had married, command would have passed to her husband. It was the way of the world.

But it rankled when the person issuing orders and decrees was Freddy. He did not have any jurisdiction over her. He was not her father, or her brother, nor yet her husband, or even the man with whom she had an understanding. He had no right to dictate her future, and the fact that he had tried had completely overset her. How dare he?

However, Eliza was honest enough to acknowledge there was something else, another reason for her objections. It had nothing to do with what Freddy had done or said, or how high-handed he had been. No. This reason had only to do with herself. For Eliza knew, deep down, that what Freddy had offered her—marriage, a lifetime with him—those things were exactly what she wanted to take.

It could never be. She knew that, and, deep down, Freddy knew it, too. It was all very well for him to say she was a gentleman's daughter, but Freddy was the son of an earl. Granted, he had no title himself, but he would still be expected to marry well, and a country vicar's daughter would not be the choice his family would approve of. Just as a man who cultivated a reputation as a rake and stayed in the country to avoid gambling debts would never be approved by Eliza's family.

"If only I hadn't agreed to drive with him to Weninghope," she muttered as she reached her front door. The drive, and the long day in his company, would only complicate things and make her want what she could not have. She would write to him as soon as she was inside, and cancel tomorrow's trip. And then she would take great pains to avoid him for as long as he was in Rotherton.

Satisfied with her plan, she walked into her house, removed her bonnet and coat, and asked for tea to be served in her parlor.

****

At Rotherton Hall, Freddy bathed and changed his clothes, then went downstairs to the library, where he found the earl writing a letter. He sanded the paper, folded and sealed it, then asked Freddy if he'd had a good day.

"On the whole, I would say so," Freddy answered, and he helped himself to a brandy from the tantalus in the corner. The library was darker than most of the rooms in the Hall, for although its windows were as large as in any other room, these had heavy dark red drapes hung at them, which didn't quite pull back to the walls. Floor to ceiling shelves of books, many bound in morocco leather in dark colors, didn't help, nor did the furniture in the room—a dark-wood desk, and armchairs upholstered in dark red leathers. Occasional tables matched the desk, and the carpet picked up the reds from the chairs. Even at the height of the day one would need a lamp or candle in here to read by, and David, the earl, had an oil lamp on the desk beside him now. The fire was lit, which did much to lift the atmosphere, though it also highlighted how dark and chill the room was, since no fires had been laid in the other rooms, which were lighter and airier.

"I didn't find what I was looking for," Freddy continued, and he sipped the fine brandy, "but the day was pleasant in itself."

David studied him for a moment as if trying to discern any hidden meaning behind Freddy's blasé comment. Freddy moved in a deliberately slow and relaxed manner to a chair, sat down and crossed his legs, determined not to show any discomfort at his friend's scrutiny.

After what seemed an eternity, David nodded. "Do you have plans for this evening?"

"No. Nothing. You?"

"Actually, yes. I'm abandoning you, I'm afraid. I have a dinner engagement with a…friend. I may stay overnight, should it grow too late." He lowered his eyes and studied his desktop, and his cheeks darkened slightly.

Freddy nodded and fought the smile that threatened. Lord Rotherton always seemed reticent around the ladies in their Society. He conversed easily enough with them, but only in the way he would have conversed with a sister or an aunt, and he rarely asked a lady for a dance. He was clearly a private man, and Freddy would respect that. All he said in reply to the earl's announcement was, "Enjoy your evening."

"Will you be all right here, alone?"

"I will be fine. In fact, I do have something I need to do. Tonight might be the perfect time to do it."

He thought about the strange cry he'd heard when he was in the churchyard at Saint Simon and Saint Jude's Church in Crompton Hadlow. It could have been an animal, but he'd been certain it came from the grave nearest to the church wall. Freddy didn't believe in ghosts, and the sexton had hinted at a phenomenon which science could explain, but that hadn't answered Freddy's question at all.

"You will keep out of trouble, I hope?" grinned David, his color back to normal and his equilibrium restored.

"I'll do my best." Freddy laughed, then told David where he intended to go.

"I'm sure you know what you're doing," said David. "Though I'm not so certain that Silas Burgess will take kindly to your snooping about his church in the dead of night."

"Then the man should open it during the day. It's always locked, and he's never at home to unlock it."

"Do you think you'll find what you're searching for in there?" David looked skeptical.

Freddy shrugged. "It's more…to satisfy my curiosity."

"I wish you luck then." David stood and put his letter into his pocket. "Take care, though. The locals are convinced that place is haunted, you know."

"I'm not surprised." Freddy thought again about the strange sound, so convincingly like a child's cry.

"If it's all the same to you, I would rather not have to explain to Fremont why you were swallowed whole by a demon from hell while I was enjoying an evening elsewhere. It would be very bad *ton*, and he would never let me forget it."

Freddy laughed again. "I will endeavor to do nothing that will cause you embarrassment or inconvenience, my lord, as long as you don't do anything to embarrass me."

"No need to worry about that. All my demons hide behind closed doors." For a moment, he looked wistful, sad even. Then he smiled, brightly, and went to change his clothes.

Freddy enjoyed an excellent, if lonely, dinner of chestnut soup, followed by freshly caught mackerel cooked with fennel and mint, and a rich meat pie with vegetables, before finishing with poached pears in fruit compote, all washed down with a fine red wine. The footman who cleared away the final course put a decanter of brandy on the table beside Freddy, but he decided not to imbibe. He had no love of drinking alone, and besides, he had better things to do.

All through the meal, he thought of Eliza and what she had told him about the children being stolen and sold to who-knew-what in America. The kidnappers were clearly ruthless, as evidenced by Claire's dead nurse, which indicated there was a sizeable profit in their enterprise. He hated the idea that Eliza might come across these people when she was alone. She was undoubtedly a strong, capable, and determined woman, but she would be no match for desperate and violent criminals. There would, almost certainly, be more than one of them, too, making her situation even more dangerous. He wanted to run to the danger for her, neutralize it, spare her the risk. If he knew where to look for it, he would go right now and take the burden from her.

Would you believe I suspected Mr. Burgess might be involved?

Her words from earlier played in his head. She had laughed, embarrassed by what she saw as a ridiculous idea.

But why was it ridiculous? As Freddy had pointed out, Burgess was as flawed as anyone else. He would not be the first follower of Christ to sacrifice his ideals for a few pieces of silver.

He had, she'd said, a nicer conveyance than most clergymen could afford. That was not, in itself, proof of wrongdoing. His family might have money, or there might be a benefactor, or perhaps the man might just be frugal in other areas, saving enough for the most comfortable vehicle he could manage.

There were certainly no other indications that he lived beyond his means. True, his home contained a lot of things, more furniture and knickknacks than the space really allowed, but none of it was particularly remarkable. The furniture in the parlor was good quality, and fairly new; it would have cost more than most of his parishioners could spend, but, at the same time, it was not of the quality and style one might expect to find in an aristocrat's townhouse. If Freddy had to guess at its origin, he would say it had probably been given by a variety of well-wishers and had then been kept by the Burgess siblings because of their desire to please all the givers rather than because of avarice or a tendency to hoard on their part. The same went for the ornaments displayed in the curate's cottage. Such a collection could not have come from only one source, for nobody with any taste would put together such an assortment. None of the pieces had stood out to him as overly valuable, although none were particularly cheap, either.

Still, Freddy could not shake the doubt that took root in his mind. It was a what-if kind of thought: what if Eliza's suspicions were right? What if there was something nefarious happening in Crompton Hadlow?

Freddy didn't think for a moment that the Reverend Mr. Burgess and his sister were kidnapping children. But, nonetheless, something about them seemed to him to be "off." He couldn't say what it was, but it was definitely there, and it behooved him, for both his own peace of mind and for Eliza's, to discover it.

He didn't want anyone other than David to know what he was doing, so he waited until the Hall was quiet, all the servants having retired for the evening. Then, dressed in his darkest clothes, he sneaked downstairs and out through the French windows in the dining room, since that was the only door he knew of which would close behind him without locking him out.

Silently, he made his way across the flagstone terrace and down the stone steps onto the manicured lawns, taking care to avoid the graveled paths where his footsteps might rattle the stones and alert people to his presence.

After leaving the earl's estate, he moved swiftly along the lanes, circling the outskirts of Rotherton, where a few hardy souls were still awake, carousing in the inn. Then he traveled on to Crompton Hadlow, whose inhabitants seemed to be tucked up in their beds, for the entire village was in darkness, save for a small lantern that hung underneath the sign over the tavern's front door. In the distance, a fox barked, its sharp, rasping cry answered by a lone dog, whose bark was quickly silenced. An owl swooped low, its silent form momentarily illuminated by the tavern's lantern as it searched for prey along the street.

At the church, the lych-gate was open; it was probably always open, for it looked as if it had not been swung shut in an age. Freddy thanked the Lord for small mercies, then grinned at the irony of thanking God for making it easier to steal into His house.

"For saintly reasons, Lord, I promise," he whispered, although he still felt strangely guilty. If he had been a Catholic, he might well have crossed himself at this point. Even as an Anglican, he was strongly tempted to do just that.

The church was silhouetted, black against the navy-blue sky, a dozen stars surrounding its spire like a crooked halo. The tiny sliver of moon gave just enough light to discern shapes and find his way, but not enough to let him see things properly, and he needed to concentrate as he moved along the path to the church porch.

The heavy wooden church door was securely locked. It didn't budge even a fraction of an inch when he pushed against it. The lock was huge, its cold metal smooth against his gloveless fingertips as he felt it. There wasn't a lockpick in the set he carried that would be up to the job of turning those tumblers, so he headed around the side and to the back of the building, where he found another door. This door was smaller than the front one, but just as sturdy, its lock as impossible for him to open.

On an exasperated sigh, he looked at the walls of the building. The windows were high, but not so high that a man couldn't climb the buttresses and access them. However, they were not made of large panes of glass that he might remove, crawl through, then try to replace, but small squares of leaded lights that nobody would be able to climb through without badly damaging them. He could also see immediately that none of the windows were made to be opened.

A complete circuit of the church did not reveal an outside entrance into the crypt, or anywhere else, so it looked as if this place was going to remain unbreached tonight. He didn't like the feeling of defeat that washed over him at that thought, but he told himself it didn't matter, since there had only been the longest shot of finding anything of use in there anyway. The odds of the Reverend Mr. Burgess and his Bible-quoting sister being involved in anything untoward were too long to calculate. Considering how difficult Freddy was finding it to gain entry, the chances of other people, smugglers, for instance, using this church for their evil deeds without the deliberate help of the curate were even longer.

On that thought, he turned to leave.

He had taken two steps when he heard the cry again. Heartbreaking in its plaintiveness, it seemed to echo through the air. The hairs on the back of his neck stood to attention and a shiver slithered down his spine. He shuddered and tensed his shoulders.

The cry sounded again. It wasn't coming from inside the church itself. At least, it didn't sound as if it was. It sounded as if it came from the graveyard. The graveyard which, Freddy could clearly see, was completely empty of living souls other than himself. He swallowed and fought the urge to retreat at a run. There was no such thing as ghosts.

And so he would keep telling himself.

Perhaps, he thought, it was a smuggler's device, designed to keep away inquisitive villagers. He knew the gangs of the last century had employed similar tactics at Herstmonceux, just a few miles down the road from here. There, it was said, a ghostly drummer had often been heard, and tales abounded of him walking the castle ramparts, fully nine feet tall and glowing, an evil and terrifying snarl on his face. The specter had worked well, and those smugglers had gone about their business completely undisturbed for years.

Could this cry be an attempt at something similar?

It sounded again, and he steeled himself to go closer to the graves, searching for whatever made the noise. "I'm going above and beyond, Fremont," he muttered. "You'd better appreciate this."

He reached the grave where he had stopped the last time he heard the cry, though he couldn't fathom how this could be the source of it. It looked solid enough.

The grave was well maintained, its plot devoid of weeds, the gravel over the surface raked evenly. A small wall, no more than six inches high, bordered the actual grave, and a chain surrounded it, looped between four posts, effectively fencing it off from the rest of the graveyard.

But something was wrong. For a minute, Freddy couldn't have said what it was, although he knew there was something about this grave that wasn't right.

He looked around at the nearby graves and realized

what was troubling him. They were all old, their surfaces overgrown with grass and weeds, the headstones leaning drunkenly where the shrinkage and shifting of the graves' earth had undermined and moved them. But the headstone on this grave was straight and smart.

That was what had bothered him. The graves nearest to the church walls were the oldest ones in the churchyard. Newer graves were farther away, and the better tended were all near the wall between the churchyard and the road. That stood to reason: the people buried in those plots were recent enough to have friends and family who were still alive to mourn them. The graves near the church itself were old, so old that most of the mourners would themselves be dead by now, or else they would be too old and decrepit to keep up the work of tending them. That was why all the nearby graves were unkempt.

So what was different about this one, that it should be so well loved?

He stepped over the low chain and approached the grave, where he crouched down on his haunches to look closer. It wasn't easy to read the headstone in the thin moonlight, but he peered hard through narrowed eyes, and traced the carved letters with his ungloved fingers, until, eventually, he managed to make out the inscription: *Molly Mae Mavers, 1685-1743.*

This woman had died some seventy five years ago, yet somebody still kept her grave in good condition? That did not ring true.

Intrigued, Freddy ran his hand over the gravel on top of the grave and realized the stones were only shallowly applied, over a solid base. A base that was not mud or soil, nor yet concrete, but wood. He could clearly feel the rough texture of it, felt the warmth that wood always held and stone never could. And then his fingers hit metal.

It was a ring, thick and solid, some four inches in diameter, attached to the wooden surface of the grave, like a door handle on an old-fashioned door. It turned in his hand with a graunching sound.

He let go of it and stood up, scratching at the back of his neck as he tried to make sense of what he'd found. This was far more than he'd been looking for, and clearly too big for him to tackle on his own. He should leave now and return tomorrow, during daylight hours, bringing Lord Rotherton who, as magistrate, would have the power to dig up poor Molly Mae Mavers. If, indeed, the lady was under here in the first place. Rotherton could also demand answers, such as, who was Molly Mae Mavers, and why would she need a door on her grave? Who tended her plot so long after her death? And what the deuce was going on?

Freddy stepped back over the chain, intending to leave for now. Then he heard it again. The plaintive sound, so like the cry of a child. And it was, most definitely, coming from beneath this grave.

Horrified, he stared at the grave for several long seconds, while he tried to make sense of what he heard. Surely, there could not be a living child in there? What kind of a monster would do such a thing as that? To leave anyone, child or adult, to lie terrified and trapped in the cold dark ground would be beyond sadistic.

Which was when another thought struck him: only another monstrous sadist would leave whoever was under there for a single moment longer than was necessary.

There was no way Freddy could ever live with

himself if he walked away now and waited for daylight, knowing somebody was very likely buried alive here. He had no choice: he must open this strange door now, tonight, dig through whatever was under it, and rescue the poor soul who cried, then stopped for a few moments, before crying again.

Briefly he thought of Eliza. Could the child he heard be her niece? Or, if not her, might it be someone who could lead them to Claire?

This grave, and its still-living occupant, could well be the answer to Eliza's prayers and the end of her search. The idea of not only rescuing some tortured soul but also reuniting Eliza with her niece filled him with warmth and made his heart beat faster with hope. A smile played on his lips as he pictured her hugging the child, then hugging him.

And after that, after she could bear to let go of the child for an instant, she would kiss him. He could almost feel her soft, full lips on his, her warm breath, tasting of chocolate and mint and happiness, her arms around his neck, her fingers in his hair…

"Easy, Finch," he whispered. "First things first." There could be no victory kiss if there was no niece rescued. "Let's get whoever is in here out, and get the job done."

He moved back to the graveside again, grabbed the metal ring, and pulled with all his might.

The door was heavy, its angle, or the earth's gravity, or both, working against him, and he had to strain every muscle and sinew to lift it. When it finally reached the point of no return, it jerked out of his hands and fell back with a loud clatter, followed by the rattle of stones falling onto the stone surround. The door hung on its hinges over the chain, revealing the deep, dark hole beneath it.

Freddy leaned over and peered into that hole. All he saw was the darkness. Everything was absolutely silent. Nothing moved inside the grave. Out here, no leaves stirred in the trees. No small animals scuttled to and fro through the undergrowth. No fox barked. Yet there was a tension in the silence, as if the world waited with bated breath for something to happen. More, there was a quality to the stillness that was different to the silence one felt in an empty room. This space did not feel empty. He could sense the aliveness of whatever, or whoever, was hiding at the bottom of the hole.

"Hello?" His greeting was whispered but it was the loud whisper of an actor on a stage. "Is anybody there?"

Nothing. No movement. No sound.

"I'm here to help you," he tried.

Some sixth sense warned him he was no longer alone at the graveside. He heard nothing, but, somehow, he knew there was someone behind him. He started to straighten, to turn to see, but he wasn't quick enough. Something big and heavy connected with his head, thudding loudly against his skull and making the world spin. He swayed and put out a foot to steady himself.

The heavy object hit him again, and this time he fell, his knees buckling and his feet sliding from under him.

He thought he whispered Eliza's name. Or was that just in his head? He would never know, he told himself, as he pitched forward into the dark, dank hole.

Chapter Fourteen

Freddy came to with a pounding head and a bruised aching that spread through his body, into his shoulders, and down one arm. He opened his eyes and saw nothing but darkness. His face was pressed into the cold, packed earth, the dampness of it chilling his skin and seeping through his shirt. He remembered leaning over what looked like an empty grave, before the excruciating pain of being hit. Clearly, he had fallen into the grave and lost consciousness, though he had no way of knowing if he had been out for hours or just a few minutes.

Gradually, his senses began to work properly. He realized the darkness wasn't complete; there were small pin holes of dim light pricking it, although he could see nothing specific from where he lay, save a sheer wall of earth. The pounding in his head subsided a little, reducing the deafening whoosh in his ear, and he became aware of other sounds: sniffling, a reassuring shush, and a child's voice asking fearfully, "Is he dead?"

Freddy wanted to say that no, he wasn't dead, but he wasn't entirely convinced that was the truth. Absurdly, it seemed to matter to him that he answered the question truthfully. Was he scared that telling a lie now would have Saint Peter barring the gate to him? The thought forced a bubble of hysteria up through his chest to his throat, where it lodged, apparently unable to go any farther and break free.

"No, he's not dead," said another voice. It sounded older than the child's but was not that of a fully grown adult.

"How do you know?" asked another young voice. "I can't see him breathing."

"He's dead, isn't he?" sobbed the youngest child.

"No," said the older voice. "I don't think so. I don't know. Go and fetch the lantern."

"But Jeannie is scared of the dark," said the third voice.

Exasperation filled the oldest voice. "Then Jeannie will have to come here with you, won't she?"

"She doesn't like it in here."

"None of us like it in here. Go and get the lantern."

The third voice muttered something but they must have done as they were told, because the pinpricks of light suddenly became a wall of brightness that really hurt Freddy's head, and he had to close his eyes against it. He groaned. The noise hurt. It also made someone cry out in alarm, and the oldest voice told whoever cried to be quiet. Now. The owner of this voice clearly had authority, because all the others fell silent too.

Slowly, with difficulty, Freddy pushed himself up onto his hands and knees, his head down, the pain throbbing through him, making him unwilling to lift it straight away. The cold of the earth made his knees ache.

"Sir?" asked the oldest voice.

Freddy groaned again, the only response he could manage at the moment.

"You will have to move for yourself, sir, for we cannot carry you, and I do not think you wish to stay here."

"We have blankets inside. And bread," said someone

else.

"He's not having mine," objected another child.

"Jeannie!"

"It's a long time till supper comes again," argued Jeannie. "And even then they forget sometimes."

With a gargantuan effort, Freddy raised his head so he could see the people speaking. Nausea roiled his stomach and his skull throbbed. The light stabbed his eyes and he shut them tight, swallowing hard as he willed himself not to vomit.

Behind the light, he made out a group of people, though he could not see enough to know who they were, whether they were all children, or all female, or even how many of them there were. He held up a hand to shield his eyes and almost toppled over.

"Annie, the light's hurting his eyes," somebody said.

"Sorry." Annie must have turned, or moved the lantern in some way, for the light dimmed and the pain of it lessened a little.

"Get back, everyone," commanded Annie, whose voice he recognized as the oldest of those who had spoken when he first came to. "Give him space." There was some shuffling as the others did as she said.

Freddy took several deep breaths, until he was certain he was not going to be sick, and then he felt for the wall of the grave and leaned into it as he pushed himself to his feet. It was slow going, and he had to pause several times when his head spun, but finally he was on his feet and upright. Almost. He still clutched the wall of earth so he didn't collapse again. Soil came away in his hands, trickling over his fingers and clogging the ends of his nails. He could taste the damp earthiness of it, mixed with the musk of unwashed bodies, and the cloying sweetness of his own cologne.

"Come, sir. Through here."

Freddy turned his head and saw Annie gesture at an opening on the other side of the grave, leading into what looked like a low-ceilinged, narrow tunnel. He saw the thick, wooden beams holding up the roof of the tunnel, like the struts in a coal mine he had once had to visit. They reduced the likelihood of cave-ins, but they couldn't take away the terrifying claustrophobia brought on by being in an underground space.

Annie and her little band entered the tunnel and walked away from the grave. Unless he wanted to be left alone in this darkness, Freddy had no choice but to follow, although he dreaded the very idea, as even Annie had to bend slightly to avoid hitting her head on the roof of the space. Somebody Freddy's size would be bent almost double. As it was, he was having trouble keeping himself from falling down. His feet were too heavy for him, and his knees felt like jelly.

Not having any other choice, he moved forward, head down, legs bent. Several times, the arch of his back scraped the ceiling, and he grabbed each wooden strut as he passed.

The tunnel was not long, although in Freddy's state, it felt as if it went on for miles. He was grateful when they turned a corner and exited the tunnel into what looked like the undercroft of a church. Once he could stand upright, his head cleared a little and the nausea subsided, although the pains that racked his body did not dissipate, and the blacksmith in his head wielded his hammer like the very devil himself.

The first few feet of this taller space was nothing more than rubble, the old stone walls of the church's foundations, jagged and uneven, loose stones having fallen to the dusty stone floor. The children continued, past the ruined walls and through a narrow doorway. Freddy followed, and found himself in the main part of the crypt. This area was also made of stone, but here it was sturdy and well kept, and brick pillars held up a low roof. The sides of the room were lined with carved stone shelves, each about three feet high, and holding several coffins. Most were thick with dust, and covered in cobwebs so big and grey they looked solid. One coffin was made of a wood that still held its sheen, and the brass handles were still bright, with only the thinnest layer of dust on it. Freddy crossed to this coffin and touched the name plate with a regret-filled caress, while he silently apologized to Bertie for the desecration of this, his final resting place.

"I'll make it right," he murmured, then grinned down at his friend's remains. "You can help, though, by putting in a good word for me up there." Because, locked in a secure crypt, with his head threatening to explode at any moment, and who knew how many villains aware that he was here and prepared for any action he might try to take, Freddy realized he was in sore need of a miracle.

Annie led the group of children to the wall at the back of the crypt, where they sat on the floor, huddled together around her. In here, the light was more evenly spread and he could see more clearly. There were seven of them, all girls. Annie looked to be the oldest—he would guess she was about fifteen. Her hair was long and straight, and stringy, her face pinched, her features sharp. She had a long-standing malnourished look but, despite that, he could see a strength and determination in her. This girl, he knew instinctively, was a survivor.

The others ranged in age from about twelve, to the youngest, who was about four. All of them looked as if they hadn't been well fed for some time, their cheeks hollow, eyes too big, hair hanging limp and lifeless. Their faces were smudged with dirt, their fingernails caked with thick grime, while their dresses were torn, hems hanging, seams parted and frayed. None of them wore stockings, just shoes that looked big and clumsy on their otherwise bare feet. They watched him, some with suspicion, all with fear.

He lowered himself onto the floor beside Bertie's coffin and leaned back. His head felt heavy and he found it increasingly difficult to concentrate. The idea of sleep was very tempting at this moment, but he knew he must not give in to it; he had learned in his time on the peninsula that somebody with a head injury should never be allowed to sleep, for there was a danger they might never wake again. As well as which, he didn't know if and when the person who had hit him was going to return. If he was asleep, he would be vulnerable, and that would not be of use to these girls at all. He concentrated on staying awake and studying the little group, who all continued to stare at him warily.

With what he hoped was a benign smile, he studied the youngest of the girls. Her torn dress was made of good quality material, and her little half boots were a better fit than the shoes worn by her friends. Her hair was a plain mouse brown, but her eyes, for all their hungry width, were striking, their irises an arresting light blue surrounded by a narrow rim of indigo. There was no mistaking this girl's lineage.

"Miss Claire Russell, I presume?" he said, keeping his voice light.

The child climbed into Annie's lap. Annie held her, protectively, but at the same time, she encouraged her to speak to him. She lifted her chin in a way she must have seen the adults in her life employ and spoke in a haughty tone far older than her years.

"Have we been introduced, sir?" Her accent was refined, betraying a privileged background.

"No, we haven't," he said, shaking his head, which hurt and caused the room to tilt and spin. "I am a friend of your Aunt Eliza's."

At least, he hoped they were still friends. They hadn't exactly parted on the best of terms earlier today…yesterday? He had completely lost track, and being in here, in this windowless room, was not helping.

The child frowned in answer to his statement. "Aunt Eliza was coming to take care of Mama after her accident."

"Yes. Yes, she was. She did so. And when she realized you were missing, she left your mama and came to look for you instead."

"Truly?" A world of hope was in that word. The other girls gasped and sat straighter too.

"Truly." He smiled again. "She is a very determined lady, your aunt. You look like her, you know."

Claire's face scrunched, skeptically. "I look like my mama."

"Then your mama must be very like her sister."

The little girl's thumb found its way to her mouth, and she clung to Annie.

She really was a sweetling. Her eyes were big and, although there was a wariness and fear in them, he thought he also saw remnants of innocent trust. He prayed it wasn't too late to restore that for her, and cursed the evil people whose greed would take it from a small child. Her hair fell limply about her face, but even without the curls, and with the hungry, hollow look that was clearly a legacy of her ordeal, the resemblance to Eliza was startling. It made Freddy wonder if this was what Eliza's own children would look like.

He closed his eyes and rested his head against the stone shelf on which Bertie rested. In his mind, he pictured Eliza, walking along beside him in the lane, laughing at the antics of the small children running ahead of them. He saw two little girls with light brown curls and blue eyes ringed with indigo, and two little boys with his honey-colored hair and grey eyes. He felt the smile tug at his lips as he watched them, then took their mother's hand in his own, savoring her warmth, welcoming the shock of electricity that passed from her to him and back again, while he thanked his lucky stars that she was finally his.

"Sir?" called one of his children.

Freddy frowned. His children should not call him "sir." He had been forced to address his father thus, and he had hated it. He wanted his own children to feel comfortable with him, to call him "Papa"...

"Sir?" The child was insistent "Sir?"

He startled awake and stared, stupidly, at the children, who watched him closely. One of them looked to be waiting for an answer from him.

"How can I help?" he asked her, and was shocked at the grogginess in his voice.

The child blushed deeply and he smiled to put her at her ease. She bit her bottom lip and, for a few moments, he thought she would change her mind and say nothing. She was, however, made of sterner stuff than that.

"Excuse me, sir," she said, at last. "Are you here to take us home?"

Freddy swallowed hard, then forced his smile back into place. "That is my intention." *As soon as I figure out how to get myself out of here, that is.*

With more determination than actual physical strength, he struggled to his feet and walked to the door of the crypt. It cost him to move in a straight line and with no sign of the weakness washing through him, but he had the feeling these girls needed someone to believe in, and that would not be him if he looked as if he might collapse at any second. When he got to the door, he put his hand on it and leaned his weight against it, under the pretense of examining it. Like every other door he had encountered about this church, it was made of oak, grey with age but still sturdy, large metal hinges holding it firmly, and a lock that he could not pick.

"Perhaps when they open the door…" he mused.

"The man is a lot bigger than you," said one of the children, in that dismissive way youngsters had of destroying an adult's ego.

"And sometimes, he has a mate with him," said another.

"They only come just inside the door anyway," added Annie. "You can't overpower them from there."

"We tried," said the second oldest child.

"They kicked Matty in the head," said Claire, her tone suggesting she could not believe such cruelty. "They knocked one of her teeth loose."

Matty opened her mouth and pulled down her lip, proudly displaying the gap that proved how brave she had been.

"But then," argued a child of about seven, "we are

only children. He's a grown-up. They never put anybody grown up in here before."

"Except for Annie," said Claire.

"Annie's not a grown-up," retorted the seven-year-old.

"I'm sixteen!" objected Annie.

"That is grown up enough," decided Freddy, hoping to fend off what looked like the start of a bitter argument.

"It's not as grown up as you," insisted the seven-year-old. "You're a proper grown-up. You're really old."

"Thank you very much." At this moment, Freddy couldn't argue with the child's assessment. He felt old. In fact, he felt positively ancient.

"You won't do as a 'dentified servant," said Claire nodding her head as if to agree with her own pronouncement.

"Indentured servant," corrected Annie, gently.

"That's what I said. And he won't, will he? He's much too old."

"Let's not dwell on me being old," he answered.

"The nasty lady said Annie was too old," continued Claire. "She told the man nobody would buy her because she would be too much trouble to train."

"But the man said someone would pay a pretty penny for her to do other things for them," said the seven-year-old.

Annie shuddered.

Freddy studied her for a long moment. "I will get you out of here," he promised her, adding silently to himself, "or I will die trying."

"Sir?" asked Matty. "I was wondering. Hoping, really. Will your wife have missed you yet? Perhaps she has set up the hue and cry. Did you tell her where you were coming?"

Freddy smiled, sadly. "Alas, I have no wife."

Although, he had told David, Lord Rotherton, what he planned to do. David would know to come straight to this church once he realized Freddy was missing. All they had to do was listen for the search party, then shout…except David had gone away for the night. Who could say how late it would be before he returned home tomorrow? If, indeed, he didn't stay away longer. He had clearly been going to be with a lover, so might well delay his return. By the time he learned Freddy was gone, it might be too late, not just for him but for all of them.

His heart heavy, Freddy sat down again and tried to think of a way he and the girls might escape this situation which did not involve a rescue that might never come.

Chapter Fifteen

At ten o'clock in the morning, Eliza sat in her parlor, wearing her nicest dove-grey dress, waiting for Freddy to arrive. She had thought to cry off this journey to Weninghope after yesterday's conversation and the way they had parted, had even gone as far as writing him a note thanking him for his kind offer but graciously declining it. She had then crumpled the note into a ball and thrown it into the wastebasket beside her desk. She had told herself then, and would continue to tell herself now, that it was pragmatism that changed her mind. Eliza needed to get to Weninghope, and the sooner the better, and Freddy Finch offered her the best—if not the only— chance of getting there.

Her about-face had nothing whatsoever to do with the desire, deep within her, to see him again and try to put right the damage done to their friendship by all that had happened yesterday.

Eliza's cheeks heated at the very thought of her actions yesterday. She had been wanton beyond belief, but she could not regret it. Even if the whole world and his wife learned of it and turned their backs to her, even should she find herself with child, her sin plain for all to see, still she would not wish the time with Freddy to have been any other way. The image that came to mind of her father's rheumy eyes filled with disappointment gave her pause, but even then the second thoughts were fleeting.

The time she had spent in Freddy's arms had been…wonderful. Magical. Incredible. Eliza did not have the words to adequately describe how she felt, even after a full night of thinking of nothing else. She had lain in bed last night, listening to the creaks and snaps as the cottage settled around her, and she'd smiled, inanely, into the darkness. Hugging herself tightly and letting the thought of him chase the butterflies that fluttered through her stomach, she had known two things.

Firstly, she would never again have that wonderful feeling, unless it was with Freddy. No other man could ever come close to making it happen. She would forever remain an old maid, for were she ever to marry anyone else, she would be settling, and having experienced how wonderful things could be, she would never again be satisfied or happy with less. It was Freddy or nobody, and she loved Freddy far too much to force him into a marriage he didn't want and would regret for the rest of his life.

Which was the second revelation that had come to her during the night. She loved him. Although, revelation was perhaps not the right word, since deep down she had known she loved him almost from the first minute she saw him at Catherine Ashton's wedding.

He had stood in the churchyard, resplendent in his elegant jacket, bright white cravat tied in an intricate style, a smile lighting his face as he spoke to Miss Potter, the bridesmaid with whom he had been paired. Then he had been so charming to Prudence, who had shouted across the garden to him like a common fishwife. Not by the merest flicker of an eyelid had he betrayed any mortification he might have felt, but had continued ever the gentleman.

Then there had been his visit to Eliza, to show her the primer he had found and to offer to show her the other treasures in the Hadlow estate chapel. And the kiss they had shared there. And yesterday...

She sprang to her feet and paced the room, wringing her hands in front of her waist, biting her bottom lip with her top front teeth. She must put aside all thought of what they had done yesterday, for surely, if she did not, it would show in her face and the whole of society would know her for the fallen woman she was. Although, if falling from grace felt as wonderful as she had felt yesterday... No! Enough!

She really should have sent that note to cancel today's trip.

Speaking of which, where was Freddy? It was now half past ten, and he was fully thirty minutes late. Eliza didn't think his manners would allow him to keep a lady waiting in this fashion, so what had happened?

For a moment, her mind pondered dire scenarios... He had fallen downstairs at Rotherton Hall and broken his leg. He had overturned his vehicle on the way here and was, even now, lying in a ditch. He was...

"Oh, stop it, Eliza Louisa Rolfe!" She scolded herself, then grimaced. "Rawlins," she corrected. Freddy Finch might know her true name now, but nobody else did, and it would be better if it stayed that way.

Which was by the by. She sighed, walked to the window, and peered along the street. She could see her neighbors out and about, walking arm in arm with their bosom bows, chatting and laughing as they made their ways to Rotherton's shops. A carter jiggled the reins to encourage his horse to plod along the road. His cart looked empty; he must have made his delivery. The

Potter's barouche went by at a sedate pace, Mrs. Potter looking well pleased with herself, while her daughter looked as if she would rather be anywhere else, doing anything else. Remembering the plan the Potters had to bring her out next season, Eliza felt some sympathy for the girl. Eliza had never had a season of her own, of course, but she had known girls who had, and they had told tales of endless visits to dressmakers and milliners, mantua makers and boot makers, where they were measured and tutted over, poked and prodded, fitted into half-finished garments and pulled and pushed into unnatural positions, as if they were mannequins, without feelings or the ability to experience discomfort. Some had loved the experience, but others, the quieter ones, had hated every minute. For a young lady like Miss Potter, it would be pure torture.

There were two other vehicles on the road: two elderly ladies rode sedately through the town in their landau with its top down so they could enjoy the weather and be seen, and Silas Burgess tooled his vehicle along the road toward Mereham, in the opposite direction. Visiting another parishioner, she mused. The man's sermons were notoriously boring, but when it came to caring for his flock, he was second to none.

Of Freddy and the carriage that would take her to Weninghope, there was no sign.

Perhaps he had taken her at her word. When he had said he would pick her up today, she had told him that it would not be wise. Had he accepted that as her cancellation of their plans? Surely, he would have said something? Not simply assumed?

She huffed impatiently. Men! They really were very different to women. A woman would have asked the questions, made sure all parties understood the conversation fully. They wouldn't just take it as read in the way a man clearly did.

Another fifteen minutes. She would give him another fifteen minutes. Then, if he still hadn't come, she would find somewhere else to search, so this day wouldn't be a complete loss.

In the end, she waited until past eleven o'clock. Then, feeling thoroughly uncharitable toward Freddy for not turning up, and guilty about her churlishness, since she had as good as told him not to do so, she rang the bell for her coat and bonnet, and set out, alone, into the fresh air.

It was a lovely day. The sun was bright, making the shop fronts gleam, bouncing off their windows so that it was impossible to see inside. The sky was a flawless blue, and the leaves on the trees seemed a brighter green. Even the road seemed cleaner. Eliza greeted her neighbors as she made her way through the town, exchanged pleasantries with most of them, and stopped to say more than a sentence or two to a few. Finally, she left Rotherton behind and strode purposefully along the narrow lanes, past fields of corn and wheat that already grew tall, and sloping meadows of cows and sheep, and the occasional horse. Little copses of oak and birch broke up the landscape, with here and there a more substantial wood shading the lane. The sun's warmth beat down, scorching her through her pelisse. The dried mud that covered the road's surface made walking unsteady, acting almost like cobblestones beneath her feet. Birds chirped and chattered, and in the distance, a cuckoo called out for attention while, closer by, leaves rustled on the gentle breeze.

Before long, she came to Crompton Hadlow. She hadn't meant to come here. Since she had seen Silas Burgess driving in the opposite direction, she reasoned there would be no way to get into the church today, so there was no reason to come. It was as if her feet had carried her along automatically, while she hadn't been concentrating.

Now that she was here, she supposed she should call on Prudence. She could have a cup of tea in the shadowed cool of the curate's cottage, stay the requisite half hour, then make a more deliberate attempt to go elsewhere. Or, one never knew, perhaps Silas would return home and allow her to look inside the church at long last. Not that she expected to find anything of use in there, but she had to satisfy herself that she had left no stone unturned, and the constant denial of entrance to Saint Simon and Saint Jude's was like a stone in her boot: it demanded attention.

She changed direction to go into the cottage garden.

The front garden was pretty. Hedges and bushes in varying shades of green provided a backdrop against which there was a riot of color, coming from sweet peas and larkspur, delphiniums and pinks, snapdragons and clematis, lavender and mint. The strong scents mingled, making the air smell clean and contrasting with the fresh-cut green of the tiny lawn and the silver-grey dustiness of the flagstone path. The walls of the cottage were white, and trails of ivy clung to them here and there, dark and ragged. The roof hung low over the upstairs windows, giving the place a sleepy, droopy-eyed look that added to its charm. If only it weren't so dark and cluttered inside, this cottage would be perfect, she decided, then chided herself for being judgmental. No doubt it already was perfect to Silas and Prudence.

Eliza was almost at the front door when she heard voices coming from the side of the cottage. A man was complaining that something hadn't been his fault, and what else was he to do, for he'd had to stop him snooping, or else he would have found everything.

Eliza frowned. Who had been snooping, and what would they have found? All her senses on alert, she moved away from the porch and stepped quietly toward the side of the house. Her first thought was that she had interrupted something villainous. Perhaps the men planned to rob the curate's cottage, and they had hurt Silas when he discovered them?

Not Silas, she realized, since she had seen him driving through Rotherton earlier and he had been hale and hearty then. His manservant, perhaps? Did Silas have a manservant? Eliza didn't know, but she did know there was a sexton here. A surly fellow, to be sure, but he didn't deserve to be attacked and hurt.

She crept around the side of the house and realized the voices came from a small shed, the sort where gardeners kept their tools and supplies, and put up their seedlings until they were strong enough to brave the outdoor weather. The shed was big enough for two people to stand inside it together, perhaps even three, if they were small and skinny. The door was open, and its width provided a screen, which meant those inside were hidden from anyone approaching from the front of the house. Luckily, it also meant the people inside would not be able to see her as she crept up on them.

Eliza moved as close to the shed as she dared, and listened, carefully. If she needed to report anything to the constable, it would be well to have as many facts as possible.

"It wasn't my fault," insisted the man. His voice was familiar, although Eliza couldn't quite place it. Perhaps it would come to her and she would be able to give the constable a name.

"Of course it was your fault!" answered an angry and scornful woman. Eliza gasped in shock, for that was a voice she definitely knew. Prudence. What on earth was Prudence doing, arguing with somebody in a potting shed? There was, so far as Eliza knew, no law against it, other than society's strictures about unmarried ladies meeting, unchaperoned, with a man for even the most innocuous of reasons. Still, this seemed a little havey-cavey, all the same.

Now that she knew the man talked to Prudence, she was able to identify his voice, too, as that of the church sexton. The realization made her breathe more easily, since there could be any number of legitimate reasons for the curate's sister to meet with the sexton. Relieved that she had not interrupted a burglary, or some such crime, Eliza decided she would creep back to the corner of the house and call out a hello, to alert them to her presence. They need never know she had eavesdropped on them, and all would be fine.

"Honestly," said Prudence, as Eliza turned to leave, being careful not to let her skirts rustle as she moved. "You don't have the brains God gave to a thistle! You could have ruined everything!"

"I didn't know what else I was supposed to do," answered the sexton. "He was that close to discovering everything."

"You didn't have to hit him with your shovel. You could have killed him, and then we would all be in the soup."

That stopped Eliza in her tracks. That was not something she would expect Prudence to say. Her tone was coarser than normal, too. Eliza was used to Prudence's refined voice, full of concern, and a certain practiced calm. Now, she sounded—angry. Exasperated. Dangerous.

"If I had killed him, he couldn't have told anybody, could he?" retorted the sexton.

There was the sound of a slap, flesh meeting flesh. Eliza winced.

"And we would have had a dead man in the crypt. How do you think I was going to explain that? Especially him. His father is the Earl of Seaford. A powerful man. Can you imagine the wrath he would bring down on us if he tied us to the death of his son?"

Eliza's jaw dropped and her eyes widened. For a moment, she couldn't breathe. She couldn't think. She simply stood, stock still, shock and horror raining down on her, threatening to drown her. *Freddy* was the youngest son of the Earl of Seaford. The sexton had, for some reason, hit Freddy and concealed him in the crypt!

Oh Lord! What do I do?

"Vengeance is mine, saith the Lord," quoted Prudence.

"We're the Lord's instruments," the sexton argued. "You said so. So did your brother. He said the Lord will deliver our enemies into our hands."

"And He has. But a fat lot of good that will do us if Mr. Finch is found dead in our church. If you'd killed him—and it is only by grace that you did not—if you had killed him, we'd have had to get him out before he could be discovered. Do you know how heavy a dead body is?"

"I should. I've buried enough," muttered the sexton.

"It's better for us if he can use his own shanks to walk out of there. Then we can get him…" Her voice trailed away for a second, before she continued in a stronger, happier tone, "get him on the ship with the cargo."

"Aye," said the sexton. "That sounds good." He chuckled. "He'll fetch a good price, I daresay."

A good price? They were going to ship Freddy to somewhere and sell him? And what on earth was this "cargo"? Eliza began to think the unthinkable, and it made her feel ill, in the pit of her stomach. Was this why Saint Simon and Saint Jude's Church was always locked? Why there had been so many excuses not to open it?

Another thought struck, like a lightning bolt—Was Claire in there?

Poor little Claire. She would be terrified, locked in a cold, dark crypt, not knowing what was happening, where her mother was, or why these terrible people had taken her in the first place. Not that Eliza would wish such a fate on anyone, but she hoped, if the little girl was in there, she was not alone. Especially if she had witnessed one of her captors doing violence to Freddy.

Prudence had said the sexton hit Freddy with his shovel. Did that mean he was hurt? *Stupid question, Eliza!* Of course he was hurt. A shovel being swung at anyone would be bound to hurt them. But how badly? She prayed his brains weren't scrambled, or his wits knocked about… *Lord, let him be all right.*

"He won't fetch any price, you idiot!" Prudence's voice sharpened as she answered the sexton's last comment. "Don't be stupid all your life."

"But he's strong—"

"He's from the Quality. You think buyers won't see that? You think they won't listen to his tale? They will. And when he tells it, we will hang."

The sexton moaned his despair.

"Unless…"

"Unless what?"

"Unless we kill him before he can say anything."

Eliza clamped her hand across her mouth to stop the cry she nearly let out.

"But you said—"

"I said I didn't want him killed here. But once he is away from here, once he can't be connected to us…halfway across the ocean would be perfect, would it not?"

"Throw him overboard? Like Jonah?"

"No, not like Jonah," she snapped. "Jonah was sent to do the Lord's work, and the Lord saved him. Mr. Finch is working against the Lord, so he will sink, with no interfering big fish in sight."

"And if his family should come looking…"

Prudence's voice became sweet and full of concern as she rehearsed her words to Freddy's family. "I cannot imagine where he could be, your lordship. He did say he was going back to London. Have you looked there? I have no idea what else to suggest. I will pray you find him."

"You think of it all," said the sexton, sounding happier, and a little awed.

"That's why the Lord put me in charge." Prudence laughed, softly. "He does move in mysterious ways, does He not?"

"Eh?" The sexton sounded as confused as Eliza felt.

"The Lord is protecting us and His enterprise delivered through us. In doing so, He will also bless the service the Earl of Seaford has given to Him. I have heard the earl is a good man. Having a rake and a wastrel for a son must be a constant source of disappointment and embarrassment to him. Thank God the older brother is hale and hearty, because the younger is neither use nor ornament."

"You think the earl'll be glad to see the back of his own son?" The sexton laughed. "You're deluded. One thing I do know, the nobility keeps what's theirs. Mr. Finch may be of little use, but he's Quality, and they do not give up on their own."

There was a silence. Did it mean Prudence was pondering the sexton's words? Or was the conversation finishing? If it was the latter, the two would leave the potting shed and close the door, leaving Eliza exposed. She could not allow them to see her. She would be no use to Freddy or Claire if she was taken by the villains, too.

She picked up her skirts and tiptoed around the side of the shed, ducking down and walking in a strange crouch so as not to be seen through the windows. Once she was hidden, she knelt and breathed a sigh of relief, although it was unfortunate that, in her new position, the voices were not as clear as they had been, and she had to strain to hear them.

"Don't you think I know that?" Prudence asked the sexton after several moments of quiet. "They will come looking for him, of course they will. But he won't be here to be found, will he? He'll be halfway to the Americas, feeding the fish."

The sexton said something Eliza did not quite catch. Whatever it was, it upset Prudence, for her answer was shrill. "The one thing I have always been able to rely on," she berated him, "was your ability to make a mess of the simplest task."

"That's not…" he started, his own anger growing.

"We do the Lord's work! Sacred work. Entrusted to us. And you, with your disobedience of God's ordinances, and your stubborn reliance on your own strength and limited intellect—"

"Hey!"

Prudence continued as if he had not interrupted her. "You have endangered that work, and the Lord's rescue of those poor benighted innocents." Her footsteps sounded on the wooden floor of the shed, and the whole building creaked softly. Eliza pressed against the wooden wall and tried to make herself smaller. If Prudence looked out of the window, if she saw Eliza there… Eliza prayed she would not see her.

"Do you think," said Prudence, "that God wants those children to remain in their lives of suffering and deprivation, when we can make them useful in His sight?"

The footsteps sounded again as she moved away from the window. Eliza breathed out the breath she had been holding.

"Of course He doesn't. He wants to bless them. He made us His instruments, His hands for this work. Mr. Finch, by his very presence here, is aiding the enemy in trying to thwart the will of God."

"That's why I stopped him."

"Stopping him is not enough!" There was an end-of-her-tether-ness about Prudence now. "He must disappear. There must be no chance of him ever being found, or of being connected with us. If he is discovered in the crypt, the Lord's work through us would, at best, be delayed, at worst stopped permanently. Do you understand?"

"Yes, Miss Burgess." The sexton was defeated. It sounded in his weary voice.

"Good. I have an errand to run for Silas while he is in Mereham. You find Norris and Hunter and tell them it is time to move the cargo. We will meet at the usual time."

"Yes, miss."

A few seconds passed. "Well? Go on!"

Eliza heard the sexton's lumbering footsteps. He left the shed, which bounced and shuddered as it was relieved of his weight, and stumped up the path. The gate latch opened, then closed behind him.

"Lord," said Prudence, "why do you send me such useless helpmates for the tasks you set for me? I try to remember, not as I will but as Thou wilt, Lord, but I am only human, and it is very hard."

She moved, her sharp, neat footsteps a contrast to the sexton's heavy, blunt ones. Eliza heard the door shut, the rattle of the lock, then the click, click, click of Prudence's heels on the garden path.

Eliza sat for some minutes, working through what she had heard. The sailor in Rye had been right, the church in the Rotherton area was involved, although never in a thousand years would Eliza have guessed Prudence might be part of it. Prudence, who referred to the Bible for her every thought, every situation; whose faith was rock-solid and all-encompassing.

She had called it the work of God! Surely, she could not believe God would want children to be stolen from their families and—what? Sold? But then, if the woman could cynically manipulate her faith to justify this, she could have no true faith at all. Was her piety a façade? If it was, it was a good one. Eliza, who had been brought up in an evangelical household, had been completely fooled.

And what of Silas? Was he involved? Eliza did not see how he could not be. He lived here, worshipped in the church—how could he not realize something was amiss? And had not the sexton implicated him?

We're the Lord's instruments. You said so. So did your brother.

Eliza needed to stop them. If she fetched the constable—no, she could not do that. This year's constable had recently been arrested himself, and was now in Hayward's Heath jail, awaiting trial. His replacement had not yet been appointed.

"I go my entire life with no need of a constable, and then when I do need one, there isn't one," she muttered, crossly.

The magistrate, then? That would be Lord Rotherton. But his home was some way from here. By the time she got there and alerted him, then brought him back here, it might be too late. Freddy, with Claire and any other children, would be gone.

That left only one course of action available to her. She would have to rescue them herself. They could fetch the magistrate later.

But how was she to get into the church? It was sturdily built, with solid doors. She had seen no way in on her previous visits, although, to be fair, she hadn't been looking for chinks in the walls, or windows to break. Not that she could climb to the windows, even if she did break one.

The constant answer to her requests to see inside had

been that Silas held the only key, and he seemed never to be at home. Now, though, Eliza questioned that. If Prudence was involved in storing stolen children inside the church, she must have some way of accessing it when Silas was not here. Ergo, there must be a key she could use. If Eliza could find that key…

She peered around the side of the shed and stared at the cottage. The sexton had gone to find two other men, while Prudence ran an errand. Silas was also out. This was her best opportunity. Provided the maid was not in the house, or was at least working where she could be avoided, then perhaps Eliza could get in, find the key, get out, and free Freddy and the others before Prudence and her men returned.

"Lord, help me," she whispered. "I know I am probably committing a crime myself here, but I am preventing a bigger one. And I promise never to do it again, if You see me through, this once." She sent up a second prayer, apologizing to Him for trying to bargain with Him, then got to her feet and sneaked around the shed to the cottage.

Chapter Sixteen

It didn't take long for Eliza to realize that luck was not with her. The Burgess's maid, Milly—or Mildred as Prudence insisted on calling her—was not only in the cottage, but was happily moving to and fro between the kitchen and the family part of the house. There would be no sneaking in through the back door without being seen. If Eliza was going to get into the cottage, it would have to be via the front door, with Milly's full knowledge.

She supposed it could be done, if she was quick and judicious in her search.

Where would Prudence hide the key? It would have to be somewhere she could access quickly but where others were not likely to see it. Eliza quickly ruled out anywhere in Prudence's bedchamber, for the maid would have more access to everything there than Prudence could control. She would want it to be near her, where she could see it was safe, which meant it would not be in any of the outside buildings.

There were really only two places where it might be: Silas' study, or Prudence's parlor. Having narrowed the possibilities, Eliza took a deep, fortifying breath and strode to the front door.

Milly answered. "Morning, mum," she said, and she did a quick and clumsy curtsy.

"Good morning, Milly." Eliza stepped inside before the maid could refuse her access.

"Neither Mr. Burgess nor Miss Burgess is available right now, I'm afraid, Mrs. Rawlins." The words were stilted, delivered by rote, and doubtless learned in the same manner.

"Oh, that is a shame," said Eliza. She was not proud to hear her regretful tone was quite convincing. "Will they be long?"

"Well, Mr. Burgess will be, for certain and sure. He's gone out to Mereham to see old Mr. Padwick." She adopted a grave look. "He doesn't have much time left, you know. Mr. Padwick, that is, not Mr. Burgess." Milly clapped her hands to her mouth, her eyes wide. "Oh, lor', Mrs. Rawlins. I wasn't supposed to tell anyone that." She repeated another lesson Eliza suspected had been drummed into her: "A visit from a clergyman is private and coincidental, and not to be gossiped about."

"I think you mean confidential," Eliza answered with a friendly smile.

"Sorry," said Milly. "Mr. Burgess has been teaching me the long words, but I do get muddled. He's ever so kind about it, though. Just corrects me, and doesn't get cross."

"What about Miss Burgess?" Eliza walked toward the parlor.

"She gets cross sometimes. Says I exacerbate her."

Eliza hid her smile. "I meant, when will she return?"

"Oh, I see. Um, I can't honestly say, madam. Shouldn't think she'll be long, though. She didn't say not to do nuncheon, so I expect she'll be back for that."

"I'll wait in here for her for a while, if I may?"

Milly bit her bottom lip. "Thing is, begging your pardon, Mrs. Rawlins, Miss Burgess doesn't like people in her parlor if she's not here. Says it's private."

"Would you prefer I come back another time, then?" Eliza shot arrow prayers to God that Milly would relent.

Milly shook her head. "I'm sure she didn't mean you couldn't go in, Mrs. Rawlins."

That was quick, Lord. Thank you!

"I'll make you some tea, madam."

Eliza went into the parlor. Milly shut the door. The minute she was gone, Eliza set to, looking in all the likeliest hiding places, as well as some unlikely ones. She found hidden drawers in three occasional tables, and a special compartment in the bureau, but no key, and it was a flustered and thwarted Eliza who sat on the edge of a sofa when Milly returned with the tea tray.

"Do you know, Milly," said Eliza, hoping she didn't sound as breathless as she felt, and that the heat in her cheeks hadn't led to a rise in color, or a light sheen on her face. "I have just remembered I am promised to Mrs. Potter at four o'clock. If I hurry, I won't be late." She smiled in a way she prayed was conspiratorial. "I would hate to displease that lady by being late."

"Um, yes, madam. I mean, no, madam," said Milly. She looked down at the tea tray, as if wondering what she should do with it.

"I can leave Miss Burgess a note," continued Eliza. Her tone was deliberately imperious, brooking no argument. It was not a tone she had ever used before, and she felt guilty for using it now. "I will need a pen and paper." She stood and walked past the maid to the parlor door. "Will I find some in Mr. Burgess's study?"

"I—nobody's supposed to go in there," said Milly. She followed Eliza along the hallway, tea tray still in her hands, the cups rattling together as she walked.

"I'm sure he won't mind," said Eliza, mentally

crossing fingers, for she was reasonably certain Silas would mind a great deal, especially if he was involved in his sister's dealings, but needs must.

She opened the study door and peered inside, relieved to see it was unoccupied. A neat room, it held a desk with a clear and tidy top, several shelves of books, and two chairs for visitors. It seemed sparse indeed for a busy clergyman—not at all like the cluttered, lived-in office her father had used.

"Madam," said Milly. "I'm not sure, that is, I mean…"

"I'll be two minutes," Eliza assured her. "You take that tray back to the kitchen and by the time you return, I will have written my note." She leaned toward the maid. "And I won't tell Miss Burgess if you drink the tea yourself. Shame to let it go to waste."

Milly looked shocked, then bit her bottom lip, clearly tempted. After a moment, she nodded. "I'll be back soon, Mrs. Rawlins," she said, and she moved away toward the kitchen.

You will never get to heaven, Eliza Rolfe. Eliza closed the door and started her search. She had been looking for less than three minutes when she found a large key on an iron ring. She shoved it into her reticule, said a silent prayer of thanks, then took paper and a pen, dipped it in ink that was on the verge of congealing, and wrote a rather splodgy note lamenting having missed Prudence, and promising to return another day. She stepped back into the hallway, folded note in hand, just as Milly returned. A minute later, she hurried down the garden path and out onto the road. A quick glance back to make sure Milly wasn't watching her, then she turned right, toward the church, instead of left, the direction to the Potters' house.

"Please, God, let me get this done before Prudence returns," she whispered as she raced through the churchyard. "And let Claire be here, Lord, I beg of you."

Hopeful, she pushed the key into the lock on the church door. It didn't fit. She pulled it out and tried again, thoughts racing, heart even faster.

The key was too small. The lock swallowed it whole.

"No," she murmured. "No, no, no!" She tried it once more, as if the lock might suddenly have shrunk. Of course, it had not.

Now what? She could try the back door, see if the key fitted that lock. But if it did not… She would have to find Lord Rotherton. But time was moving on. Even if he came immediately, it could be too late.

Mayhap she could find help at the inn along the street? But would they listen to her? Silas and Prudence were respected members of society, pillars of the community. It would probably take more than Eliza's uncorroborated accusations to bring them out. She must, she was certain, face this alone, and unaided. On that sobering and unedifying thought, Eliza ran to the rear of the church, praying the key would fit the door there.

It did not. The back door was smaller than the front, its lock correspondingly smaller, but the key still slid in too easily, and turned without touching the tumblers. She muttered a very unchristian, extremely unladylike word, then raised her eyes skyward and apologized. Although, this situation might have made an Apostle swear.

"Please, show me the way in," she whispered. Her eyes filled with hot tears, and a heavy lump, like a large rock, pressed on her chest, making it difficult to breathe.

Swallowing was almost impossible, and the tip of her nose itched with a despair that threatened to drown her. Prudence would be back soon, along with the sexton and the men he had gone to find, and she had no idea what to do to stop them.

Something touched her shoulder. She jumped and gave a little shriek of alarm, then whirled round, ready to fight her way out and run for help. But it wasn't Prudence, or the sexton. It was Ned Fellowes. He stood, a look of concern on his thin face, his head cocked to one side.

"Ned!" She breathed out, and put her hand to her chest. "You startled me."

He looked shamefaced. Silently, she wished he would go away. She didn't have time for him at the moment. But when he looked down at the key in her hand, and frowned, she shrugged and thought she might as well tell him. It wasn't as if he was going to gossip about it, was it?

And that was the unkindest thought she'd had all day, she told herself, promising she would make it up to him with a slap-up feast later.

"I was trying to get into the church," she said, aloud. "The key doesn't fit the door." She glared down at it, and fought the urge to throw it across the churchyard, before she stuffed it into her pocket. "I don't suppose you know of another way in, do you?" She grinned. "Without climbing through the windows, that is, or digging a hole in the roof."

She sighed. Here she was, having a conversation she didn't have time for, with a man who could not answer her even if he understood. This day was certainly taking a toll on her.

Ned beckoned her to follow him.

"Have you seen Mr. Finch?" she asked. She hadn't planned to, but the question slipped out. Eliza cursed her stupidity. Ned couldn't tell her, even if he had.

A second later, she realized she was wrong about that, too. The boy straightened and adopted a pose of indolent arrogance that was exactly like Freddy's. He kicked up one side of his mouth in a cocky, come-hither grin. Despite the gravity of the situation, Eliza chuckled. The boy was an excellent mimic. He had Freddy to a T.

"Do you know where he is?" she asked. She hoped against hope that the boy would let her know Freddy was not in the crypt, despite what she had heard.

Alas, Ned pointed at the church. Not only that, but he mimed Freddy peering at something, before being coshed on the head and falling.

Eliza's heart skipped a beat. Her mouth was dry and her breath caught in her throat. It took two hard swallows before she could ask, "Is he hurt?"

Ned shrugged. He gestured again that she should follow him, and this time she did.

He led her around the building, threading a path through the old graves, most of them overgrown with weeds and grass, their headstones leaning precariously, the engraved words almost worn away by years of wind and rain. Finally, he stopped at a grave that was lovingly tended. The stone told her it was the resting place of one Molly Mae Mavers. It wasn't a name Eliza knew, and she had no idea why Ned thought it was significant. She couldn't see what it had to do with Freddy at all.

Perhaps it was Ned's mother? No. It couldn't be. This woman had died in 1743. Ned would have to be at least seventy-five years old for this to be his mother. A great-grandmother, perhaps? Was this his only known family? Or somebody he had chosen to be his family? Had he kept up the care of the grave? It made her sad to think of him, so lonely that he would claim a long dead woman in this way. Under other circumstances, she would sit with him and try to comfort him, to befriend him. But not today.

"It's lovely, Ned, but I must find Mr. Finch," she said, and hoped her exasperation didn't sound in her voice.

Ned nodded and pointed at the grave again. Then he sighed and rolled his eyes as if he despaired of Eliza's stupidity, bent and scraped away the gravel stones that covered the grave. She opened her mouth to tell him to stop. There was no call for him to desecrate the poor woman's grave. Before she could say a word, though, she saw what he was trying to show her: a wooden panel with a large metal ring embedded in it.

He reached down and pulled at the ring. He was clearly stronger than his skinny frame suggested, for the wood panel shifted slightly before falling back into its place. He pulled again with the same result.

Eliza stood beside him and wrapped her own hands around the ring, next to his. She had no idea if her small strength would make a difference, but she prayed it would.

"When I am weak, Lord," she muttered, "then I am strong."

She and Ned tugged in unison. The wood shifted, then fell back with a clatter.

"My strength is made perfect in weakness." The last word was strained as they pulled again. Again the wood moved, then fell back.

She wrapped her hands more tightly around the ring, and murmured, "He giveth power to the faint; and to them that have no might He increaseth strength." She tried not to dwell on the fact that she was emulating Prudence Burgess now, filling her speech with Bible quotes. Only, in her case, the quotes were prayers, reminders of her limitations, and supplication for His help.

"Please, Lord," she whispered. "More strength." Then she pulled again. This time, the wood panel came away from its bed enough for Ned to get his hands underneath it. He pulled and it creaked as it moved past the point of no return and fell back over the wall surrounding the grave. There was a rattle as loose stones fell from the panel to the stone around the outside of the grave.

Underneath where the panel had been was a deep, dark hole. About ten feet deep, it had sheer walls made of mud, and a mud floor where Eliza could just see a puddle glistening. Of Molly Mae Mavers, there was no sign.

"Ye gods!" she whispered, then glanced guiltily at the church and silently apologized for what could be construed as blasphemy. "Freddy—Mr. Finch—is down there?"

Ned nodded and once again mimed Freddy being coshed and falling.

"It's quite a way to fall," she said, more to herself than to Ned. "He may be badly hurt." She glanced at Ned. "We have to go down there."

Ned's eyes widened in shock and horror. He stepped back from the grave and shook his head, vehemently.

"He may need our help."

Ned took another step back and shook his head again. Eliza realized he was a hair's breadth from running away, leaving her to do it all alone. Which would make the job almost impossible.

"You stay here then," she told him. "I will go."

He looked at her, uncertainly.

"Will you wait up here for me? I may need you to help pull me out."

Ned narrowed his eyes. He looked from her to the grave, then back, before he nodded.

"Right," she said, with more confidence than she felt. "Firstly, how do I get down there?"

His answer was to lay on his front beside the grave, his arms dangling into it, his face grimacing as if something heavy hung from his hands.

"You will lower me?"

He nodded.

"Let's get it done."

The worst part was the beginning of the maneuver. Eliza sat on the edge for several seconds, her feet dangling over the hole while she gathered her courage. Lowering herself into a grave, albeit a false one as this clearly was, went against every instinct, and she wanted nothing more than to abort this rescue and go for help instead. So, before she could change her mind and talk herself out of it, she held out her hands. Ned gripped her, his clasp strong and firm, giving her hope that he could hold her weight, and she wouldn't plunge to the bottom and break her leg, if not her neck.

She closed her eyes as she slid off the graveside and into nothing but air. Automatically, her feet scrambled for purchase, while her heartbeat rose to a painful speed and a whooshing sound filled her ears. Ned held her wrists, just above the hemline of her gloves.

Her feet found the wall and pressed against it, giving her stability and stopping the swing of her body. Gingerly, she walked herself down. With her height, plus the length of her arms, which felt as though they would be pulled from their sockets at any moment, together with the long skinny arms Ned stretched down to her, she reached to just a couple of feet from the bottom before she had to jump. Her feet jarred against the hard-packed earth as she landed, but she was unhurt and remained upright. She looked up at Ned.

"Don't go away," she said. He gave a yip, like that of a small dog. Eliza hoped that meant he would stay.

To one side, the wall of the grave had been carved away, leading to a low and narrow tunnel shored up with thick wooden beams. Eliza could see only a few feet into the tunnel before it disappeared into a darkness so complete it seemed solid. The last thing she wanted to do was enter it, but since there was no other entrance or exit, she had no choice.

She shivered. The cold damp on her skin was like a clammy hand, and her breaths were so shallow and rapid she thought she might faint. Her knees were suddenly no more solid than pease pudding and she had to reach out and touch the wall to stop herself from sinking to the floor. It took her several seconds to muster the courage to bend down and take the first step into the tunnel.

"Please, don't let there be spiders," she whispered. Or anything else that crawled.

Surprisingly, the tunnel never became completely dark once she was inside it. The light coming into it from the grave was meagre, but it dispelled some of the shadow and allowed Eliza to see roughly where she was going. She stumbled on the rough flooring once or twice, but it could have been much worse.

And if she told herself that often enough, she might even believe it.

At last, she turned a corner, climbed over rubble and found herself in the church crypt, where light from a lamp glowed dimly. It showed shelves of coffins, a small area at one end where she suspected services had once been held for the souls of the dead, and a wooden door at the other end.

Freddy sat propped up against one of the shelves. His loosened cravat was stained with blood, which had also darkened and matted his hair. His coat was torn and there was a hole in the knee of his breeches. He blinked at her. "Please, tell me you are real." His voice was raspy, dry, his speech slightly slurred.

"I am real," she replied.

A small smile kicked up one side of his mouth. His eyes closed and he struggled to open them again. "Can anyone else see her?" he asked. He made no effort to move.

"She's real," said a voice, startling Eliza, who whirled to see a group of girls come out from behind the altar table. The oldest was about fifteen years old, and the youngest...

"Claire?" breathed Eliza, hardly daring to say the name, terrified she would be wrong.

"Are you my aunt?" asked the child. She clung to the oldest girl, half hiding behind her.

"I am, if you are Miss Claire Russell."

"No doubt of that." Freddy chuckled. "She looks like you."

"She looks like her mama," answered Eliza, smiling

and fighting back tears at the same time.

"That's what I said." The child glared at Freddy triumphantly.

"I stand corrected," he said, then turned his attention back to Eliza. "Where's David? Did he send men?"

Instead of answering him, Eliza turned to the girls. Her smile was too wide and bright, and it made her face ache, while her voice was full of a confidence she did not feel. She hoped the girls did not see through her.

"We're going to get you out of here and back to your families," she said. Hidden by her coat she crossed her fingers and silently prayed it was the truth.

"How?" asked the oldest girl.

Eliza was about to say they would climb out of the grave, pulled up by Ned, when it occurred to her there might be an easier way, one that didn't involve climbing or dark tunnels. She moved to the door and examined the lock, then felt in her pocket, breathing a sigh of relief when she found the key was still there.

Holding her breath, every muscle tense, every nerve on edge, she put the key into the lock. It fitted perfectly and, a moment later, the door opened onto stone steps that led up to a light which was, presumably, coming from the main body of the church.

Freddy struggled to his feet, though it was clear to Eliza his strength was fading and he would not get far. She pushed herself under his arm in an attempt to help him, although she knew if he keeled over now she could not stop him, and she'd probably go down with him. It was all they had, though, so it would have to do.

"Where is David?" he asked again. "Rotherton," he clarified as he stumbled on the steps.

"Less talking, more walking," she ground out, his

weight squeezing her voice.

"You didn't come alone?" When she didn't answer, he cursed.

"I do have help," she said.

"Who has come with you? Why are they not here?"

"They are outside."

He stumbled up the last two steps, following the girls, who looked around the church, trying the doors and peeking into every nook and cranny.

"There's no way out of here," said the oldest girl. Claire began to cry. Eliza wanted to pull her close and tell her all would be well, but she could not. For one thing, if she let go of him, Freddy would likely topple back down the steps and break his neck. For another, how could she reassure the child when she wasn't actually certain herself?

"Who waits outside?" insisted Freddy.

Reluctantly, Eliza said, "Ned Fellowes." Freddy groaned, and she went on, quickly, "He showed me the way in, and he'll help us all out if we need to go that way."

Freddy blinked at her, slowly. She suspected the only reason he did not berate her for coming here without the Watch was that it would hurt him to do so.

"Pot, kettle, black," she whispered. "At least I have Ned. You came entirely alone." So had she, if she was completely honest, but he did not need to know that. Mentally, she crossed her fingers against the dissemblance.

He grunted his reply.

"There are loose boards here," called one of the girls from behind the table. "Mayhap it's a way out."

Everybody moved to the altar. An area in the floor,

about two feet square, was loose and ill-fitting. It would not be seen unless someone came behind the table, which made it virtually undiscoverable; even a clergyman would never stand between the communion table and the altar itself. If it turned out to be a hole, the girls might escape that way, although it would be a squeeze for Eliza, and Freddy would not fit into it at all.

The oldest girls lifted the boards.

"A storage space," said one. "There's a chest in there."

"A chest?" Freddy moved forward, his movements awkward. "Annie?" The oldest girl opened it, and everyone gasped at the sight of gold coins spilling from velveteen bags. Freddy sighed. "I might have known."

"Known what?" asked Eliza. Then she shook her head. "Tell us later. We don't have time now. Prudence and her cohort are coming."

Some of the girls cried out in fear and dismay, but all redoubled their efforts, looking for a way out of the church. It didn't take long to realize there wasn't one.

"Right. Through the tunnel," ordered Eliza.

Freddy pulled away from her and sat down in the preacher's chair beside the quire. "You go. I will follow in a minute."

"But—"

"Get the girls to safety. Fetch help."

"I won't leave you," said Eliza, and she meant it. Leaving Freddy would be like leaving a piece of herself. "If they come, you won't stand a chance if you are here alone."

"I am not dead yet."

No, but he soon would be if he stayed here. Eliza didn't think she could bear that.

"I can't get out that way in my current state," he whispered to her. "Get the girls out."

He made sense. Eliza knew that. Ned might be strong enough to haul the girls out, but he could not lift Freddy, especially if Freddy couldn't use his own strength to help. And if they didn't rescue the girls now, chances were that the villains would take them all.

"I will come back for you," she promised, and she touched his cheek, lovingly.

He smiled. "Go."

She led the children back down the steps and through the tunnel to the grave. Ned peered over at them, nothing more than a silhouette now. The sky above him had changed color, from the bright blue of the sunny day to a darker, duskier hue. Clouds tinged pink and orange showed against it, reminding Eliza time was running out.

"Hurry," she told them. "When you get out, hide until Annie comes. Then get across the road. There's a tavern. Go in and tell the landlord, and everybody else in there, what has happened to you. Tell them to send for Lord Rotherton."

"What about you?" asked Annie.

"I'll be along shortly. I need to help Freddy—Mr. Finch, and then I will come."

"Will you take me to my mama?" asked Claire.

Eliza hugged her. "You'll soon see all of your family again, sweetling."

"Not Uncle Donald." The child looked scared. "He hurt Rowena."

"Rowena?" Eliza frowned. She didn't know anybody named Rowena.

"My nurse. He hit her when she wouldn't let him take me away. She fell and she didn't get up. And then he gave me to the bad man."

Eliza felt sick. Charlotte's brother-in-law was behind Claire's abduction? What with Prudence's crimes, and her suspicion that Silas may also be involved, Claire's revelation about Donald was almost more than she could take. Her head spun and the world tilted, and it took all her willpower to right it again.

"We will deal with Uncle Donald later," she promised. "Let's get you out of here first."

The first four girls were easy. With Annie and her friend Matty to steady them, each small child climbed onto Eliza's shoulders and reached up. Ned grabbed them and hauled them up out of the hole and onto *terra firma*. The last three girls proved more of a challenge, being bigger, but they were determined and, after a couple of failed attempts, all except Eliza and Annie were out.

"You can't lift me, miss," Annie said. "I'm too big."

"I will bend down, and you can climb on my back. Ned should be able to reach you, then."

"No, miss. I can't let you do that."

"You can and you must. I need you to care for those girls until Lord Rotherton gets here. They're too little to do it alone."

Annie bit her lip, uncertain.

"Get to the tavern. If anybody should try to stop you, yell and holler for all you are worth. Attract every person in Crompton Hadlow. Wake the dead. Do you hear me?"

Annie nodded. She threw her arms around Eliza, her eyes glistening. Eliza's own vision was blurred. She blinked a couple of times to dispel the tears, then bent over so Annie could climb onto her back. Her arms, shoulders, and ribs felt bruised, and she made no doubt she would be black and blue by tomorrow, but if these girls were rescued, it would be worth it.

As soon as Annie had scrambled over the rim of the hole, Eliza ducked back through the tunnel and made her way to Freddy. He had moved and now sat beside the hole in the floor, his fingers toying with coins from the chest.

"I've been looking for this."

"Was it stolen from you?" Eliza sat beside him and pulled up her knees, then wrapped her arms around them.

He shook his head. "It's contraband. Traitor's gold."

She studied him for a few moments. Suddenly, the answer to the enigma that was Freddy Finch was blindingly obvious. "You work for the government."

He gave her a sidelong look and a crooked smile.

"Don't worry. I won't tell anybody."

"That's good. I would hate it to ruin my reputation as a rake and a ne'er-do-well."

"I am beginning to think rakes and ne'er-do-wells are preferable to pillars of the community."

He chuckled. "I don't know. Pillars are not all villains."

"Aren't they?" She counted on her fingers as she listed them. "Prudence. Possibly Silas. And now, Donald Russell." She told him what Claire had said.

"The dastard!" he said. "Sorry for my language."

"Don't be sorry. I was thinking it."

"I look forward to planting him a facer."

"I'll hold your coat."

"And after I've hit him, I'll—" He stopped speaking as a racket started up outside. Children screamed and wailed, girls shouted, men cried out. A dog barked, setting off other dogs, farther away. Then a cockerel crowed, and finally…

"A wolf?" Freddy's face said he was completely confused. "I didn't think there were any wolves in England."

"It's Ned." Eliza sprang to her feet. "Ned and the girls." She grinned. "I told them to wake the dead."

"All the way to Hastings, by the sound of it." Freddy struggled to his feet and leaned against the altar table.

The church door rattled and opened, and Prudence and the sexton rushed inside, then pushed against it, slammed it shut, and locked it. Immediately, there were thuds and bangs against it, and the sound of angry people shouting. Prudence's bonnet was skewwhiff, and her chest heaved with the exertion. When she turned to face them, her eyes were bright and her skin a mottled red.

"You!" She pointed at Freddy, her hand shaking. "You abomination! You tool of the devil!" She saw Eliza and her face darkened. "So he has corrupted you as well."

"Forget them," said the sexton. He pushed his disheveled hair back from his forehead, then glanced nervously at the door. "Let's get the gold and get out while we can."

"That gold belongs to the government." Freddy's voice was calm and even. He didn't move. Eliza worried that was because he could not. His eyes were hooded, and she suspected it was only sheer willpower that kept him conscious.

"That gold belongs to God!" argued Prudence. "God led me to where it was hidden. He wanted me to have it, so it could be used in furtherance of His work."

"What work would that be?" asked Eliza, her disgust plain. "Stealing children? Taking them from loving families so you can profit from them?"

"Loving families?" Prudence laughed. It wasn't her usual titter, but something far more sinister. "Loving families? Ha! Their families could not and would not care for them. Mothers soused in gin! Fathers who spend every farthing on drink. We save those children from their debauched origins."

"We haven't got time for this," said the sexton.

"You stole Claire!" Eliza's hands fisted at her sides. She had never, not once in her life, hit another human being deliberately. Right now, it took everything she had not to hit Prudence.

For a moment, Prudence looked nonplussed. "Claire? What is she to you?"

"My niece." The words came out through gritted teeth, which hardened Eliza's tone and made it more dangerous. The shouts outside the church grew louder.

"Then you should thank me. Her uncle told us how she was neglected and unloved. He paid well for us to take her. In fact, his money bought the new baptismal font here."

"You bought it with the devil's money," said Eliza.

"Blasphemy!" Prudence pointed at Freddy, who leaned more and more heavily onto the table. "I warned you not to associate with him. He has corrupted you." She glared at him. "Horror monger! Gambler! Villain!"

Freddy gave a chuckle. The pain on his face said his nonchalance cost him dear. "I am a sinner. I readily admit it. But at least I am an honest sinner. You, dear lady, are in a class all your own."

Prudence's eyes widened. "I am an instrument of the Lord."

The banging on the door increased.

"I'm getting out of here," said the sexton. He pushed past Freddy, grabbed a bag of the gold, then turned to leave. Freddy stuck out his foot and the sexton fell. Coins flew from the bag and rolled across the floor. Prudence cried out and bent to gather them up. The sexton took the bag and what coins he could grab, and ran down the stairs to the crypt.

"You will burn in hell for what you have done," Prudence shouted. "Destruction shall be to the workers of iniquity! If it be of God, ye cannot overthrow it!"

The banging at the door stopped, suddenly. The silence rang in Eliza's ears.

Prudence laughed. "God shall wound the head of his enemies, and the hairy scalp of such a one as goeth on still in his trespasses. But the salvation of the righteous is of the Lord: he is their strength in the time of trouble."

A key turned. The church door flew open. Lord Rotherton rushed into the church, followed closely by Silas Burgess. Other men crowded the doorway behind them. Two of them held the sexton, his arms pinned to his sides.

"What the deuce—? Prudence?" Silas looked bewildered. He took in the sight of his sister, standing in the aisle, clutching several gold coins to her chest. Then he glanced at Freddy, listing heavily to the side, his cravat and shirt stained with blood, his face ashen and clammy. Silas looked from Freddy to Eliza, his mouth open, forming a perfect O. Eliza suddenly became aware of the sight she presented. Her dress was filthy and torn, her hair no longer confined beneath her bonnet. She would bet her face was dirty, too.

Lord Rotherton raised one eyebrow. "I take it you found what you were looking for, Finch?"

Freddy huffed a quiet laugh. "Good to see you, my lord. Take over, will you?" And with that, he pitched forward, unconscious.

Chapter Seventeen

The sexton and his men were arrested and taken to the jail in Haywards Heath, where one man quickly told his jailers everything, agreeing to testify to keep the noose from his neck. Lord Rotherton decided that Prudence was mad, a verdict Eliza could not dispute, for who in their right mind would do what Prudence had done, and twist Scripture to justify it? Even as she was taken away, she quoted the Bible and cursed her enemies for impeding the Lord's work.

Silas was heartbroken. He spent several days ensconced in Rotherton's study along with the earl and the Right Reverend John Buckner, Bishop of Chichester. He had, Lord Rotherton told Eliza a few days later, known nothing of his sister's deeds.

"Nothing?" Eliza was surprised and more than a little skeptical.

"I, too, had my doubts," said Lord Rotherton. "But he has satisfied me, and the bishop, that it's the truth. He is mortified. He said Prudence was always a little extreme in her beliefs, but he never thought her zealotry could cause any real harm."

"Poor Silas," said Eliza. "He's as much her victim as the children she stole."

Lord Rotherton smiled. "You are truly a heaven-sent angel, my dear. Few would be as forgiving as you. Including himself. He feels the need to put right, insofar as is possible, all of her wrongs. To that end, he has resigned his living here and intends to go to America, to find those she sold, so he can restore them to their rightful families."

"That is a big task."

"I said that when I tried to talk him out of it. He's been a good minister to the flock. His sermons are a little dry, I grant you, but… He's probably right. It would be difficult for him to continue here." The earl sighed. "Which means I now have the task of finding his replacement. Honestly," he rolled his eyes, "when these people commit their crimes, I don't think they spare so much as a thought for the work they create for people like me. As if I didn't have enough to do."

Eliza chuckled, as he meant her to, then sobered again. "How is Mr. Finch today?"

"Much as he was when you asked me yesterday. His skull is cracked and will take time to heal, but the doctor has high hopes. Apparently, Finch has a hard head, which stood him in good stead when somebody bashed it. On top of which, I am told, there wasn't anything important filling the inside of his skull, so it shouldn't affect him too much."

"That's unkind."

"The sentiments are not mine. They're his father's. Seaford arrived yesterday and has been at his bedside since."

"I thought they had quarreled."

Lord Rotherton smiled. "Seaford's exacting in his expectations. But he is also a father. And like any father, he will not stand by idly when his son needs him." The earl sniffed. "It probably helps that Freddy's days of working for Fremont are in the past now."

Eliza was glad. She did not like the thought of Freddy putting his life on the line at Lord Fremont's behest, even if it was for the good of king and country. To her mind, Freddy had played his part. He deserved a peaceful retirement, reconciliation with his family, and the right to show, publicly, the truth of his character. Mayhap he would even take a wife now, and set up his nursery. A pain shot through her at that thought, which was selfish of her. Freddy had earned his happiness.

"As soon as the doctor tells us he is fit for travel, Seaford will take Finch home to recover. I doubt we'll see him around here again. Pity. I shall miss him."

Eliza's heart cracked at the thought of never seeing Freddy again, although it was probably for the best. They both needed to move on with their lives. He needed time to heal. So did she, although she would never admit to that. Her wounds were invisible to the eye, and she would nurse them in secret. And if, when she sat alone, she chose to press on the bruise by recalling the feel of his lips on hers, the warmth of his arms around her, the scent of his cologne, and the crooked smile meant only for her…well, that was her business.

"I must leave, too," she told Lord Rotherton, and she tried to be glad of it. "I must take Claire to her mother. I've had a letter from my sister. She is leaving her home in Leicestershire and coming to Surrey, where my father is taking a house big enough for all of us. It will do her good to get away from the Russells. And Claire will be more comfortable if she doesn't have to see her uncle Donald."

"Lord, I nearly forgot," said Lord Rotherton, and he smacked his palm against his forehead. "Anybody might think it was me with the cracked skull. I had a missive from the magistrate in Leicester. Donald Russell has been arrested and held for the murder of the nursery nurse. He also will be tried for the abduction of his niece, and various offences to do with his business. They're investigating his role in the death of his brother, and the attempted murder of your sister."

"Oh, my!" Eliza slumped a little and massaged her forehead with her fingertips.

"Donald's actions were, to say the least, nefarious. Your brother-in-law discovered it and withdrew from the business, which put Donald in a financial bind. Jonathan also threatened to go to the authorities."

"So Donald killed him?" Hot tears burned Eliza's eyes. What a terrible thing to do. Why were people so wicked?

Lord Rotherton continued, "Jonathan had invested in a number of other enterprises, which had made him very wealthy. In his will, Jonathan left the bulk of his fortune in trust for your niece. Donald tried to gain guardianship of her, so that he could control the money, but he failed."

"We should be thankful he didn't simply kill her," said Eliza. Her stomach turned at the thought.

"I don't think he could stomach the thought of murdering a child himself. So he hatched a plan. He sold the child. She would be gone, hopefully to die in her new, harsh environment. Then he planned to say your sister wasn't fit to handle the trust and it should be given to him." Lord Rotherton shook his head. "The love of money, as I am sure Miss Burgess would tell us, is at the root of most, if not all, evil."

Eliza wanted to cry. So much pain, so much suffering, all for twisted desires and greed. It was good that Charlotte and Claire would now live with Papa. The values he held dear would comfort Charlotte, and give a good grounding to Claire.

When Lord Rotherton had gone, Eliza went upstairs to finish packing. She and Claire would leave on the morrow. The sooner she could deliver the child safely to her mother, the better.

****

July 1818

It was one of the warmest summers Eliza could remember. The sun beat down, the only clouds the occasional thin and feathery ones that brightened the sky's blue and refused to bring rain. At times, the days were uncomfortably hot, although today there was enough of a wind to make it balmy.

Eliza sat beside Charlotte on the terrace of their father's house, watching Claire play in the shade of a tree with her new nursery nurse, Annie, the only one of the rescued girls who had had no family to return to. Papa was in his study, working on the treatise on the book of Romans he had been threatening to write for years. The study window was open, and doubtless he enjoyed the sound of Claire's laughter on the gentle breeze. Before too long, she knew, he would leave his work and come to play with the child he doted on.

Charlotte held a pad of paper and a piece of charcoal and drew lines, which would form the basis of her new painting. She wouldn't let anyone see it until it was finished, although Eliza knew it would be a portrait of Claire. All of Charlotte's drawings these days were of Claire.

Eliza was supposed to be embroidering a handkerchief, although she hadn't laid a stitch in several minutes. Both sisters wore cotton dresses in dark lavender, in half mourning for Charlotte's husband.

"Are you all right?" asked Charlotte.

Eliza turned from watching Claire play to look at her sister. "Of course."

"Are you certain?"

Eliza could recite the next words Charlotte would say, for she said them daily.

"You are much subdued since your return from Sussex."

Eliza prepared to say, as she always did, that it had been a busy time and it had tired her, but Claire bounded over to them, Annie trailing behind her.

"Aunt Eliza saved me, Mama," beamed the child.

Charlotte smiled and held out her arms for Claire to come in for a hug. "I know she did, my darling." Over the top of the child's head, she glared meaningfully at Eliza, who concentrated on her embroidery so she didn't have to meet her sister's eye. "But what of herself?"

Claire giggled. "Silly Mama. Aunt Eliza wasn't 'ducted. She didn't need saving."

"That is correct. I didn't." Eliza smiled at Claire.

"Why don't you and Annie go to the kitchens?" suggested Charlotte. "I'm sure Dory has made biscuits and she'll need you to try them."

The child ran off, Annie behind her.

Eliza sighed. *Here we go again.* This happened almost daily. Charlotte sent Claire to the kitchens for biscuits. As soon as the child was out of earshot, she would lean forward in her chair and fix Eliza with a knowing, older-sister look and ask her what happened in Sussex. Eliza would mention Prudence Burgess, and Charlotte would wave her hand as if swatting a fly.

"Not that. What else happened?"

"Nothing else happened. I followed the clues, stayed in a cottage, met some people."

I met a man and fell in love, and then we went our separate ways.

"Then," she continued aloud, "we rescued everyone, and I brought Claire home."

And he went to his family where he has probably forgotten me completely.

Eliza knew she would never forget him, though. The smiles he had given her, the friendly banter, their wonderful kisses, even the times when they argued. All were precious to her, and always would be.

"You are determined not to tell me," said Charlotte. "But I am equally determined to… Now what?"

A loud, childish squeal sounded in the house. Charlotte threw off her lap blanket, grabbed her walking stick, and struggled to her feet. Eliza stood, too. Part of her wanted to run and make sure Claire was safe, though the squeal had sounded more joyous than alarmed, and Papa was there, as well as Annie, Dory, and the other servants, should the child need protection. Besides, Claire was Charlotte's child, and Charlotte should be the one who responded to her.

Before Charlotte could move far, Claire ran to them, shouting, "He's here! He's here!" at the top of her voice.

"Who's here?" asked Charlotte, bewildered.

Eliza said nothing. She could not. She had been rendered speechless by the man standing in the doorway. Her heart skipped and pattered, and her breath caught, while a thousand butterflies took flight in her stomach.

She swallowed. It didn't help. She swallowed again.

"Mr. Finch has come!" shouted Claire.

"Mr. Finch?" Charlotte glanced at Eliza, then smiled and held out her hand toward Freddy, who strode across the garden to them. He bowed over Charlotte's hand and kissed the air above it.

"Forgive the intrusion, ma'am," he said.

"You could not be an intrusion, sir." Charlotte smiled. "Not after you saved my daughter."

Freddy laughed. "Alas, that was not me. All I did was get myself into trouble so that I, too, needed rescue. The true hero of the piece, or rather, the heroine, is your own sister."

Eliza felt her cheeks warming. Charlotte looked from one to the other of them, then smiled.

"You must have much to discuss," she said. "I will ring for tea. Eliza, why don't you show Mr. Finch the gardens while we wait?"

"Charlotte!" hissed Eliza. Could her sister be any more obvious?

"I can come, too. I'll show you where I climb the tree," cried Claire, and Charlotte grabbed her hand to stop her running off.

"You can stay here with me."

"Mama!" moaned the child.

"I should very much like to see the garden, Miss Rolfe," said Freddy.

"All right," said Eliza. Her mouth was dry and the words sounded raspy.

Claire argued that she wanted to go with them. Eliza was tempted to tell her to come, so afraid was she of this man and his reason for being here. Charlotte would never allow it, though, so Eliza conceded defeat and led him from the terrace, across the lawn and to a small wilderness on the far side, where an apple tree and a plum tree grew, surrounded by brambles and long grass.

"You look well," she said after an awkward silence. "Are you fully recovered?"

"I still tire easily, and I have headaches, but, on the whole, yes, I am recovered."

"And reconciled with your father?"

Freddy gave a tiny smile. "Reconcil*ing*. It looks promising."

"I am glad."

He cleared his throat. "They found some boys. Did you know that? In a disused building outside Crompton Hadlow. And babies near Rye. Twenty-three children, in all."

Eliza shook her head and said nothing. What could one say?

"I went back, "Freddy continued. "To Rotherton. As soon as I could travel. You were gone."

He'd gone back? He'd looked for her? "I had to return Claire to her mother, and…"

"David—Rotherton—gave me your direction. I rode all day yesterday, and since early this morning."

Her eyes widened. Was he mad? Had he no care for his own wellbeing? "You rode? You daft man. You could have damaged yourself."

"Eliza—"

"You could have set back your healing—"

"Mrs. Rawlins…"

"Or re-opened the wound, or…"

"Miss Rolfe." His stern tone got her attention. He huffed and closed his eyes, frustrated. "I don't even know what to call you." He opened his eyes again and watched her. A small smile twitched his lips. "I know what I would like to call you, but I don't know how you'll feel about it."

She frowned, uncertain. "What would you like to call me?" she asked, and braced herself. Whatever nickname he had coined for her, she hoped it wasn't too bad.

He swallowed, nervous, flexed his neck muscles as if his cravat was too tight, and straightened his shoulders. "I'd like to call you 'Mrs. Finch.' "

It took Eliza a few seconds to realize what he had said. When she did, she stared at him, astounded.

"If you would do me the incredible honor of agreeing," he said as he took her hand in his and caressed her fingers, "I would like to call you…'wife.' "

For a moment she stood, too stupefied to answer. A million thoughts raced through her head. She didn't catch any of them. Then one returned to torment her. It danced around inside her mind.

A sunny day in a meadow. A picnic. Kisses. And more.

I took your maidenhead. We will marry.

"Why?" she asked.

He frowned. "Why?"

"Why do you want to marry me?"

He watched her for a long moment. She was terrified he'd mention obligations and responsibilities. The air hummed with the lazy drones of bees flittering from plant to plant. The sun warmed her skin. Or was that the thrum of her blood? The breeze caressed her. A stray strand of hair tickled across her cheek, and she trembled.

Finally, he spoke. "Why? Because I love you, Eliza Rolfe, more than I ever thought I could love anybody. I can't stop thinking about you, and I want to spend the rest of my life showing you."

Eliza nodded. "I see," she said, schooling her face into an expression she hoped was bland and thoughtful.

His smile faded, and she couldn't keep up the pretense.

She laughed. "I love you, too, Freddy Finch. Not a day has gone by this last month when I haven't thought about you, missed you, wished you were here. I love you and, yes, I will marry you."

He pulled her to him and kissed her, long and slow and very, very thoroughly. Eliza prayed he would never stop.

And over on the terrace, Claire cheered and clapped her hands, loudly.

A word about the author…

Caitlyn Callery lives in Sussex, southern England, near the Regency towns of Brighton and Tunbridge Wells. She is passionate about writing and suffers withdrawal symptoms when she takes a few days away from her work.

Before becoming a full-time writer, she worked in banking, as a waitress, in the motor repair industry, in a call centre, and for a charity. As part of this last job, she helped build a school in Kenya, and drove a vanload of wheelchairs from the UK to Morocco.

She also loves reading, knitting, walking by the sea, the theatre, and spending time with her family.

CaitlynCallery.com

Thank you for purchasing
this publication of The Wild Rose Press, Inc.

For questions or more information
contact us at
info@thewildrosepress.com.

The Wild Rose Press, Inc.